CHARLOTTE FAIRLIE

CHARLOTTE FAIRLIE

By

D. E. STEVENSON

COLLINS
ST JAMES'S PLACE, LONDON

FIRST IMPRESSION   OCTOBER 1954
SECOND IMPRESSION   OCTOBER 1954

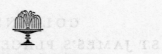

PRINTED IN GREAT BRITAIN
COLLINS CLEAR-TYPE PRESS: LONDON AND GLASGOW

Contents

Contents

PART ONE

Saint Elizabeth's

1

"THE LONELIEST JOB IN THE WORLD". Charlotte Fairlie read the article with interest (it was all about light-houses and was beautifully illustrated with shiny pictures) but when she came to the end she shook her head thoughtfully and put the paper on the table beside her. No she could not agree. Caring for a lighthouse was not the most lonely job in the world. The three lighthouse-keepers lived together, sharing the work, eating their meals in company, talking about their hobbies and laughing at one another's jokes. They were friends. Charlotte's job precluded friends; she lived and moved and had her being in a sort of —a sort of glass-case, thought Charlotte, smiling rather sadly at the fantastic idea. She was surrounded by people but she could have no friend. There was nobody to whom she could speak her mind freely, nobody with whom she could be herself. To make a friend led to trouble and jealousy. Yes, her job was the loneliest in the world. No king, no dictator set high upon a pinnacle, was as friendless as the headmistress of a girls' school.

Charlotte Fairlie was proud of her position, and would not have exchanged jobs with anybody, for Saint Elizabeth's was a fine school with great traditions. *The school stands upon gently sloping hills,* said the prospectus. *Its position is healthy and bracing; it has wide parks with fine old trees and splendid playing fields. The school buildings have been added to and*

modernised, they are placed round a quadrangle of well-kept turf.
Although Saint Elizabeth's is in the country (in a district justly
famous for its beauty and seclusion) it is by no means difficult of
access for it is only four miles from the ancient and interesting town
of Larchester where there are good shops and comfortable
hotels. . . .

The prospectus said a great deal more. It gave a record of
the school's achievements in scholarship and sport and it
was illustrated with pictures of dormitories and classrooms
and playing fields.

The suite of rooms allotted to the headmistress of Saint
Elizabeth's was at the back of the main building and com-
prised a sitting-room, bedroom and bathroom, there was
also a small office for her secretary. The sitting-room had
a french window which opened on to a stone terrace with a
carved stone balustrade. Beyond this was the park and the
swimming pool and a view of woods and fields.

It was no wonder that Charlotte Fairlie was proud of the
school. She was proud of the girls and in some ways she was
proud of her staff. The members of her staff were conscientious and extremely competent—if they had not been she
could and would have replaced them—but sometimes they
were so foolish and petty that they almost drove her mad.
(Too many women, all herded together, thought Charlotte.
That's what's the matter. It would do us all good to have a
few men . . . and then she smiled at the idiotic idea, for of
course a few men would disrupt the whole place; the foolish-
nesses and jealousies would be multiplied a hundredfold—
a few men, indeed!)

In spite of the pinnacle upon which she sat Charlotte knew
a good deal about what went on in the school. She kept her
finger on its pulse and any irregularity in the beat was
promptly investigated. She knew of the quarrels amongst
her staff which flared up for no reason at all—or at least for

no reasonable reason. Sometimes she ignored them until they died down and sometimes she summoned the antagon-ists to her private sitting-room and had it out with them. Miss Pinkerton was usually at the bottom of the trouble (she was a trouble-maker if ever there was one) but she was senior maths mistress and exceedingly capable and she had been at Saint Elizabeth's for years so there was no excuse for getting rid of her. Besides Charlotte was sorry for Miss Pinkerton; she was aware that if *she* had not applied for the post of headmistress Miss Pinkerton would have got it. Miss Pinkerton knew this too, and although neither of them had ever mentioned the subject it lay like an abyss between them.

Then there were the girls. Charlotte made it her business to know all the girls and, as there were over three hundred of them, it was not very easy. It was not easy to remember every face and every name when all the faces were young and fresh and nearly all were round and innocent and assumed expressions of holy awe when one spoke to their owners. The only safe way was to keep a private file with the par-ticulars of every girl in the school—of her appearance, her scholastic abilities and her family background.

This file was so extremely private that it was kept under lock and key and not even Charlotte's secretary was allowed access to it. Miss Post was loyal in her own way but she was inquisitive and she would have given a good deal to see that file and to know what Miss Fairlie thought about everyone. Of course one would not tell, but just to *know* would give one satisfaction . . . it would also give one power. Miss Post had suggested that the private file should be typed out neatly—it would be easier for Miss Fairlie to read—but Miss Fairlie had refused the offer saying that she would not like to give Miss Post so much extra work. Miss Post was about to reply that she did not mind the extra work but she hesi-

tated with the words unspoken for although Miss Fairlie's
face looked perfectly serious there was an odd little twinkle
in her wide grey eyes.

How very good-looking she was, thought Miss Post (not
for the first time by any means) how very attractive and
young! She looked absurdly young for her responsible
position. If only she did not wear her hair smoothed back
and gathered so tightly into a knob at the nape of her neck
she would look even younger. Miss Post wondered if she
knew that everybody in Saint Elizabeth's called her "The
Old Girl".

As a matter of fact Charlotte knew. The name had been
bestowed upon her when she was appointed to her position
by the Board of Governors. Sir Joseph Spinner, introducing
her to the whole school on Parents' Day, had finished the
list of her qualifications by pointing out that she was a
former pupil of Saint Elizabeth's—"An Old Girl, if I
may be allowed the expression," said Sir Joseph smiling—
and the audience, assembled in the big school hall, had
awakened from its stupor and clapped. Naturally Miss
Fairlie was "The Old Girl" and would remain so for as long
as she remained at Saint Elizabeth's. One might have
thought that the name betokened a lack of respect but such
was not the case. Saint Elizabeth's used it with awe and
bated breath . . . you had to mind your P's and Q's with
the Old Girl.

It was when Charlotte was on her way home from America
that she had seen the advertisement in *The Times* inviting
applications for the post of headmistress of Saint Elizabeth's
School and her first thought had been: I wonder who will
get it. Her second thought had been: Why not me? It
seemed absurd but there was no harm in trying so she sat
down then and there and wrote out a list of her qualifications: her First Class Honours in Modern Languages at

Oxford, her two years in Paris at the Lycée and her year in Philadelphia. Last but not least the fact that she had been a pupil at Saint Elizabeth's and Captain of the Cricket XI. It looked quite impressive and as she read it over she began to have a vague hope that she might possibly be invited to appear before the Board of Governors for an interview . . . but they won't take me, she told herself firmly. They'll think I'm too young.

In due time the Board of Governors summoned Miss Fairlie to an interview and Miss Fairlie appeared before them. She had taken a good deal of trouble and without actually making up (which would have been wrong) she had contrived to look some years older than usual. One could do a lot with sedate clothes and a dowdy hat. Mr. Swayne was the only member of the board who had asked her age and Charlotte had replied that she was under forty.

" You said in your advertisement that applicants should be under forty," said Charlotte seriously.

"Oh, of course," agreed Mr. Swayne covered with embarrassment. "I never thought for a moment—I mean I thought—I thought if anything you were too young." He blushed and sat back in his chair. Mr. Swayne was not very old himself and had only just been elected to the Board (he was the headmaster of Bells Hill, the Boys' Preparatory School in Larchester).

Charlotte Fairlie said no more. She did not feel guilty of deceit for if they really wanted to know her age they had only to look up her name in the School List—but she hoped they would not bother.

"Miss Pinkerton is older," said Mr. Allnut, the Rector of Saint Simon's. " Miss Pinkerton has been at Saint Elizabeth's for twelve years—under Miss Bain—and knows all about the school—the traditions and so forth."

"Ah yes—Miss Pinkerton," nodded Mr. Walpole and he

wrote "Miss Pinkerton" on the nice clean pad of paper which lay before him on the table.

"We are interviewing Miss Fairlie," said Sir Joseph Spinner. Sir Joseph was president of the Board and filled his post with dignity. He was a fine looking man—perhaps about sixty—with silvery white hair, good features and piercing blue eyes. Having lived in Larchester all his life Sir Joseph knew everybody worth knowing and had a finger in every pie. He was The Great Man of Larchester.

"We are interviewing Miss Fairlie," Sir Joseph said. "Later if the Board wishes to do so, it can interview Miss Pinkerton."

"Yes," agreed Mr. Allnut. "I only mentioned Miss Pinkerton——"

"What are Miss Pinkerton's qualifications?" asked Mr. Swayne. "I mean she doesn't seem to have a scholastic degree—not even an M.A."

"Scholastic degrees are not everything," declared Mr. Allnut. "Miss Pinkerton is an ardent churchwoman with exceedingly high principles——"

"Degrees may not be everything but in this case I should think a degree was very important. Parents like it," said Mr. Swayne with conviction. "I mean if we were choosing somebody to be president of a Church Guild it would be different. We're choosing a headmistress for a school."

Mr. Allnut glared at him.

"Is Miss Pinkerton under forty?" asked Mr. Wise.

The Board immediately began to discuss Miss Pinkerton's age. Some of the members thought she must be over forty, others thought not.

"May I remind you that we are supposed to be interviewing Miss Fairlie?" inquired Sir Joseph Spinner rapping on the table.

"Of course," agreed Mr. Walpole. He consulted his notes

and added, "I see Miss Fairlie has a First in Modern Languages. It would look well on the prospectus."

"Have you had much experience of girls?" asked Mr.
Renfrew, speaking for the first time.

It was the first really sensible question—or so Charlotte
thought—and she answered it by explaining what experience
she had had in Paris and Philadelphia.

"French and American girls," said Mr. Renfrew doubtfully. "They would be quite different from English girls.
I can't help feeling we should see some of the other applicants
before deciding definitely. We ought to have somebody who
knows about girls."

"Miss Fairlie was a girl herself not so very long ago,"
said Mr. Walpole with a little chuckle. "I expect she remem-
bers what it was like."

"That is exactly the trouble," declared Mr. Allnut. "In
my opinion Miss Fairlie is too young and inexperienced."

Miss Fairlie was somewhat embarrassed. "Would the
Board like to discuss the matter in private?" she asked, half
rising from her chair.

"Presently, presently," said Sir Joseph hastily. "When
the Board has finished interviewing you we shall ask you to
retire for a few minutes." He looked round the table with a
quelling eye and added, "No doubt Miss Fairlie is—er—
young, but her qualifications are exceptional. I am sure we
all agree that it is better to—er—appoint a lady who has
many years of active work ahead of her rather than—er—"
he hesitated and cleared his throat.

They all knew what was in his mind. Miss Bain, the
retiring headmistress, was old. She had not been in her first
youth when appointed and, naturally enough, she had
become older and older. Yes, everybody thought of Miss
Bain. Charlotte Fairlie thought of her too. Poor old Bainie,
she thought. Bainie was too old when I was at Saint Eliza-

beth's—she must be positively senile by this time. If I get the job it will be because Bainie stayed on too long.

"Has the Board any more questions to ask?" inquired Sir Joseph. He looked round the table again and his eye fell upon Mr. Cowper. Mr. Cowper was the oldest member of the Board and had been slumbering peacefully through the proceedings. "Mr. Cowper!" said Sir Joseph loudly. "Have you any questions to put to Miss Fairlie before she retires?"

"Eh—what?" exclaimed the old gentleman, opening his eyes and looking about him in amazement.

"Any questions to ask?" repeated Sir Joseph.

"No, not at all," said Mr. Cowper, gathering his wits together. "I think we have been over the ground very thoroughly—very thoroughly indeed. We should certainly appoint Miss—er—er——"

"Miss Fairlie," said Mr. Swayne.

"Miss Fairlie, of course," agreed Mr. Cowper, nodding. "Yes, we couldn't do better."

"I second the motion," said Mr. Swayne cheerfully.

The other gentlemen looked a trifle surprised but Sir Joseph was master of the situation. He asked if there was an amendment to the motion. Mr. Allnut looked round wildly; he still hankered after Miss Pinkerton but it was obvious that nobody was ready to support him and while he was still wondering whether or not to propose an amendment the president clinched the matter.

"That's settled then," said Sir Joseph smiling happily. "The Board is unanimous in appointing Miss Fairlie. I should like to be the first to congratulate her upon her appointment and I think we should congratulate ourselves as well. Miss Fairlie will make an admirable headmistress and I feel sure that Saint Elizabeth's will—er—go from strength to strength under her management."

There was a murmur of assent.

Charlotte thanked them in a voice that trembled a little in spite of her efforts to steady it. She could hardly believe it was true. She had wanted with all her heart and soul to be headmistress of her old school. It had been her dream ever since she had gone to Saint Elizabeth's as a leggy coltish child of twelve years old and had sat at the bottom table in the big dining-hall. From that lowly position she had looked up to the table where the great and mighty took their meals and where Miss Bain—the greatest and mightiest —sat in state surrounded by her satellites. *Someday I'll be her*, thought young Charlotte who was nothing if not ambitious. The ambition to fill Bainie's shoes had waxed and waned like the moon, but—like the moon—had never actually vanished.

Charlotte's only surviving relative was an aunt who lived in Kensington and was too self-centred to be interested in anything except her own affairs. She was willing to give Charlotte house-room when necessary but she had never understood her niece, nor bothered to try. So she was not particularly sympathetic when Charlotte returned to the Kensington flat with her glorious news.

"Yes, dear," said Aunt Lydia vaguely. "Do you think you will like it? I don't care for Larchester myself—it's a provincial little town—but of course you know it. You were at school there, weren't you?"

Tepid water is more damping than a cold douche. Charlotte wished there were somebody—anybody—who would share her enthusiasm and to whom she could talk of her plans.

* 2 *

IT WAS now two years since Charlotte Fairlie had taken up her post as headmistress of Saint Elizabeth's and she was comfortably settled and happy in a quiet way. If she could have had one friend (or two, like the lighthouse-keepers) she would have been happier. One friend was all she needed—somebody to whom she could open her heart and with whom she could laugh over the funny little incidents of school life or grouse over the annoyances—but she had discovered it to be impossible. The moment you showed the slightest partiality for one of the staff the trouble began.

Charlotte sighed. It was nearly midnight and she was very tired for it was the first day of the Christmas Term. She had spent the day interviewing (or being interviewed) by the parents of new girls all of whom were firmly convinced that their chick was a swan—or should it be a cygnet? This was natural of course and Charlotte did not blame them . . . but it was tiring. She was assailed by that odd sort of tiredness which releases the subconscious mind and allows it to roam. The right thing to do was to go to bed, but she knew she would not sleep, so instead of going to bed she boiled her electric kettle and made herself some tea and sat down with a cigarette to enjoy it . . . and as she did so her eyes fell upon her latest acquisition which she had placed with care upon the centre of her mantelpiece. It was a Chinese ornament modelled in pottery or porcelain; the figure was that of a large fat Buddha in gorgeous robes, sitting with his fat hands folded across his fat tummy and a meditative expression upon his fat face. He was by no means beautiful, but there was something about him that appealed to Charlotte. She had bought him to keep her company and to be an antidote to the poison of absolute power (which is said to be so corrupting). She had bought him to remind her of this and to make her smile. She smiled now as she looked at him, for it seemed to her that she and the Buddha were alike. He could have no friend either. He was solitary and powerful. The Buddha would keep her from getting too uppish—that was the idea.

Letting her thoughts roam as she drank her tea Charlotte found herself remembering every small detail of the afternoon upon which she and the Buddha had met. She had been staying with Aunt Lydia for a few days before the term began and, having occasion to visit her lawyer in the City, she had decided to walk part of the way home. She was in no hurry so she sauntered along slowly, looking at the people and amusing herself by making up little stories about them and their affairs. Presently she got lost in a maze of little streets with tiny shops and even tinier houses. She was just wondering which way to turn when a heavy shower came on and having no umbrella she took shelter in a convenient doorway; it was the doorway of a small curiosity-shop which in Charlotte's fancy might easily have belonged to little Nell's grandfather. For a few minutes she stood there, watching the rain, and then the door behind her opened and a young man in a brown pullover and grey slacks appeared upon the threshold. He was not at all the sort of person one might have expected to see in these somewhat sordid surroundings for he was a nice, clean, chubby lad with well-brushed hair and a pleasant smile.

"Won't you come in?" he said. "No need to stand in the wet."

Charlotte thanked him and went in. He found her an old worm-eaten wooden chair and placed it for her politely. The shop was full of an odd assortment of furniture; it was mostly cheap and shoddy rubbish but there were some old brass pots upon a high shelf which caught Charlotte's eye. When the young man saw she was interested in the pots he got a ladder and brought one of them down for her to look at . . . behind the pots was the Buddha.

"What's that?" asked Charlotte pointing.

"It's an idol or something," replied the young man. He took it down and set it upon the table. "Ugly, isn't he?" added the young man cheerfully.

He was ugly. He was also extremely dirty. There was a film of London soot and grime all over him. But somehow he appealed to Charlotte.

"Is he very expensive?" she enquired.

The young man turned the figure upside down and looked at the base. "Five quid!" he exclaimed. "Phew, what a price! Fancy five quid for *that*!"

Charlotte agreed that it seemed a lot, but as a matter of fact she was not really surprised, for although she knew very little about Chinese porcelain she had a feeling that the specimen was good.

"Do you know if it is pottery or porcelain?" she asked in doubtful tones.

"I don't know anything about it," replied the young man sadly. "I'd let you have it for less, but I can't do that. You see I'm just looking after the shop to oblige—that's the way it is. If the old chap was here himself he'd probably reduce it."

The more Charlotte looked at the Buddha the more she liked him . . . why shouldn't she have him? Her salary was more than adequate and she worked hard for it. Why shouldn't she have what she wanted?

"I'll have him," she said.

"You'll pay five quid, you mean?" asked the young man incredulously and his eyebrows nearly disappeared into his hair.

Charlotte nodded. She produced five crinkly pound notes and handed them to him.

The young man found a box and packed the Buddha with some dirty old newspaper, and the transaction was complete. By this time the rain had stopped, and when Charlotte emerged from the dim little shop the sun was shining brightly and glittering with blinding radiance upon the wet streets. Somehow it seemed like fate . . . it almost seemed as if the shower had come at that very moment so that Charlotte should find the Buddha and buy him.

It was long past midnight and Charlotte was just finishing her tea, and thinking of bed, when there was a knock on her sitting-room door.

"Come in," she said, wondering who it could be at this unlikely hour.

Her visitor opened the door and looked in. It was Miss Pinkerton.

"Come in," repeated Charlotte, trying to sound friendly and hospitable.

"Oh!" said Miss Pinkerton. "I know it's very late but I saw your light, so I knew you hadn't gone to bed. I won't keep you a minute . . . no, I won't have tea. I shouldn't sleep a wink all night if I drank tea at this hour." She sidled in and sat down. "I won't keep you a minute," she repeated. "It's just that I wanted to speak to you about the new games mistress."

"She seems nice, doesn't she?" said Charlotte.

"I wish you would speak to her," said Miss Pinkerton.

"She talks and laughs far too loudly—especially for somebody who is quite *new*. When I went into the library, hoping
for a little peace and quiet, she was actually sitting in my
chair—the chair I always sit in—talking to Miss Margetson
quite loudly as if she had been at Saint Elizabeth's all her life."

Miss Pinkerton's chair in the library was a constant source
of annoyance; Charlotte was sick of Miss Pinkerton's chair
—which of course was not really hers at all except by long
usage—

"I don't suppose she knew it was your chair," said
Charlotte tactfully.

"Miss Margetson should have told her . . . but perhaps
if you were just to give her a hint. I've been here fourteen
years, so I think I'm entitled to a *little* consideration."

"Yes, of course," agreed Charlotte.

"Well, that's all, really," said Miss Pinkerton rising. "If
you could just give her a hint. Oh, where did *that* come
from?"

"What? Oh, the Buddha! He's nice, isn't he?" said
Charlotte looking at him affectionately.

Miss Pinkerton had taken the figure in her hands and was
examining it with interest. She was myopic so she had
removed her spectacles. "Beautiful!" declared Miss Pinkerton. "A representation of the Buddhist Priest in Contemplation."

"Is it real porcelain?" asked Charlotte.

"Undoubtedly," replied Miss Pinkerton. "If it were
pottery it would be a good deal heavier. I should put it as
belonging to the Ming Dynastic period—probably about
the sixteenth century. The beautiful glaze and the clear
Mohammedan blue of the robes are characteristic of the
ceramics of that period. I may be wrong, of course; you
probably know all about it," She put the Buddhist Priest
back upon the mantelpiece as she spoke.

"I don't know anything about it," said Charlotte smiling.

"You don't know anything about it!" echoed Miss Pinkerton in horrified tones. "But what an extraordinary thing to say! Fancy owning a beautiful thing like that and knowing nothing about it."

"I meant to find out," said Charlotte apologetically. "As a matter of fact I haven't had it long. I bought it the other day in a funny little shop in London."

"You bought it!" cried Miss Pinkerton. "You must be a rich woman if you can afford to buy a thing like that! And it isn't as if you appreciated it, or collected Chinese porcelain. You just bought it for a whim!"

Charlotte was somewhat taken aback. It was true that she knew very little—practically nothing—about Chinese porcelain, but she felt that she did appreciate her Buddha (or her Buddhist Priest in Contemplation, if that was what he was). She appreciated him for himself. "I liked him," said Charlotte, beginning to explain. "And he wasn't very expensive—"

"Oh, wasn't he?" interrupted Miss Pinkerton with a sneer. "He wasn't very expensive! You wouldn't get a specimen like that for nothing. It's a collector's piece. Of course it doesn't matter to *me*," she added bitterly. "It's none of *my* business how you spend your money."

"No, it isn't," agreed Charlotte gravely. "But as a matter of fact I was just going to tell you I only paid——"

"I don't want to hear!" cried Miss Pinkerton, in sudden rage. "What do I care how much you paid! It's easy for you! You sit here drawing a nice fat salary so of course you can afford to indulge your whims. It isn't fair! You've no business to be here at all! If it hadn't been for you——"

"Miss Pinkerton!" exclaimed Charlotte, trying to stem the tide.

"I can't bear it! I think of it all the time! Miss Bain said I was certain to get the post—I had been here for twelve years—and I would have got it if it hadn't been for you! "

"Please stop! Please . . . "

"I shan't stop—it's true, every word of it, and you know it as well as I do. What right had you—an outsider—a mere girl—to apply for a post like this? And how did you manage to get it? By influence—that's all! By some sort of hanky-panky with the Board of Governors! "

Charlotte was silent.

"Oh, I know I shouldn't have said it," declared Miss Pinkerton gasping with fury. "I should have gone on bottling it up; but I've bottled it up for two whole years—watching you throwing your weight about and everyone bowing and scraping to you as if you were a queen! Well, I've finished now. You know what I think of you. Of course I shall have to go. I shall have to leave Saint Elizabeth's."

For a moment Charlotte hesitated and then she said quietly, "You needn't leave Saint Elizabeth's if you don't want to. We'll forget about this if you like—we'll wash it out completely—but I think it would be much better for you to find a post elsewhere. You would be happier, wouldn't you? Don't let's say any more to-night (we're both tired) but think it over and decide——"

"I'll go! " cried Miss Pinkerton wildly. "Oh yes, I'll go! You've always wanted to get rid of me, haven't you? I'd have left long ago if it hadn't been for Miss Bain. She said ' wait and see'. She was sure you'd make a hash of it. Well, now you're going to get rid of me—you've got what you wanted. You're one of those people who always get what they want! "

The door banged behind Miss Pinkerton's retreating back and Charlotte was alone. She found herself trembling all over. It was horrible to be hated. It was frightening. For two whole years Miss Pinkerton had been full of hatred and resentment. Poor Miss Pinkerton! She must go, of course, there was nothing else for it. Miss Pinkerton had said unforgiveable, unforgettable words (words that nobody else in Charlotte's position would have been willing to overlook) but Charlotte had always felt a little guilty about Miss Pinkerton and that was why she had been willing to " wash it out ".

Charlotte sighed and decided that she really must go to bed. As she rose from her chair her eyes fell upon her Buddha—sitting upon her mantelpiece in contemplation— and she remembered what Miss Pinkerton had said: a collector's piece . . . of the Ming Dynastic period . . . you must be a rich woman! Charlotte looked at him with new eyes and realised that he really was very beautiful indeed, in a hideous sort of way, and that it was quite astounding that she could have bought him for five pounds. There must have been some mistake. Of course he had been dirty, his glory hidden beneath a cloak of grime. Charlotte had cleaned him carefully in soapy water with a paint brush and as the dirt came off she had been charmed with the glowing colour of his robes . . . but somehow it had never crossed her mind that the price she had paid was inadequate.

The truth was that once she had bought her Buddha she had thought no more about the price. Now that she thought about it she remembered that the young man had turned the Buddha upside down and discovered the price marked upon his base. She took him off the mantelpiece and looked for herself but the mark had been washed off and practically obliterated. What ought she to do? She was now perfectly certain that the young man had made a mistake—it had been dark in the little shop—yes, he had made a mistake and the only thing to do was to return the Buddha and explain what had happened. I had better write at once, thought Charlotte . . . and then she realised that she could not write because she had not the slightest idea what the shop was called nor did she know the name of the street in which it was situated. She would have to go to London and find it.

The Buddha sat and looked at her complacently. He did not care.

* 3 *

THE BEGINNING of Term was always a very busy time for
Charlotte (it was impossible for her to leave Saint
Elizabeth's for a whole day), so the matter of the
Buddha must needs wait until things settled down. Mean-
while he sat upon the mantelpiece in his gorgeous robes and
reflected upon the foolishness of mankind—or of woman-
kind, perhaps. Charlotte often looked at him but her pleasure
in his companionship was clouded. The young man would
get into trouble when the owner of the shop returned and
discovered what he had done (and Charlotte had liked the
young man) and the young man would not know she was
coming back to put things right. What a bore it was! In
addition to this Charlotte had become so attached to the
Buddha that she hated the idea of parting with him. Of
course she need not part with him; she could pay the price
—unless it was beyond her means. What would be a fair
price, Charlotte wondered. Miss Pinkerton might know, but
it was impossible to ask her, and Charlotte did not know
anybody else to ask.

Charlotte wished she had never seen the Buddha—he was
a thorn in her flesh—but this was a little unfair for the
Buddha had done her a good turn. It was he who had goaded
Miss Pinkerton into unwise speech and forced her to send in
her resignation. No more had been said about the midnight
talk which had ended so disastrously but Charlotte had been

27

informed by the Board of Governors that a letter of resignation had been received from Miss Pinkerton; the matter was
on the agenda of the next meeting.

These things worried Charlotte, but only off and on, for
she had so much to do, and so many things to arrange that
there was little time for thought.

The new girls (there were twenty of them) were much the
same as usual. Charlotte, as usual, saw each of them
separately and talked to them about their homes and about
the school. It was difficult to make much headway with
them for they were shy and tongue-tied in the Presence—
or occasionally, if their nerves betrayed them, regrettably
pert—but Charlotte remembered her own feelings in the
same circumstances and was able to make allowances for
them. There was one new girl, however, for whom no
allowances had to be made. Tessa MacRynne was friendly
and pleasant and quite obviously enjoyed her chat with her
headmistress. Tessa's father was a Highland Laird and her
mother was an American. Perhaps that odd mixture of old
and new accounted for her poise.

Mrs. MacRynne had brought Tessa to Saint Elizabeth's
on the first day of term and had asked for an interview with
Miss Fairlie. They had had a very pleasant talk. Mrs.
MacRynne was beautiful to look at, with a pale creamy
complexion, dark eyes and raven-black hair. She had
elegance and grace and a natural charm of manner which
was all the more delightful because it was unexpected. For
some reason or other very few parents displayed charming
manners when they were interviewing the headmistress of
Saint Elizabeth's; they were usually too anxious to tell
Miss Fairlie all about Rosemary or Sylvia or Joan and to
make sure that Miss Fairlie understood how fortunate
Saint Elizabeth's was in having such a very unusual and
interesting young lady amongst its pupils.

Mrs. MacRynne had quite a different approach, she seemed interested in Miss Fairlie, and as she was going away she said in her charming voice with the very slight American accent, "Would it be any good asking you to come and have dinner with me in the hotel, Miss Fairlie? It would give me very great pleasure if you could manage it."

Charlotte could not accept, it was impossible for her to go out to dinner on the first day of term, but she liked being asked. "Perhaps some other time when you come to see Tessa," she suggested.

She had expected Mrs. MacRynne to agree to this vague arrangement but Mrs. MacRynne did not. She hesitated and then said, "I was afraid it was pretty hopeless but it was worth trying. You never get much in this world unless you go out and try for it, Miss Fairlie."

Charlotte smiled and agreed. Mrs. MacRynne looked as if she usually got what she wanted. "I'd come if I possibly could," added Charlotte.

"I know that," nodded her visitor. "You've got to stay put. I'm not the only mother who wants to talk to you." She hesitated again—as if she wanted to say more—and then held out her hand. "I've taken up more than my fair share of your time. Good-bye, Miss Fairlie. I'm glad you're you. Tessa will need a good friend."

Charlotte was slightly puzzled by this odd little speech but she decided it did not mean much. All mothers expected the headmistress of Saint Elizabeth's to be a good friend to their daughters.

Mrs. MacRynne had interested Charlotte so she was interested to see the daughter. Tessa was not beautiful, but she was attractive. She was rather small for her age but slim and straight with swift graceful movements. Her face was thin and brown; her mouth was rather large; her hazel eyes were lively and intelligent. She had dark brown hair with reddish lights in it, and it curled naturally about her ears. Very attractive indeed, thought Charlotte, looking at her approvingly.

"Sit down, Tessa," said Charlotte smiling at her new pupil.

Tessa sat down at once and smiled back in an engaging manner.

"I hope you'll be happy here," said Charlotte.

"I expect I'll be a bit homesick at first," replied Tessa frankly. "You see I've never been away from Targ before except for holidays. It's all so different. There are so many girls for one thing, and I'm not used to girls."

"Not used to girls?"

"No," said Tessa shaking her head. "There are no girls at Targ. I had a governess."

"You're very fond of Targ?"

"I adore it. Anybody would adore it. Targ is the most beautiful place in the world."

"It's an island, isn't it?"

"Yes, it's an island off the west coast of Scotland. You have to cross the sound in a boat. There's a village on the island and the old castle where we live. Sometimes in the winter we're cut off from the mainland for days on end but we're practically self-supporting so it doesn't matter much —in fact it's rather fun——" She stopped and smiled apologetically. "But I don't suppose you're interested," she added.

"Of course I'm interested," said Charlotte, "Some day, when we've more time, you must tell me all about Targ. I want to talk to you about Saint Elizabeth's to-day."

"About lessons, I suppose," agreed Tessa. "I'm backward in some subjects but I'm fairly intelligent so I expect I shall catch up. You see, there were always so many interesting things to do at home that lessons used to get shelved. Daddy used to come into the schoolroom and tell us to shut up the books and go for a picnic," said Tessa with a mischievous grin. "So of course we did."

"You will have to work hard here——" began Charlotte, somewhat shocked.

"Oh, rather," agreed Tessa. "But everybody else will be having lessons so it will be quite easy."

The term was a fortnight old before Charlotte could make a free day for her expedition. She drove to Larchester in her little car and leaving it in the garage near the station took the ten o'clock train to London. Her plan was to retrace her steps, starting from her lawyer's office in the City. After some difficulty she found a maze of little old-fashioned streets with tiny shops and began her search. Unfortunately it was not as easy as she had expected; there were quite a lot of junk-shops in the district, sandwiched between tiny restaurants and even smaller tobacconists and draper's stores, but none of them seemed right. As a matter of fact she had forgotten what the place looked like. She had a vague idea that there had been a large round brass tray in the window, but that did not help much; the tray might have been sold. For two solid hours Charlotte walked up one street and down another searching for the shop where she had bought the Buddha and becoming more and more muddled and doubtful, and more and more tired. At last in despair she stopped a young policeman and explained her predicament.

"You mean you paid too little for the ornament?" he asked incredulously.

"Much too little."

"Well, that's a funny one!" he exclaimed. "We often get complaints from people that have been done—paid too much, I mean—but you're the first to complain you've paid too little."

"It was a mistake," Charlotte said.

"Look here, miss, are you sure? These junk-shop owners are pretty spry."

"The owner was away and there was a young man in charge of the shop."

The policeman looked perplexed. "What do you want me to *do* exactly?" he inquired.

"I thought you might ask."

"Ask what? Go about asking if someone sold an ornament for less than it's worth? Why, you'd get a dozen junk merchants clamouring round before you knew where you were! You'd land yourself in a fine old mess."

"Well, what do you sugggest?"

"Keep it and say nothing," he replied, smiling down at her.

"But it's worrying me."

"I shouldn't worry, miss. Honestly I don't see what we can do. Of course I *could* go round some of the junk shops and make inquiries, but I wouldn't know if I found the right one. You mightn't know the right one yourself."

"I think I would," said Charlotte, but she said it doubtfully and the policeman was not impressed.

"Forget it, miss," he said, shutting up his book in which he had begun to take notes. "That's my advice. You don't know the name of the shop and you don't know where it is—seems pretty hopeless to me. If it's any comfort you can be sure he'd have done you if he could; there are no flies on these junk merchants, I can tell you."

Charlotte was not satisfied but she could do no more.

4

THE MEETING of the Board of Governors was on the following Wednesday afternoon and Charlotte had been summoned to attend. It was a beautiful day, bright and sunny with a slight nip in the air; the trees were golden and red with Autumn colours and amongst them stood hawthorn bushes, clad in brilliant scarlet berries and elder-trees heavy with their purple fruit. Charlotte had been tethered to her office chair, dealing with business letters, so she was delighted to be out in the fresh air. She was not looking forward to the meeting but the drive to Larchester was most enjoyable.

Saint Elizabeth's was four miles from Larchester; the school was situated upon a ridge of hills and the town lay in the valley upon the banks of the river. The road was hilly for the most part; it wound its way through woods and past little farms. When it reached the Thornbush Inn it tilted suddenly into the valley and Larchester lay spread before one's eyes. Charlotte loved this view and if she had time she always stopped at the inn or a little beyond it. Fortunately she had plenty of time to-day so she stopped and switched off her engine and looked her fill.

The town lay snugly on the banks of the river and the river flowed into the distance between green meadows full of contented cows. It was very quiet and peaceful, but it had not always been peaceful. Larchester was an ancient

Roman fortress and its narrow streets were still encircled by a wall. Within the wall was the Old Town with its Cathedral, its shops and queer old-fashioned houses; outside the wall there were pleasant modern houses—some large, some small—with gardens and trees.

From the Thornbush Inn it was easy to see the plan of the town, to follow the winding of the encircling wall which was built of stone and was as strong and solid as the day it was finished. Along the top of the wall there was a wide pathway with buttresses and bastions. The citizens of Larchester used this as a pleasant walk on Sunday afternoons. There was a splendid view of the surrounding country from this path and for those who were more interested in people than in landscapes there were splendid views of their neigh-bours' houses and gardens.

The striking of the town-clock, borne faintly upon the breeze, warned Charlotte of the time so she drove on into Larchester and made her way to the Town Hall where the meeting was to take place. In spite of her delay she was early and the only person present was Mr. Swayne who was walking about the board-room examining the pictures of dead and gone mayors which decorated the walls.

"Hallo, Miss Fairlie," he said. "Come and look at them. Aren't they beauties?"

"Not exactly beauties," said Charlotte laughing. "But I must say I like the one with the whiskers."

"Do you admire whiskers?" inquired Mr. Swayne, strok-ing his shaven cheeks in a reflective manner.

"Passionately," declared Charlotte.

"I prefer a beard—in fact I'm thinking of growing one in the Christmas holidays. It would give one confidence and authority and it would impress parents. Are your parents absolutely unbearable, Miss Fairlie?"

Charlotte was aware that Mr. Swayne was not inquiring

about her own progenitors but about those of the girls. "They are a little troublesome sometimes," she admitted cautiously.

"Mine are absolutely unbearable," declared Mr. Swayne. "I wish to goodness all my boys were orphans. It would be rather fun to have a school for orphans only. Think what a free hand you would have!"

"But what about the holidays?" asked Charlotte.

Mr. Swayne nodded. "I see your point," he said gravely. "Yes, you've got something there. A school for orphans is out of the question, you'd never get rid of the little brutes."

This interesting if somewhat fruitless conversation was interrupted by the arrival of the other members of the Board and everyone sat down at the table. As usual Sir Joseph Spinner was in the chair.

The first few items on the agenda were matters of routine; there was an apology from Mr. Cowper for his inability to attend (but he was not much loss) and the minutes of the last meeting were read by the secretary and approved. Charlotte did not pay much attention; she was worrying about the third item on the agenda, the matter of Miss Pinkerton's resignation, for she had no idea what Miss Pinkerton had said in her letter nor what reason Miss Pinkerton had given for her decision to resign.

Fortunately Miss Pinkerton had been discreet; her letter, which was read out by the secretary, merely stated that she had been at Saint Elizabeth's for fourteen years and would like a change. She would look for a post which would give her more scope. She had always done her work to the best of her ability and hoped the Board of Governors would give her a testimonial. She added that she was in no hurry to leave and was willing to stay on at Saint Elizabeth's to the end of the scholastic year if the Board considered it advisable.

"This is a *disaster*," declared Mr. Allnut. "There is no other word for it. I cannot think why Miss Pinkerton should want to leave."

"More scope?" said Mr. Renfrew. "What does she mean by that, I wonder?"

They all looked at Charlotte, but Charlotte remained silent.

"There are as good fish in the sea——" began Sir Joseph.

"Not in this case," interrupted Mr. Allnut. "I happen to know that Miss Bain thinks *very* highly of Miss Pinkerton's abilities."

"Miss Bain is a back number," said Mr. Swayne.

"Miss Bain has the welfare of the school at heart." said Mr. Allnut.

"So have we all," retorted Mr. Swayne.

"Oh, of course," agreed Mr. Renfrew.

"Miss Pinkerton is a woman of high principles," declared Mr. Allnut. "I feel she has a stabilising influence."

"Stabilising?" inquired Sir Joseph, raising his eyebrows. "What do you mean by that, exactly?"

"Exactly what I say," replied Mr. Allnut crossly. "In my opinion it is essential to have a woman of experience at Saint Elizabeth's."

They all knew what he meant of course. Mr. Allnut had never made any secret of the fact that he considered the present headmistress too young.

"There's something in that," said Mr. Wise doubtfully. "Perhaps Miss Pinkerton might reconsider her decision ..."

"If she were given more scope," suggested Mr. Renfrew looking at Miss Fairlie.

Miss Fairlie said nothing.

"What does she mean by more scope?" asked Mr. Wise looking round the table.

Nobody seemed able to reply to this question.

"We could raise her salary of course," suggested Mr. Walpole.

"I don't think that alone would tempt her," said Mr. Allnut.

"It would tempt most people," remarked Mr. Walpole with a little chuckle. "But the point is, do we want her to stay on? What do you think about it, Miss Fairlie?"

"I have no fault to find with her work," said Miss Fairlie primly.

"I think that would be a frightful mistake," declared Mr. Swayne. "It's always a mistake to crawl to people and ask them to stay on. They think they're indispensable if you do that. I know it only too well from my own experience. Not very long ago one of my masters said he wanted to resign and I asked him to stay on and raised his screw and he agreed, making a favour of it. The consequence was he got too big for his boots and eventually I had to sack him. It was all very unpleasant and I made up my mind I'd never do it again. If people want to go let them—that's what I say."

The Board had listened to this interesting little sidelight upon the inner working of Bells Hill School with attention. Some of the members seemed impressed, but Mr. Allnut was not.

"This is quite a different matter," said Mr. Allnut. "Miss Pinkerton is extremely conscientious. She would never dream of—er—taking advantage——"

"She wants more scope," said Mr. Renfrew for the second time—or was it the third? He added, "Might we ask exactly what scope she has at present, Miss Fairlie?"

"Of course," said Miss Fairlie readily. "At present Miss Pinkerton has a completely free hand in her own department. She is the senior mistress in mathematics. She arranges her own classes and her wishes are consulted when a junior mistress is engaged."

"That seems fair enough," nodded Mr. Walpole. "What more does she want?"

Mr. Allnut seemed to know; he said, "I think she would like to be consulted about matters of school policy and to have her position as senior mistress properly recognised. I think she would welcome a little more responsibility."

"Would that be possible, Miss Fairlie?" asked Mr. Wise.

"Quite possible," replied Miss Fairlie. "I am at Saint Elizabeth's to carry out your wishes. But I should like Miss Pinkerton's position and duties to be clearly defined. Perhaps the Board will discuss the matter and let me know exactly what responsibilities Miss Pinkerton should be given." She looked round the table with a pleasant smile and waited.

The Board of Governors was silent.

"Well, as a matter of fact," said Mr. Allnut at last. "There is one thing . . . I happen to know that Miss Pinkerton would appreciate the opportunity to take prayers occasionally. Saint Elizabeth's opens the morning session with prayer and a short reading from the Bible—an admirable practice. In Miss Bain's time Miss Pinkerton conducted the little service. I feel sure that this would mean a great deal to her and——"

"Oh, no!" exclaimed Charlotte impulsively. "I'm sorry, but I couldn't—it means a great deal to me—it's important——"

"When I was in the Navy," said Mr. Walpole. "It was in the First War, of course, the captain of the ship always took prayers."

"That's right," nodded Sir Joseph. "The captain of the ship takes prayers."

"Oh well—er——" said Mr. Allnut rather uncomfortably. "Perhaps some other duty could be allotted to Miss Pinkerton. There is no need for us to define—I mean I feel sure we can leave it to Miss Fairlie."

"I should prefer something definite," Miss Fairlie declared.

"But how can we say anything definite?" asked Mr. Wise.

"Miss Fairlie is right" declared Sir Joseph in a judicial manner. "The Board must define exactly what duties Miss Pinkerton is to be given or else leave the whole affair to Miss Fairlie. It must be either one thing or another."

"I don't see how we can define her duties," grumbled Mr. Wise.

"Aren't we wasting our time discussing it?" inquired Mr. Walpole. "I mean we haven't asked Miss Pinkerton whether or not she would be willing to stay on."

"She won't unless you give her more scope," said Mr. Renfrew. "We've got to decide what inducement we can offer Miss Pinkerton. Haven't we?"

"We've got to decide whether we want her to stay on." said Mr. Swayne. "That's the first thing to decide."

"I thought we had agreed upon that," said Mr. Renfrew.

"We haven't agreed upon anything," Sir Joseph told him.

"I propose that Miss Pinkerton should be asked to stay on," said Mr. Allnut hastily.

"I second the proposal," said Mr. Renfrew.

"Is there any amendment?" inquired Sir Joseph.

"Yes," said Mr. Swayne. "I propose an amendment that Miss Pinkerton's resignation be accepted but that in view of her long service she should be given a—well, a sort of bonus or something—and, subject to Miss Fairlie's approval, a good—er—testimonial."

"I second the amendment," said Mr. Walpole. "We can easily find someone else——"

"Not as easily as you think," said Mr. Allnut.

Everybody began to talk at once and Sir Joseph was obliged to call the meeting to order. He rapped the table and

announced that he would take a show of hands. "First for
the amendment," said Sir Joseph. "That Miss Pinkerton's
resignation be accepted and that she shall be given a bonus
and a testimonial."

Mr. Swayne and Mr. Walpole held up their hands.

Mr. Allnut and Mr. Renfrew voted for the proposal of
course; Mr. Wise abstained from voting. It was left for
Sir Joseph to give the casting vote; he voted in favour of
the amendment. The secretary was instructed to write to
Miss Pinkerton accepting her resignation with regret and
acquainting her with the Board of Governors' decision.

"She says she will stay on until the end of the scholastic
year," said Mr. Renfrew. "We ought to thank her for that.
It will give us more time to look about and find somebody
else."

"Thank her by all means," agreed Mr. Walpole.

Charlotte was not too pleased at the idea of having to bear
Miss Pinkerton until the end of the Summer Term—it would
be most unpleasant—but she could do nothing about it so
she held her peace and the Board heaved sighs of relief and
moved on to the next item on the agenda.

The meeting was over and Charlotte was getting into
her car when Mr. Swayne came up to speak to her.

"What a lot of talk about nothing!" he said. "Fortunately
I have a keen sense of humour so I get some fun out of it,
otherwise it would be a complete waste of time. Come and
have a cup of tea, Miss Fairlie."

This seemed a good idea so they went into the Golden
Hind Hotel and sat down in the lounge together. Charlotte's
head was aching—it had been stuffy in the Board-Room—
so she took off her hat and put it beside her on a chair. Her
golden-brown hair was a little untidy, it curled on her
forehead and round her ears . .

"Why do you wear that awful hat?" asked Mr. Swayne.
"Is it awful?"

"It's frightful! Where on earth did you get it?"

Charlotte did not answer. Tea had appeared and she was busy pouring it out, but she could not help smiling to herself. As a matter of fact she had got it at a Jumble Sale for sixpence. It had been left over at the end of the sale and the harassed stall-keeper had been only too glad to get rid of it. Charlotte glanced at the hat, lying beside her on the sofa. It was a particularly ugly shade of brown, large and floppy and trimmed with brown petersham ribbon. Yes, it certainly was rather awful.

"You look ten years younger without it," added Mr. Swayne.

Charlotte knew this already. "Do you take sugar?" she inquired.

"Two lumps," he replied, "and lots of milk."

There was a short silence.

"It's a good thing you're getting rid of Miss Pinkerton," said Mr. Swayne at last. "A woman like that can create hell."

"Do you know her?" asked Charlotte in surprise.

"Lord, no! But I knew she must be a wart when you said you were perfectly satisfied with her work. It's an absolutely damning thing to say about anyone. Somehow I just seemed to *see* the woman . . . with spectacles and a thin pointed nose and a tongue like a serpent. Am I right?"

"You aren't far out," said Charlotte smiling. "Anyhow I'm very glad she's going and very grateful to you for what you said."

"Think no more of it," said Mr. Swayne cheerfully.

"But I do think of it," Charlotte declared. "If it hadn't been for you——"

"Oh, that's rot!" interrupted Mr. Swayne. "You'd have got rid of the woman without me raising a finger. You've got Sir Joseph eating out of your hand. I like Sir Joseph— he's worth all the rest of them put together. He doesn't say very much but he manages everybody and always gets his own way."

"It's a good way," said Charlotte, sticking up for him.

"Usually," agreed Mr. Swayne.

They were silent for a few minutes but it was a companionable silence; they were both tired and it was pleasant to relax in a comfortable chair, to drink tea and smoke cigarettes.

"How would you like a maths master?" asked Mr. Swayne suddenly. "I know a fellow who wants a job. He's pretty good."

"No, definitely not," replied Charlotte. "I have enough trouble already without a man to complicate things—unless he's over seventy, of course."

"He's twenty-seven," said Mr. Swayne laughing.

"Then it's no," said Charlotte firmly.

They had finished tea by this time and Charlotte began to put on her gloves.

"Oh, I say, don't go yet!" exclaimed Mr. Swayne viewing the process in dismay. "We've only just begun to talk. Do stay a bit longer."

"I've got a lot of work waiting for me, and I expect you have too," replied Charlotte, rising.

"There's always lots of work," agreed Mr. Swayne. "It gets worse and worse but I suppose one shouldn't grumble."

He looked at his watch and added, "Yes, I'll have to get back, worse luck! Professor Eastwood is coming to see me about his boys. He isn't satisfied with their progress—well, neither am I, really, but I can't make silk purses out of nit-wits, and neither of them ever does a stroke of work.

By the way he has a daughter at Saint Elizabeth's, hasn't he?"

"Yes," said Charlotte. She thought of Dione Eastwood as she spoke. Dione was a dreamy creature—not exactly a nit-wit, but so inattentive that she sometimes appeared so. It seemed odd that a clever man, like Professor Eastwood, should have three unusually stupid children.

"So the professor is your parent too!" exclaimed Mr. Swayne. "That makes us brother and sister, doesn't it? Tell me, Miss Fairlie, how do you get on with our father?"

"I never discuss my parents," replied Charlotte hiding a smile.

"What a pity! It would have been so interesting," said Mr. Swayne sadly.

"I have to be discreet," Charlotte told him. "It's different for you. I mean Bells Hill belongs to you, so you're your own master and can do and say what you like, whereas I'm the servant of the Board of Governors. Good-bye, Mr. Swayne, thank you for the tea . . . and for everything."

"Good-bye," said Mr. Swayne. "And be sure to give my love to Miss Pinkerton."

5

CHARLOTTE THOUGHT about Mr. Swayne as she drove home. She liked him; he was natural and friendly and very amusing—if somewhat indiscreet. It was a pity they could not meet sometimes and chat, for of course they had a good deal in common. As a matter of fact Mr. Swayne had suggested another meeting but Charlotte had refused. To have a cup of tea together was one thing but to make a habit of meeting him was another. Larchester was a gossipy little place.

She had reached the Thornbush Inn by this time so she stopped and looked back. It was getting dark and lights were springing up all over the town—here there and everywhere—some of them were reflected in the river. The sky was cloudless, it was pale green in colour and looked translucent, like glass. Even as she looked the light faded; objects which, a moment ago, had been clearly visible became indistinguishable, other objects seemed to take a different shape. There was something unreal about the twilight, it was like a scene in the theatre when the lights are gradually dimmed.

Suddenly Charlotte heard footsteps coming along the road; she switched on her headlights and immediately a small figure dodged into the shadow of the trees . . . but Charlotte's eye had caught sight of a maroon hat!

It was possible that she was mistaken of course. Other

people besides Saint Elizabeth girls sometimes wore hats of that colour . . . but Charlotte felt pretty certain that she was not mistaken. Here, on the main road to Larchester, was one of her girls where one of her girls had no right to be.

There was no time to be lost; Charlotte leapt out of the car and dived into the shadow of the trees. The girl—for certainly it was a girl—climbed a fence and sped across a field; Charlotte followed and after a short sharp chase she managed to corner the fugitive in the angle of a hedge, which was impenetrable to everything except a rabbit.

Charlotte, who was somewhat breathless, seized the girl by the arm and held her firmly. " What are—you doing? " she gasped . . . and then, looking more closely at her captive, she saw that it was Tessa MacRynne. " Tessa—it's you! " she exclaimed in dismay.

" Yes, it's me," said Tessa. " I'm going home."

" But you can't go home! "

" You can't stop me going home, Miss Fairlie."

" I have stopped you," declared Charlotte, tightening her grip. " Oh, Tessa, I thought you were sensible! " She was really disappointed and the sincerity of her voice seemed to get through to the child and melt her defiance.

" I'm sorry," said Tessa in quite a different tone. " Truly I'm sorry—but I must go home to Targ."

" But you haven't given it a trial! Lots of girls are homesick at first. You must be brave."

" You don't understand! It isn't because I'm homesick."

" What is it, then? "

" It's just—just that I must go home. I'm sorry I had to run away. I thought of coming and telling you, but I was afraid you wouldn't let me go."

" I can't let you."

" But you must! " cried Tessa in agonised tones, " You must let me go! I'm not a prisoner! "

"Tessa, be sensible!"

"I *am* being sensible. Please let me go, Miss Fairlie."

"Listen, Tessa," said Charlotte quietly. "Your parents have put you in my charge and until they tell me that they are removing you from my charge it's my duty to keep you at Saint Elizabeth's."

Tessa had begun to sob.

"You aren't feeling ill, are you?" asked Charlotte anxiously.

"No—yes I am," sobbed Tessa. "I mean I've got a frightful headache but that doesn't matter."

"Come," said Charlotte. She took the child's hand, just in case there was another attempt at escape (though as a matter of fact she did not think there would be) and together they walked back across the field to the road. The car was standing there with its headlights on, and Mrs. Spurling who was the wife of the innkeeper, was standing beside it.

"Oh, it's you, Miss Fairlie!" she exclaimed. "I wondered who 'ad left their car 'ere with the lights on."

Charlotte answered at random. Her one idea was to get rid of the woman as quickly as possible and take Tessa back to Saint Elizabeth's. Perhaps by this time her absence had been discovered and she was being sought for high and low, but there was just a chance that nobody had noticed her absence.

She pushed Tessa into the car and got in herself. "Yes, Mrs. Spurling," she said vaguely. "It was silly of me to leave the lights on, but I was in a hurry. I must get back to the school. I'll see you again soon, I expect. Good-bye."

Tessa had controlled her sobs and was sitting beside her quietly.

"You must tell me about it and then I shall understand," said Charlotte as she let in the clutch and drove off.

"But I don't think I *can* tell you," said Tessa in a choked voice. "It's so dreadful—everything has gone wrong—frightfully horribly wrong——"

"Somebody is ill?"

"Not ill—it's Mummy—she's going away! But she can't—she can't go away! Mummy belongs to us—she belongs to Targ—she *can't* go away and never come back any more!"

Charlotte found the cold little hand and gave it a reassuring squeeze. "I understand now," she said. "We'll talk about it presently; the first thing is to get back to school before you're missed."

It was pitch dark when they reached Saint Elizabeth's so it was not difficult to avoid observation. Charlotte took the child to her private sitting-room and left her there while she made some necessary arrangements. She hurried to the classroom (where Tessa should have been) and found Miss Pinkerton in charge. The girls were doing prep. and Miss Pinkerton was knitting. Charlotte explained briefly that Tessa MacRynne had a bad headache and was being sent to the sick-room to rest.

"Oh, isn't she here?" asked Miss Pinkerton, looking round in surprise.

There was no need to answer this purely rhetorical question and Charlotte retired before Miss Pinkerton had time to collect her wits and ask any other questions which might have been more awkward. Having made sure that all was well Charlotte felt more comfortable; she found one of the maids in the corridor and sent her with a message to Sister Ferguson warning her to expect a patient. Then she returned to Tessa.

Tessa had been crying bitterly; she was huddled in a little heap in the corner of the sofa. Her face was blotched with tears and her eyes were red and swollen; she looked the picture of misery.

"Now," said Charlotte, sitting down beside her and taking

her hand. "Now then, supposing you tell me the whole thing? Stop crying—there's a dear! Look, here's a nice clean handkerchief. Tell me when you heard about it."

"It was a letter—yesterday—" said Tessa, taking the handkerchief and drying her eyes. "I didn't sleep all night. I must go home—I must! Here's the letter, Miss Fairlie." She produced a crumpled letter from her pocket.

"Do you want me to read it? Are you sure it isn't private?"

"Well, perhaps it is," said Tessa miserably. "I don't know really whether it's private or not. Anyway it doesn't say much. It's from Mummy and she just says she's going back to America and there will be a divorce. She says Daddy understands and she hopes I'll understand too . . . and she says she still loves me and someday she'll come and see me and I'm not to worry about it. Not to worry! " said Tessa, her tears beginning to flow again. "Not to worry! "

Charlotte put her arms round the thin shoulders and Tessa yielded to the embrace. "You *are* kind," she sobbed. "I know I'm being a baby but I can't help it. Think of Daddy! Oh, Miss Fairlie, I must go home! "

"What good could you do? "

"I could persuade her—not to go——"

"But she wouldn't listen, would she? This can't be a sudden idea, you know. They must have talked it over and made up their minds. It would only complicate things if you went home. Nothing you could do or say would make any difference."

Tessa was quiet for a few moments. At last she said, "Do you think they sent me here to be out of the way? "

Charlotte was sure of it. She remembered her talk with Mrs. MacRynne and became even more certain. She felt very angry with Mrs. MacRynne. No wonder Mrs. MacRynne had said that her daughter would need a good friend; (but she might have warned me, thought Charlotte.

If only she had warned me instead of speaking in riddles . . .)

"Do you think so?" asked Tessa. "Do you think they sent me away on purpose?"

"Darling," said Charlotte, running her hand through the tangled hair. "Darling Tessa, we don't know, do we? It's no good thinking about it——"

"Nothing is any good."

It was difficult to know what to say but at least she could listen and after a little prompting and a few leading questions the flood-gates were opened and the whole story came rushing out. Charlotte, piecing the bits together and filling in the background, began to get a clear picture of the MacRynne family and its problems. Colonel MacRynne loved his island home and was perfectly contented to look after his farms and his people; to go out on the moors and shoot, or to fish in the river; but Mrs. MacRynne was not so happy at Targ; she liked gaiety and the companionship of her kind. There were two aunts, sisters of the Colonel's father, who had made their home at Targ and had their own suite of rooms in the east wing of the castle; there was Mrs. Fraser the cook, who had been at Targ all her life and was almost one of the family, and there was Euan who was a foster-brother of the Colonel's and looked after the yacht and did anything else that needed to be done.

"We were all so happy," explained Tessa. "Targ was so—so complete. Daddy never wants to leave Targ. We went to Edinburgh one winter for a few months because Mummy wanted to, but it was very expensive and Daddy was miserable—so after that Mummy always went for holidays by herself. Sometimes she went to Paris or to Rome and one year she went to Cyprus. We got on all right without her but it was lovely when she came home—and she liked coming home, I know she did—and now she's never coming home any more! Oh, I love Mummy!" declared Tessa with a sob of despair. "I love Mummy—and I love Daddy—and I love Targ. I want things to go on just as they are."

What was there to say? Charlotte had no idea how to comfort Tessa.

"Think of Daddy!" cried Tessa. "Oh, poor Daddy, he'll be so miserable! He'll be so—so ashamed—I know he will! He'll be so lonely. There'll be nobody to cheer him up —not even me. Don't you think I ought to go home, Miss Fairlie?"

"Why not write and ask him——" began Charlotte.

"I've tried to write," declared Tessa. "I tried to write to Daddy this morning but I didn't know what to say, so then I thought the only thing to do was to go home."

"Shall I write to him?"

"Oh yes!" cried Tessa. "Oh yes, that would be splendid. Write and tell him I want to come home—or if I can't come home that he must come to Saint Elizabeth's. I must see Daddy. I must talk to him! Oh please write at once and tell him."

Charlotte regretted her offer the moment she had made it, but she saw that she could not withdraw it now. "Very well," she said, " I'll write to him and tell him how you feel; then, if he wants you to go home he has only got to say so." She rose and took Tessa's hand. "Come along," she added. "You're going into the sick-room to-night."

"The sick-room!"

"Yes, it's all arranged. You must never tell anyone that you tried to run away."

"Do you mean nobody knows?" asked Tessa incredulously.

"Nobody knows and nobody will ever know. You must promise me faithfully that you will never tell anybody."

"Oh, yes," said Tessa, "I promise. I don't want anybody to know."

"That's right then," nodded Charlotte. "It's a secret

between you and me. Come along, Tessa, it's time you were in bed."

Tessa was calmer now; her head was almost bursting and there was a queer lassitude in her limbs, but she had stopped crying. She followed Miss Fairlie along the corridor to the sick-room and stood there while Miss Fairlie explained to Sister Ferguson that this was Tessa MacRynne and that she was to have a glass of hot milk and a sedative and go to bed at once. Tessa heard them talking but their voices sounded unreal and a long way off. It was a curious sort of feeling. Sister Ferguson was a Scot; her voice was comfortable and sympathetic.

"Poor wee soul!" said Sister Ferguson. "She looks just miserable. Let's hope it's not measles."

"Measles! Oh no, it isn't measles," declared Miss Fairlie.

"There's measles in the town," said Sister Ferguson. "But we'll just need to wait and see. I'll have the hot milk ready in a jiffy, Miss Fairlie."

"I don't want any milk thank you," said Tessa hoarsely.

"But you'll take a wee sip just to please me," declared Sister Ferguson. "Come away now, and into bed with you. There's a nice warm hottie in the bed—that'll be nice, won't it? I'll take your temperature and give you your milk and a wee tablet and you'll be off to sleep in no time."

Charlotte said good-night and left them. She had promised to write to Colonel MacRynne, but like Tessa she found the task extremely difficult. What could one say in the circumstances? One could hardly write without saying one was sorry . . . and yet it seemed impertinent for a complete stranger to condole with him. She dealt with some other easier letters first and then started upon the difficult one; but she had not got beyond the opening sentence when there was a tap on the door and Sister Ferguson appeared.

"It was just to tell you she's sleeping like a lamb," said Sister Ferguson. "I was wondering would I sit up with her—what do you think, Miss Fairlie? The temperature is a wee bit up, but not as much as I'd expected, so maybe it's not measles after all."

Charlotte liked Sister Ferguson; she was discreet—and discretion was a virtue to be valued above rubies—"It isn't measles," said Charlotte. "I'm sure there's no need to sit up with her. The fact is Tessa has had very bad news from home."

There was a little pause.

"Her mother is leaving home," continued Charlotte. "I'm afraid there's to be a divorce—that's the truth of the matter. I know I can depend upon you to say nothing about it."

Sister Ferguson nodded. "Of course . . . poor wee soul! No wonder she's upset. It will be better to keep her in the sick-room for a day or two. After all there's no saying but what it *might* be measles."

They looked at one another understandingly. Charlotte could not help smiling and there was a ghost of a twinkle in Sister Ferguson's light blue eyes. She shut the door softly and went away.

Charlotte took up her pen and wrote quickly:

DEAR COLONEL MACRYNNE,

Tessa was very much distressed at the news in her mother's letter. She tried to write to you about it but she found it difficult to put her feelings into words so she asked me to write to you instead. Tessa thinks you will be lonely and would like to be with you, but of course it is for you to decide what is best. If you would like her to come home I will take her to London myself and see her into the plane; if you would rather she remained here I shall do all I can to help her and to make things as easy as I can for her. Tessa has plenty of courage and I think she would settle down fairly soon. If I may be allowed to make a suggestion it is that you do not visit her here— Tessa suggests this but I am sure it would be a mistake. My experience is that visits from parents prevent girls from settling down in their new life, and in Tessa's case a visit from you would be very upsetting indeed. Nor would it be a good plan to allow Tessa to come home if you intend to send her back to Saint Elizabeth's. It should be either one thing or the other. Please forgive me for stating my opinion so plainly. I have done so for Tessa's sake. I shall await your decision and instructions.

Yours sincerely,
CHARLOTTE FAIRLIE

Charlotte read the letter over. She was not particularly pleased with it for it seemed cold and unsympathetic, but she had no right to offer her sympathy to Colonel MacRynne and it might be unacceptable. Perhaps Colonel MacRynne would realise her predicament and make allowances for her. The letter was perfectly clear—that was one point in its favour—and as she did not feel she could improve upon it she decided it would have to do.

* 6 *

SEVERAL DAYS passed before Charlotte received an answer to the letter which she had written to Colonel MacRynne. She was on the look-out for it and was able to rescue it from her mail before it was opened by her secretary.

"A private letter," she explained.

Miss Post was annoyed with herself for not being a bit quicker—she had not even seen the post-mark—if *only* she had seen it in time! But it was too late now; she would never know what was in that letter, and it must be something important because, instead of settling down to work, Miss Fairlie went off with it to her sitting-room to read it at leisure.

DEAR MISS FAIRLIE,

Thank you for your letter, which I appreciate very much. You will think it strange that I did not write to Tessa myself but I did not know her mother intended to write to her. I meant to wait and let her settle down at school before telling her what had happened. Of course the news was bound to upset her and I am not surprised to hear she wants to come home but it will be better for her not to come. At school she will have the companionship of the other girls and plenty of new things to occupy her mind. One of the reasons why I decided to send Tessa to school was so that she would not be here when her mother left home. The other reason was that there seemed to be no other way to continue her education. Up to now Tessa has had a resident governess but it would be impossible for me to have a governess staying in the house now. If Tessa can settle down happily at school that will be the best thing for her.

Of course I miss her and the house seems very empty and quiet without her but I must just get used to it. I intended to go and see Tessa and explain everything to her but I shall take your advice and leave her alone.

I find this letter very difficult to write and before going further I should like to apologise for burdening you with my private affairs but I feel I must tell you what has happened. I have no idea how much you know or how much Tessa's mother explained in her letter. I will be as brief as possible. Tessa's mother has gone to America to stay with her parents and to arrange a divorce. We were married in America and apparently this makes it easier—at any rate that is what I am told. Our tragedy is that she cannot be happy at Targ and I find it difficult to be happy elsewhere. There you have it in a nutshell. I would have been willing to live in Edinburgh for part of the year if it would have saved our marriage from shipwreck but I have not a large enough income to keep up two establishments so that was out of the question. Of course I have known for some time that we were drifting onto the rocks but there was nothing I could do. I think I should explain that my wife and I have parted upon good terms. There has been no quarrel and no scandal. She is an American and takes what she calls a realistic view of life. She says I am a sentimentalist. The affair must seem strange to you—it seems very strange to me. So far nobody here knows about it but of course they will have to know sooner

or later. These things get about surprisingly quickly.
I shall leave it to you to tell Tessa as much or as little as
you think fit. The main thing is to soften the blow.
Nothing else matters. I am more grateful than I can say
for your kindness to my daughter. She is everything in
the world to me. If you could spare time to let me know
how she is getting on I should be even more grateful.

Yours sincerely

RORY MACRYNNE

Charlotte pondered over the letter. It was very restrained
but there was a good deal to be read between the lines. The
short terse sentences were those of a man who was more used
to handling a gun or a fishing-rod than a pen. It was the
letter of a man who had taken a hard knock and was standing
up to it with courage and dignity—but whether the blow
was more to his heart or to his pride Charlotte could not
tell.

There was very little in the letter that Tessa did not know
already but all the same she must see Tessa and tell her about
it; so Charlotte summoned Miss Post and told her to go and
find Tessa MacRynne.

"Oh, that's the new girl!" exclaimed Miss Post.

"One of them," said Charlotte smiling.

"Oh, I know," agreed Miss Post. "I only meant—I mean
as a rule it takes some time before anybody *notices* new girls.
You know how it is, Miss Fairlie."

"Have they noticed Tessa in any special way?" inquired
Miss Fairlie with interest and perhaps a shade of apprehension.

"She seems very popular, that's all," replied Miss Post.
"Perhaps it's because everyone thought she had measles
and then they found she hadn't."

This seemed an insufficient reason for a sudden rise to

popularity but Miss Fairlie knew a good deal about girls and therefore knew that it was within the bounds of possibility. Tessa might have become a heroine overnight simply because her indisposition had been wrongly diagnosed. Funnier things had happened.

"Well, I had better see her," said Miss Fairlie. "Tell her to come after tea."

Tessa had been having an interesting time. She had spent two nights and one day in the sick-room and as there was no other patient she had had several long talks with Sister Ferguson whose matter-of-fact outlook had helped her to get re-oriented—so to speak. Sister Ferguson's method of dealing with misfortunes was to "wash them out". You never got anywhere if you sat down and brooded and felt sorry for yourself. The thing to do was to pretend you didn't care . . . then, after a bit, you found the pretence was true.

This philosophy of life appealed to Tessa, who was courageous and proud, so she decided to adopt it as her own.

Between the talks, when Sister Ferguson was busy, Tessa had occupied herself in reading poetry—and that too had helped. By the next day she felt much better and as the doctor could find nothing whatever the matter with her she was sent back to school.

"What will they all say?" asked Tessa anxiously. "I mean everybody will want to know what's been the matter with me."

"They'll not bother," replied Sister Ferguson. "But if anybody asks what's been the matter with you, you'll just tell them the truth. You'll just say they thought it might be measles but it wasn't. Say no more and no less," added Sister Ferguson briskly.

Of course everybody asked her. Tessa, who had implicit

faith in Sister Ferguson, said her piece obediently and found it worked like a charm.

"Hallo Tessa, what's been wrong with you?"

"They thought it might be measles but it wasn't."

"Gosh! Good thing it wasn't! We'd have been in quarantine. I say, has anybody seen my gym-shoes?"

Yes, it worked like a charm.

Miss Pinkerton, the maths mistress, was the only person upon whom the charm failed to work.

"Measles!" exclaimed Miss Pinkerton in horrified tones.

"But it wasn't," Tessa reminded her.

"What was it, then?"

"They didn't tell me."

Tessa was rather pleased with this reply. It was true: they had not told her what was the matter with her. She hoped the reply would satisfy Miss Pinkerton, but unfortunately it did not. Miss Pinkerton pursued her interrogation remorselessly; she wanted to know at what hour Tessa had begun to feel ill and why she had gone to Miss Fairlie instead of to Matron. Didn't Tessa know that the right thing to do if you felt ill was to go to Matron?

"I know now, I didn't before," said Tessa.

"How do you know now?" asked Miss Pinkerton.

"Because you've told me, Miss Pinkerton," replied Tessa innocently.

This conversation was taking place in class and several girls were obliged to smother involuntary giggles.

"There is no need to be impertinent, Tessa," said Miss Pinkerton sternly.

"But I wasn't!" exclaimed Tessa in surprise. "I mean you asked me how I knew, so I told you."

"That's quite enough," said Miss Pinkerton. She hesitated for a moment and then asked another question. "Did you go straight to Miss Fairlie's room?"

This was difficult ground. Tessa searched for an answer and at last found one. "I met her outside—by accident," said Tessa truthfully.

"And you told her you felt unwell?"

"She asked me if I felt ill, and I told her I had a frightful headache," said Tessa. This also was perfectly true.

"So she took you to the sick-room?"

This was plain sailing. All the rocks were behind her. "Yes," said Tessa, heaving a sigh of relief. "She took me to the sick-room and left me there, and Sister Ferguson gave me some hot milk and a white tablet and put me to bed."

The whole class was listening with all its ears to this simple recital. They found it much more interesting than long division in which they were supposed to be engaged.

"Most extraordinary!" exclaimed Miss Pinkerton. "If you were suspected of having measles you should have been sent to the San. Did you have a rash?"

"N'no," replied Tessa. She hesitated and then added triumphantly, "But I had a temperature."

"Why did they suspect measles?"

"I don't know," said Tessa. "Sister Ferguson said they thought it might be measles—but it wasn't."

This was where they had come in and Miss Pinkerton was obliged to abandon the subject and return to long division, but she was by no means satisfied. There was a mystery here. Somehow or other she would get to the bottom of it.

One result of Miss Pinkerton's cross-examination surprised Tessa a good deal and pleased her even more. Miss Pinkerton was not popular with her pupils and they were delighted to see her routed . . . Tessa had given Old Pinkie beans! Several of Tessa's class-mates congratulated her and told her she was priceless and one of them offered her a chocolate bar. Tessa was charmed with the gift; not because she liked chocolate (she was one of those curious people who dislike chocolate in any form) but because it was a symbol of friend-ship. She ate half of it in the donor's presence, disguising her aversion, and put the other half down the lavatory. It was Dione Eastwood who gave Tessa the chocolate bar and this marked the beginning of a friendship which was to be very important to them both.

On Wednesday afternoon there was a hockey match and those who were not playing took rugs and settled down to watch. Tessa and her new friend sat together, a little apart from the others, and chatted about all sorts of interesting things.

"Dione is a silly name," said its owner. "Everyone calls me Donny—at least all the people I like. Is your name really Tessa, or is it short for something else?"

"It's short for Esther, but nobody ever calls me that," Tessa replied.

"I've got two brothers," said Donny. "They're both younger than me. Harold is twelve and Barney is nearly eleven. Barney's real name is Barnabas because Mother died when he was born. It means Son of Consolation."

"So you've got no mother!" said Tessa. "I've got no mother either."

"Oh, I'm glad," exclaimed Donny. "I mean it seems an unkind thing to say but it makes us the same, doesn't it?"

"Who looks after your house?"

"Miss Hurdstone. She's a sort of housekeeper and she's been with us for ages—ever since I can remember. I say, Tessa, would you like to come to tea on Sunday? I always go home on Sunday afternoons."

Tessa accepted rapturously.

"Now tell me about your home," said Donny.

Tessa was only too ready to talk about Targ.

They were still chatting happily when Miss Post found them and gave Tessa the message from Miss Fairlie. "Go

directly after tea," said Miss Post. "And be sure you're tidy
and clean. I shan't be there so you must just knock on Miss
Fairlie's door and wait until she tells you to come in."

"Yes," said Tessa. She knew what the summons meant.
It meant that Miss Fairlie had had a letter . . .

"I say, you *are* pale! " exclaimed Donny. "You needn't
worry—honestly. The Old Girl is quite nice. At least you
needn't worry unless you've done something awful. You
haven't have you? "

"No," said Tessa.

"The Old Girl is quite nice," repeated Donny encouragingly.

"She's absolutely marvellous," declared Tessa. "She's the
most marvellous person in the whole world . . . except
perhaps Daddy."

"I say! " exclaimed Donny in amazement. "But how——"
Tessa began to talk about something else.

It was natural that Tessa should have fallen in love with
her headmistress, but that was part of the secret, of course—
the secret which she would never divulge, not even if she
were tortured. During her short stay in the sick-room Tessa
had thought things out; she had thought of a great many
things and had made some rather curious decisions. One of
these tangled lines of thought had been unravelled without
much difficulty; Tessa realised that Miss Fairlie had saved
her from making a complete fool of herself. If Miss Fairlie
had not caught her in time Tessa would have gone home to
Targ and arrived there unwanted and unwelcome—obviously
they did not want her at home or they would not have sent
her to school—it would have made things worse, not better,
if she had walked in unexpectedly. It would have been frightful. Quite possibly she would have been sent straight back
to school (since she was not wanted at home) and that would
have been frightful too. She would have been branded for
life as the girl who ran away, the coward who could not

stand on her own feet but ran off home like a silly baby. (Tessa could almost hear the comments of her school-mates upon her behaviour: "That's Tessa MacRynne. You know what the little fool did, don't you? She ran away. Of course they sent her back again. They didn't want her at home." Yes, that was what they would have said.) Tessa would never have been able to live it down—never.

Miss Fairlie had saved her from worse than death. Miss Fairlie had covered up her foolish behaviour and made everything all right. Tessa had no idea how it had been managed but obviously the truth had not been told. Miss Fairlie had lied for her! Probably it was quite a small lie (more not-telling-the-truth than an actual lie) but Miss Fairlie was not the sort of person who told lies easily—Tessa was sure of that.

In the last few days Tessa's admiration and adoration of Miss Fairlie had grown and grown. When Miss Fairlie stood upon the dais in the school hall, beautiful as an angel and remote as a star in the evening sky, Tessa looked at her and remembered the softness of her shoulder and the firm clasp of her arm and the kindness of her voice. *She kissed me, thought Tessa.* It was a wonderful secret. It was almost too much bliss to bear.

And to-day—only this morning—when Tessa was standing in the corridor with a group of other girls, Miss Fairlie had passed them and had paused for a moment and said, "Hallo, Tessa, are you feeling better?" and she had replied, "Yes thank you, Miss Fairlie." Just as if it was quite ordinary and nothing at all had happened. Somehow that made it even more blissful.

After tea Tessa brushed her hair and washed her hands and made her way to Miss Fairlie's room. Miss Fairlie was writing but she turned and smiled at Tessa and they sat down together on the sofa as they had done before.

"You've had a letter from Daddy," said Tessa with a little gasp.

"Yes, it came this morning. He wants you to stay here, Tessa. It would be difficult to have a governess at home."

Tessa did not see why, but she was willing to take it on trust. "What else did he say?" she inquired.

Charlotte told her most of Colonel MacRynne's news but not quite all of it. She had been given leave to use her discretion.

"I was wondering," said Tessa turning her head and looking into the fire. "I was wondering if—if Mummy will—marry somebody else."

Charlotte had been wondering the same thing. "I don't know," she replied trying to speak in a natural matter-of-fact tone. "I only know that she has gone to America to stay with her parents."

"Sometimes people do," said Tessa.

"I wouldn't think about it if I were you. Your job is to settle down at school and try to be happy. You will try, won't you?"

Tessa nodded. "As a matter of fact it isn't as bad as I'd expected. I don't *think* about things much—there's no time—and everybody is very nice to me—and I've got a friend. She's called Donny Eastwood."

"Donny Eastwood?" echoed Charlotte. It was rather surprising that the lively intelligent Tessa had chosen Donny as her bosom friend. "I wonder——" continued Charlotte and then hesitated for it was one of her rules not to discuss one girl with another.

"You wonder?" asked Tessa, looking up with a frank open gaze.

"I was just going to say I wondered why Donny doesn't do better at lessons. I'm sure she could if she tried . . . but of course it's nothing to do with you."

"No, of course not," said Tessa thoughtfully.

"Well, it's good to hear you're beginning to settle down." Charlotte told her, changing the subject.

Tessa nodded. "I've got things—sorted out. Sister Ferguson was awfully kind, and she gave me a book of poems to read which helped a lot. Do you know a poem called *The Forsaken Merman*?"

Charlotte knew it well.

"I liked it so much that I learnt some of it off by heart," said Tessa. "It's like Daddy in a way . . . ' Here came a mortal but faithless was she: And alone dwell for ever the kings of the sea ' . . . but of course in another way it's not a *bit* like Daddy because Daddy will *never* call to her to come home—he's too proud. He's proud of being MacRynne of Targ. If Mummy wants to leave Targ and go away she can go; Daddy won't call her back and neither will I. That's all really."

And quite enough too, thought Charlotte in some dismay. She had not expected this reaction. Pride was all very well; it could sustain you and help you to take the hard knocks of life with dignity—as Charlotte knew by her own experience —but this sort of pride in a child of thirteen was rather alarming.

"It's almost as if Matthew Arnold knew Targ," continued Tessa dreamily. "Especially the last bit of the poem:

When soft the winds blow;
When clear falls the moonlight
When spring tides are low;
When sweet airs come sea-ward
From heaths starred with broom;
And high rocks throw mildly
On the blanch'd sands a gloom:
Up the still, glistening beaches,

Up the creeks we will hie;
Over the banks of bright sea-weed
The ebb-tide leaves dry.

That's Targ, Miss Fairlie. It really is—and the story about the mortal who went away and deserted the merman and the children is *nearly* right. It was horrid of her, wasn't it? "

"Yes," said Charlotte, "but I always feel sorry for the mortal. She was torn in half, wasn't she? Half of her wanted to go back to the merman and the children and the other half wanted the cosy, comfortable life she was used to. It wasn't easy for her."

Tessa turned a stricken face to Charlotte. "Don't—please," she whispered. "I can't bear it that way. I've got to—to bear it my own way if I've got to bear it . . . "

"Yes, all right," said Charlotte quickly. "I'm sorry Tessa; it was silly of me. Bear it your own way."

They sat for a little while in silence with Charlotte's arm round Tessa's shoulders and then Charlotte kissed her lightly on the forehead and told her to go. "If you're unhappy you must come and tell me," said Charlotte. "But you aren't going to be unhappy, are you? "

"No, I don't think so," Tessa said.

* 7 *

WHEN HER visitor had gone Charlotte sat on beside the fire, lost in thought. She was comparing herself and her own childhood with Tessa's; like Tessa's her own childhood had been broken by a tragedy, though it was of quite a different nature. Like Tessa she had had to re-orient herself; but she had tackled the problem in a different way. Charlotte had intended to tell Tessa a little about this and was on the point of doing so when Tessa had stopped her by saying, "I've got to bear it my own way if I've got to bear it." Perhaps Tessa was right and everybody had to find their own way of bearing things. Certainly Tessa's drastic way seemed to have worked.

Charlotte's mother had died when Charlotte was four years old. Sometimes she had a feeling that she remembered her mother but it may have been just imagination, helped out by the painting of the beautiful woman with the calm eyes which hung upon the wall of her father's library. The house where they lived was in a quiet crescent in Bayswater; Mr. Fairlie was a director of a large and flourishing export firm. He was away all day and the child was looked after by a nurse, but when he came home she was brought downstairs to the library and they would play games together and he would tell her stories until it was time for her to go to bed. Charlotte looked forward to this playtime all day, and as she grew older she looked forward to it even

66

more. Her father was her adored companion. On Saturday afternoons they always went out together for expeditions in the car; or perhaps to the Zoo; or sometimes, if it were wet, to a picture house.

When she was old enough Charlotte went to a day school a few minutes walk from her home; she liked school immensely; the girls were friendly and lessons were no trouble to her. She told her father everything that happened at school—all the funny little jokes—and he was always ready and eager to listen. He was very proud of her progress at school and often told her that he would take her on as a partner in the firm and rename his business, "Branding, Fairlie and Daughter." This was just fun (Charlotte knew that) but sometimes she wondered if perhaps it might come true . . . not the name of the firm, of course, but the partnership. Women were doing all sorts of interesting things nowadays and there seemed no reason why a woman should not hold an important position in an export business. With this aim in view she worked harder than ever at her lessons and encouraged her father to talk about his business affairs and discuss them with her.

At twelve years old Charlotte knew a good deal about the firm; she had visited the huge warehouses near the Pool of London and had seen the ships from far-away lands loading and unloading their cargoes. There was nothing she enjoyed better than these visits, not only because of the interest and the romance of the great ships with their varied merchandise, but also because she felt so proud of her father; he knew all that was happening and could explain it to her, and he knew all the men who worked in the warehouses. To Charlotte he seemed a king.

The life they led was quiet and in some respects uneventful. It was a safe, solid, sheltered life and Charlotte envisaged no change; she felt things had always been like this and would go on like this for ever. But soon after Charlotte was twelve years old a change came. Mr. Fairlie told her that he was going to be married.

At first Charlotte felt pleased about it, for she knew Miss Price and liked her immensely—she was pretty and gay and amusing—it would be fun to have her living in the house. Also Charlotte was quite old enough and sensible enough to realise that the house needed a mistress to run it properly; she and her father were at the mercy of incompetent house- keepers who served up uneatable meals and cheated them right and left. Yes, Charlotte was pleased and everyone was happy—life was going to be fuller and more interesting than before.

Unfortunately however things did not turn out as was expected for the new Mrs. Fairlie seemed different from Miss Price; she seemed like a different person altogether. Miss Price had been fond of Charlotte and chatted to her and taken her out shopping—they had had all sorts of jokes together—but all that was altered when Miss Price became Mrs. Fairlie. The young Charlotte could not understand what had happened nor why her new stepmother had suddenly become so disagreeable, so irritable and unkind.

It was jealousy, of course. Mrs. Fairlie wanted all her husband's attention, she did not want to share it with another woman's child. It was torture to her to see Charlotte and her father together, laughing at some joke or talking about "The Firm," and it was no good when they explained the joke to her, or tried to explain the working of the business: Mrs. Fairlie had very little sense of humour—ex- cept for her own kind of jokes—and she was not interested in business matters.

At last it was decided that Charlotte had better be sent to boarding school and as Saint Elizabeth's happened to have a vacancy in the immediate future her outfit was bought and packed and she was taken to the station by her father. Mr. Fairlie felt very unhappy and embarrassed in his daughter's company. He did his best to talk cheerfully, telling her that she would like school and he was sure she would get on splendidly. Charlotte agreed to all he said.

"We shall see you in the Christmas Holidays, you know," he told her.

"Yes, of course," said Charlotte.

"Perhaps things will be—be easier then——"

"Yes," said Charlotte. She flung her arms round his neck and burst into tears. "I've tried!" she sobbed. "I *have* tried—really."

"I know," he said uncomfortably. "Don't cry, Charlotte." They kissed one another good-bye.

Charlotte never saw her father again. He had said that they would see her in the Christmas Holidays but, instead of going home to Bayswater, she was sent to her uncle (her mother's only brother) who had a farm in Devonshire.

Uncle Tom was a bachelor and lived by himself with an old couple to look after him; it was an odd sort of household with a free and easy atmosphere and although it was somewhat lonely for a child Charlotte managed to content herself in it. She would have been happier if she could have seen her father—she loved him so dearly, they had been so near one another, such good companions—but he showed no desire to see her and when she wrote to him his replies were impersonal and cold.

"I shall see Daddy at Easter," she said to Uncle Tom. "It seems a long time until Easter, but——"

"Well, I don't think so," replied Uncle Tom uncomfortably. "That woman doesn't seem to like you, Charlotte."

"You mean I'm not to go home for the Easter Holidays?"

"No," he said. "The fact is—well, apparently you don't hit it off with that woman. I don't blame you either—quite a different sort of woman from your mother—can't imagine what your father was thinking of. But don't you worry, Charlotte, you can depend upon your old Uncle Tom."

"Do you mean Daddy doesn't want to—to see me ever again?" asked young Charlotte in horrified tones.

"You're quite happy here, aren't you?" asked Uncle Tom, fumbling for words of comfort. "We get on all right, don't we? I thought I'd look about and find a pony for you. Easter would be a good time for you to start riding. You don't want to go back there if they don't want you. I like having you here—you're Mary's daughter. I was very fond of Mary. You've got Mary's pretty hair and eyes—and I've nobody else belonging to me, or at least nobody I care for. Your Aunt Lydia and I never hit it off. Well, there it is, Charlotte."

There it was. Later, by dint of questioning, Charlotte discovered that Uncle Tom had adopted her; he had made himself responsible for her education and intended to make her his heir . . . and all this had been arranged by her father without her consent. Perhaps it was the best way out of the mess—certainly Uncle Tom was very kind—but for a long time Charlotte could not see beyond the fact that Daddy did not want her, that he had given her away, handed her over like an unwanted piece of furniture.

Charlotte was wounded to the heart, she was utterly wretched. She sat down and wrote to her father then and there. It was a hysterical letter, which began by begging for a meeting (" If I could only see you just once! ") and went on to reproach him for his unkindness and to remind him of the happy times they had had together. It was a tear-blotched letter, written in haste, and certainly most unwise; few people have attained much wisdom at the age of thirteen.

There was no reply to her letter and after some weeks

Charlotte ceased to expect one and settled down to remake her life as best she could. It seemed to her that her life was cut in half with a gigantic pair of scissors for nothing at all remained to her of her childhood days. Fortunately she was happy at school and was able to forget her troubles in work and in play. The ambition to become a partner in "The Firm" was abandoned but another ambition took its place: someday she would be headmistress of Saint Elizabeth's and rule in the place of Miss Bain.

From Saint Elizabeth's Charlotte went to Oxford and while she was there her uncle died. She had been fond of Uncle Tom, they had got on extremely well together, but he was not the sort of man to inspire deep affection, so although Charlotte felt very grateful to him for all his kindness to her she was not heart-broken at his death. He had left everything to Charlotte, as he had promised to do, but when the farm was sold and the estate was settled there was surprisingly little money left; fortunately there was enough to complete her education and the remainder, safely invested, brought her about a hundred pounds a year.

It was a long time since Charlotte had thought of the past —Tessa's trouble had raised the ghost of her own trouble— and as she sat and pondered over it she was surprised to find that all the pain of it had gone. She could think of it objectively as if it had happened to somebody else; she could sympathise with her father's predicament. What else could he have done? thought Charlotte. He might have done it in a different way, but, under the circumstances, it was the only thing to do.

* 8 *

THE EASTWOODS' house stood just outside the Old Wall of Larchester, in fact the wall towered up at the end of the garden—a great strong bulwark made of uncut stone. In a way it was useful to the Eastwoods as a shelter from the wind but on Sunday afternoons the path along the top was thronged with people who gazed into the garden and violated their privacy. The Eastwoods' house was a square Georgian brick building which had weathered to an unobtrusive pink; it was well-proportioned and the windows were high but trees had been allowed to grow too near the house and their heavy foliage shut out the light. There were thick curtains in the windows and dull old-fashioned furniture in the rooms and the woodwork was an ugly brown which produced a gloomy effect.

It was a house which would have driven a person of taste to despair but the Eastwoods had no taste and never noticed their surroundings. Professor Eastwood had written one book upon the subject of economics and was now engaged upon another which was to be even more weighty than the first; all he wanted was a quiet room, a good fire and a comfortable chair; Donny lived in her dreams (if only people would leave her in peace to dream them) and Harold and Barney accepted things as they were and had no idea that their surroundings might have been different or more pleasant.

72

Harold was a tall thin boy with a pale skin and dark hair. Barney was brown; he had brown eyes, brown freckles on his snub nose and brown hair which was usually very untidy. The boys went to Bells Hill School daily—except on Sundays and holidays of course. The fifth member of the household was Miss Hurdstone who had been with the Eastwoods ever since Barney was born. She cooked and cleaned and catered and looked after the whole family in a comfortable if somewhat unimaginative manner.

It was Sunday. The boys had been out all afternoon on some ploy of their own and were returning to Hatton Lodge to tea.

"I wonder if Donny's here yet," said Barney as he opened the garden gate.

"What? Oh yes," said Harold vaguely. "I'd forgotten she was coming."

"She always comes on Sundays."

"I know."

"Well, why did you say you'd forgotten?"

"Because I had. I mean I'd forgotten it was Sunday."

"I don't see how you could," Barney declared. "We went to church this morning, and we've been out all the afternoon. I like it when Donny comes."

"So do I," said Harold.

"Well, you can't have been looking forward to seeing her or you wouldn't have forgotten she was coming."

They had reached the front-door by this time and continued their argument in lowered voices for they were aware that their father disliked being disturbed.

"Don't you understand?" said Harold. "I hadn't forgotten Donny was coming. I had forgotten to-day was to-day."

"You *had* forgotten."

"I hadn't."

"Well anyhow, you'd forgotten she was bringing that girl to tea."

"What girl?"

"There—you *had* forgotten!" triumphed Barney.

"Oh, you mean that girl she's got such a pash on!"

"Well, of course."

"No, I hadn't forgotten."

"What's her name, then?"

"Chrissie—or something."

"No, it isn't."

"Yes, it is."

"It's Tessa, you ass!"

"Ass yourself! It's just the same, anyhow."

"It isn't the same. It's quite different."

Harold did not reply.

"It's quite different," repeated Barney.

"All right it's quite different," said Harold losing interest in the argument.

They were standing in the hall now. It was paved with big squares of black and white marble and furnished with a huge mahogany table, several chairs of the same wood and a lamentable piece of furniture consisting of a hat-and-coat-rack and umbrella-stand combined. Harold hung his cap on the rack with neatness and precision; Barney tossed his in the air. He tossed it up several times before it stuck on a peg and each time it fell he had to crawl into the corner to retrieve it. Harold watched with patient indifference. When at last the cap caught on a peg they opened the door of the dining-room and went in.

The two girls were sitting at the table having tea.

"Oh, hallo!" exclaimed Donny. "You're late, aren't you? This is Tessa. That's Harold and that's Barney."

They all said "hallo!" and the two boys hugged their sister somewhat roughly and kissed her with obvious enjoyment. (Tessa, watching this demonstration of brotherly affection, felt an odd little pain in the region of her heart. It would be rather nice to have brothers who loved you like that). Then the boys sat down and began to eat large slabs of bread-and-butter and jam.

"You haven't washed your hands," said Donny.

"We'll wash after," replied Barney, his utterance some-what impeded by a large mouthful of food. "It's a waste to wash before tea because you get sticky, so you have to wash afterwards—and that makes twice."

"It's bad for the skin to wash too often," added Harold.

"Your skin must be awfully good," said Donny seriously.

Barney grinned. His grin stretched almost from ear to ear and displayed a set of large white teeth.

"I say," said Harold addressing his guest. "How long have you been at Saint Elizabeth's?"

"Just since the beginning of this term," replied Tessa.

"She was in the sick-room for two days," put in Donny.

"What was the matter with you?" asked the two boys simultaneously.

"They thought it might be measles but it wasn't," explained Tessa.

"That's rather good," said Barney thoughtfully. "They thought it might be measles but it wasn't. You could make a song out of that."

"There isn't a rhyme for wasn't," declared Harold.

"There's pleasant," suggested Donny.

"Oh goodness, no!" exclaimed Barney in shocked tones. "That would be frightful. Let's see now . . ." He lay back in his chair and looked at the ceiling for inspiration while his three companions watched him.

"What about ain't?" suggested Harold. "They thought it might be measles but it ain't."

"There's lots of rhymes for ain't," said Donny encouragingly. "There's saint and faint and quaint——"

"Shut up," said the poet. "How can I think if you keep on interrupting me?"

"I don't keep on interrupting you——"

"Well, you are now."

They were silent for about a minute and then Barney nodded. "It's pretty good," he declared. "Just listen——"
He waved his arms and began to chant:

> *They thought it might be measles but it ain't.*
> *It's nothing but a dab of crimson paint.*
> *She put it on her chin*
> *To take the doctor in——*
>
> (Go on everybody!)
>
> *They thought it might be measles but it ain't.*

They all chanted the last line and they all laughed. Tessa was delighted with the rhyme—it was very clever of Barney to make a song out of her magic charm—"Let's have it again," she suggested.

They had it again—in fact they had it several times—and then suddenly the door burst open and Professor Eastwood appeared. He was an untidy little man with baggy trousers and carpet slippers; his eyebrows were bushy and he had iron-grey hair which grew in tufts on his unusually large head. He stood in the open door-way and looked at them . . . and immediately there was silence.

"Pray do not consider me," he said. "Continue your concert. I have come downstairs so that I may hear it more conveniently. As it is quite impossible for me to work in this house I should welcome entertainment."

"This is Tessa, Father," said Donny in a low voice.

"Oh, I was not aware you had a guest! "

"How do you do, Professor Eastwood," said Tessa politely. She was not quite sure whether the professor was "trying to be funny" or whether he was angry, but it could do no harm to be polite.

"How do you do, Miss—er——"

"Tessa MacRynne," said Tessa introducing herself. "I'm a new girl at Saint Elizabeth's and Donny very kindly asked me to tea."

It was really the duty of her hostess to explain all this of course but her hostess seemed to be afflicted with dumbness and Tessa was socially adroit. She was used to being with grown-up people and she was not in the least frightened of the untidy little man. Tessa was never frightened of anybody. Why should she be frightened? People couldn't eat you. Besides she was Tessa MacRynne of Targ.

"Ah! " said the professor looking at her.

Tessa looked straight back at him and waited. It was his turn to speak.

"And how do you like Saint Elizabeth's, Miss—er—MacRynne? " inquired Professor Eastwood.

"Better than I expected," replied his guest promptly. "I was afraid I wouldn't like it at all."

"Why so? "

"Because I knew it would be so different from Targ. We're isolated at Targ."

"Isolated? You mean your home is in the country."

"It's an island. That's why I said isolated," explained Tessa.

"You actually live upon an island? " asked the professor incredulously. "That must be extremely inconvenient."

"Oh no, we're used to it you see. We've been there for hundreds of years."

"Hundreds of years " said the professor looking at his

young guest disapprovingly. "I fear you have acquired the modern habit of exaggeration, Miss MacRynne."

"Well, we've been at Targ since 1360 for certain—that's when the castle was built—but Daddy thinks there may have been MacRynnes at Targ long before that."

Professor Eastwood looked slightly taken aback and his bushy eyebrows rose. "Dear me," he said. "That is—er—very interesting."

"Yes, isn't it?" agreed Tessa. "Of course the castle has been added to and brought up-to-date with bathrooms and electric light and all that sort of thing."

"Electric light?"

"We make it ourselves with water-power," Tessa explained.

The professor came in and sat down at the table. "I suppose this island home of yours is in Scotland," he said.

Tessa nodded.

"And your native language is Gaelic?"

"Goodness no!" exclaimed Tessa smiling at the absurd idea. "Of course I can speak Gaelic a bit."

"The natives speak Gaelic, I imagine."

"Yes, they speak it amongst themselves—in their own homes."

"Do you mean they can speak English?"

"Of course," replied Tessa laughing. "What *would* they do when they went over to the mainland if they couldn't speak English?"

Professor Eastwood abandoned the subject; he glanced at his daughter and said: "Is there no tea in your teapot, Dione?"

"Oh yes!" cried Donny starting in alarm. "I didn't know you wanted tea, Father!"

"I presume you have all been drinking tea. Why should I be denied some?"

"No, of course—I wasn't thinking. I mean you don't usually have tea with us. You're usually writing——" stammered Donny, pouring out tea and slopping milk into it with a shaking hand.

"I was writing until I was interrupted by Noise. You were singing, I believe." He fixed Harold with a piercing gaze.

Harold choked over a piece of cake and said hoarsely, "We all were. It was a sort of song."

"A sort of song!" repeated the professor with an unpleasant smile. "May I inquire what sort of song?"

"Just one I made up," said Barney. "Nothing really——"

"What modesty! Here we have a lyric-writer who proclaims his work to be nothing! Come, Barney, let us hear the fruits of your endeavours."

"No," said Barney wriggling. "It was just—just rubbish —to make them laugh. You wouldn't like it."

"You are suggesting that I am devoid of a sense of humour?"

"Yes—I mean no. I mean you'd think it silly," said the wretched Barney.

"Allow me to judge for myself," said Professor Eastwood. He assumed an attitude of expectancy and waited.

Silence fell.

"It was just a nonsense rhyme," explained Tessa throwing herself into the breach. "It was about me—they thought I had measles but it wasn't—Barney made it up out of his head in a few moments. Like Lear."

"Like Lear?" asked the Professor in surprise.

"Not Shakespeare of course," said Tessa hastily. I meant Edward Lear. I expect you know his nonsense rhymes, don't you, Professor Eastwood?"

"Nonsense rhymes are not quite in my line——"

"Oh you *must* know them!" cried Tessa. "I thought everybody knew them. Didn't you read them to Donny and Harold and Barney when they were little?"

"Er—no," said Professor Eastwood. "I cannot say I remember——"

"Daddy used to read them to me."

"I can see you are fond of poetry, Miss MacRynne."

"Oh yes!" exclaimed Tessa enthusiastically. "Of course Lear's verses aren't really poetry. I like Matthew Arnold much better."

The professor was surprised. He was accustomed to extend patronage to those with whom he conversed but somehow this extraordinary young woman refused to be patronised, indeed she seemed to be taking the lead in the conversation. She was quite polite and pleasant—in fact she was extremely polite and pleasant—but all the same the professor did not like it much.

"I suppose your favourite poet is Robert Burns," said Professor Eastwood with the ghost of a sneer.

"Burns?" asked Tessa in surprise.

"He is your national poet, is he not?"

"But he was a Lowlander! I mean we're as different from Lowland Scots as—as French people are from Germans." She hesitated. It seemed funny that a professor should be so ignorant. Professors were supposed to be clever. Tessa wondered if Professor Eastwood was pretending to be ignorant just to tease her. She had a feeling that she had been talking too much but at any rate she had managed to head him off Barney's verses. "I expect you know all about it, really," she added.

"Er—yes of course," agreed the professor. "The Highlander and the Lowlander . . . the fact that they spring from different stock had escaped my memory for the moment."

Tessa felt it was time to take a little interest in her host's affairs. "I hope your book is getting on well," she said kindly. "Donny told me you were writing one."

"It is not getting on well," he replied. "I am disturbed constantly. There is never any peace——"

"Oh, what a pity," said Tessa sympathetically. "I know you must have peace when you're writing a book. There was a friend of Daddy's who came and stayed at Targ last year and he was writing a book, so we put him in the Tower Room and nobody went near him, but even then he didn't have peace. He said the ghosts disturbed him."

"The ghosts!" exclaimed the professor in surprise.

"That's what he said. Daddy said it was owls. I don't know which it was really. The book was all about Mary Queen of Scots." She hesitated and then added, "I expect you know about *her*."

"The name seems familiar," said the professor with frightful sarcasm.

"Yes, I thought it would be," nodded Tessa, "Daddy says she's the only person in Scottish History that English people know about—and the murder of Rizzio is the only event."

There was a moment's silence while the professor tried to remember some other person or event in the history of Scotland but for some reason he could not remember any. Of course history was not in his line (any more than nonsense rhymes) but still . . .

"Er—I had no idea it was so late," declared the professor; he drank the remains of his tea hastily and went away.

The young people went out into the garden; there was a feeling of embarrassment in the air. They did not discuss Professor Eastwood of course, but they could find no other subject to discuss. Tessa felt certain that the slight chill in her relationship with her companions was due to the fact that she had been " too grown-up." Instead of treating her as a contemporary and joking with her (as they had done before the advent of Professor Eastwood) they were treating her with the respect due to an adult. Tessa was sorry about it and wondered what she could do to make things right.

They walked round the garden solemnly—together in body but not in spirit—

" Those are the roses," said Donny, somewhat unnecessarily.

" I like roses," declared Tessa. " Daddy likes them too. He bought some new ones in Inverness. They're called Miss Hogg. Isn't that a funny name for a rose? "

" Very funny," agreed Donny politely.

" The roses are nearly over now," said Harold.

" But the chrysanthemums are nice," said Barney.

" Very nice," agreed Tessa politely.

They walked on in silence.

" Oh! " exclaimed Tessa. " What a huge enormous wall! "

The Eastwoods seized upon the topic gratefully and related the history of the Old Wall of Larchester at some length. Their guest was interested; history was a subject which appealed to her.

" There are people walking along the top," said Tessa looking up.

" The steps are in the town," explained Donny. " You can go up the steps and walk along—all round the top—we do it sometimes."

" Do you ever climb it? "

" Climb it! " echoed Barney in amazement. " Nobody could climb the Wall—it's like a precipice. I mean there are no sticking out bits to hold onto."

" It isn't really very difficult," said Tessa looking at it critically.

The Eastwoods gazed at her in surprise.

Tessa laughed. "I'll show you," she said. "It's a good thing I've got rubber soles——"

Donny suddenly awoke to the fact that her guest intended to climb the Wall. "But you can't!" she cried in horrified tones. "You'll fall down and break your neck! Tessa, you mustn't——"

"I'm used to rock-climbing," said Tessa; she threw off her jacket and, before they could do anything to stop her, she ran lightly across the flower-bed and began the ascent.

The first part was not very difficult, for the Wall was broader at its base, but half way up it became almost perpendicular and the three Eastwoods watched their guest with bated breath—too terrified to make a sound. She was like a fly upon the Wall. She seemed to be flat against it. They could see her fingers searching in the masonry for a hold . . . finding a little crevice and clinging to it. A young man in a cloth cap who had come out for his Sunday afternoon walk was watching from the top with interest and apprehension.

Slowly and carefully Tessa ascended and in a few minutes she was standing upon the ramparts, safe and sound.

"Gosh, how marvellous!" shouted Barney waving to her. Tessa waved back cheerfully.

Donny felt quite weak. The strain of watching had been almost unbearable. She had expected every moment to see Tessa fall, to see Tessa roll down and lie in a crumpled heap amongst the chrysanthemums. In addition to her alarm and anxiety Donny had felt the burden of responsibility for she was a year older than her guest and it was she who had asked Tessa to come to tea. If Tessa were killed it would be her fault; she would be—practically—a murderer. When she saw Tessa standing upon the ramparts, waving cheerfully to Barney, Donny's knees began to tremble and, oddly enough, she felt rather angry . . . but she still felt responsible for her guest and the trouble and worry was by no means over. There was Tessa standing upon the top of the Wall with her skirts blowing in the breeze and her dark hair disordered and, worst of all, holding an amicable conversation with a strange young man in a cloth cap.

"How is she going to get down?" asked Donny, for it was obvious that coming down would be even more dangerous than going up.

"She could go round and come down by the steps," suggested Harold.

"I suppose she had better," agreed Donny in doubtful tones.

It was against the rules of the school for a girl to walk through Larchester all by herself—and Tessa had no hat and looked extremely untidy—and it would be even worse to walk though Larchester with that rather odd-looking young man—and probably Tessa, being new, did not know the rule. She might easily meet one of the mistresses, or even the Old Girl herself! All these thoughts chased each other through Donny's head in a moment . . . but it would be less disastrous to break a rule than to break you neck!

"It's a lovely view from here!" shouted Tessa. "I can see the river for miles and miles—winding away into the distance."

"Gosh, isn't she marvellous!" exclaimed Barney, looking up with worshipful eyes.

"A ladder would be no good," said Harold in a thoughtful tone.

"None whatever," replied Donny rather sharply.

"I could go round and meet her—we all could," suggested Harold. "Then she wouldn't get into trouble, would she?

I mean because of that potty rule about not walking about Larchester by yourself."

Donny thought this was rather clever of Harold (it certainly seemed the best solution to the problem) so they began to shout to Tessa and explain that she was to stay where she was until they came and fetched her, but the wind was blowing so strongly on the top of the Wall that Tessa could not hear what they were saying.

"All right, don't worry!" shouted Tessa, and with that she disappeared from view.

The Eastwoods looked at one another in dismay. Where had she gone? What was she doing?

Suddenly Barney pointed and exclaimed, "There she is!"

Tessa had run along the top of the Wall to a place where the angle was less acute and a small tree had loosened some of the stones. She climbed down carefully, but without apparent difficulty, and in a few moments was standing beside her friends upon level ground.

"Hurrah!" shouted the young man in the cloth cap who had been watching from above.

"Hurrah!" shouted Tessa, waving frantically.

Donny burst into tears.

"Oh Donny!" exclaimed Tessa filled with compunction. "Oh Donny, were you frightened? But it wasn't difficult—not really. You see I'm used to rock-climbing; I've done it all my life ever since I was quite small. Daddy taught me. Honestly Donny, it wasn't a bit dangerous."

"It's all right—you're safe," said Donny, blowing her nose.

Barney picked up Tessa's jacket and handed it to her. He would have liked to hold it for her while she put it on, but Harold would laugh. Harold would think it soppy—even Donny would be surprised.

"It was marvellous," declared Barney. "You looked like

a fly—but flies have sticky stuff on their feet, so it's easy for them. How do you do it, Tessa? It's simply marvellous."

"It's just practice," said Tessa.

"Could I learn?" asked Barney humbly. "You said it wasn't very difficult so perhaps you could teach me."

"No, I couldn't," replied Tessa. "You can't learn rock-climbing all in a moment. You have to start with easy climbs and gradually get on to more difficult ones. That old wall is a bit tricky and some of the stones are crumbling away. *Don't you try*," she added, looking at Barney earnestly. "If you try to climb that wall you'll get stuck and they'll have to get you down with a ladder. You'd look an awful fool, wouldn't you?"

"Yes," agreed Barney regretfully. "Yes, I *would* look a fool. As a matter of fact I know I couldn't do it; but I would like to learn."

"You must come to Targ—all of you," declared Tessa with the regal hospitality of the true Gael. "Yes, of course I mean it. You'd simply love Targ. It's the most wonderful place in the whole world . . ." and she proceeded to tell the young Eastwoods about the joys which would be theirs when they came to Targ. She told them about the old castle and about the high black cliffs where the sea-birds nested; she told them about the moors and the little burns and the bays of white sand where you could have picnics and bathe; she told them what fun it was to sail in the yacht and how you could fish for mackerel or go with the fishermen and help them to raise their lobster pots.

"Of course it rains a good deal," admitted Tessa. "But you just put on a waterproof and go out. Nobody minds rain."

"Of course not!" exclaimed the Eastwoods with one voice; who could possibly mind a few drops of rain in Heaven?

"Could we *really* come someday? " Barney asked. "I mean really and truly? "

"You *must* come. It's settled," declared Tessa with conviction.

"But what about your mother and father," asked the cautious Harold.

"I haven't got a mother—and Daddy always lets me do exactly as I like," replied Tessa cheerfully.

Her hearers were stricken dumb.

* 9 *

SOON AFTER the false alarm about Tessa MacRynne having measles there was a *bona fide* outbreak of the disease in Saint Elizabeth's. Sister Ferguson had said there was measles in the town so it was not really surprising but it was exceedingly annoying for it disrupted classes and drove the form mistresses distracted and interfered with practices for the Christmas Concert.

One day when Charlotte was shopping in Larchester she met Mr. Swayne and they stopped for a few minutes to chat.

"I say," said Mr. Swayne. "Have you got measles?"

Charlotte was used to Mr. Swayne's mode of speech so she knew what he meant. "Yes," said Charlotte ruefully. "Have you?"

"Lord, yes!" groaned Mr. Swayne. "It's measles, measles all the way. I'm sick of spotty faces. I'm fed up. Look here, Miss Fairlie, come and have dinner with me at the Golden Hind."

"It's very nice of you——" began Charlotte.

"Splendid!"

"I didn't say I'd come."

"But you will, won't you?"

At that very moment Professor Eastwood passed. He looked at them and walked on.

"No," said Charlotte firmly. "Thank you very much Mr. Swayne, but honestly——"

"Because of that gargoyle!" exclaimed Mr. Swayne bitterly.

"That—and others."

"I don't believe anybody would bother their heads about us."

"Oh yes they would. I might just as well type out a notice and have it pinned up on the school notice-board."

Mr. Swayne roared with laughter. "Why don't you? I'll do the same: *Miss Charlotte Fairlie is dining with Mr. Lawrence Swayne at the Golden Hind to-morrow night at 8 o'clock precisely.*"

"It would come to the same thing in the end," declared Charlotte smiling.

"Is that the only reason?" asked Mr. Swayne. "I mean you don't hate the sight of me or anything?"

"Of course I don't hate the sight of you," laughed Charlotte.

"Well, what about going somewhere else? Look here, Miss Fairlie, will you dine with me at Borley Manor Hotel? It's only about six miles from Saint Elizabeth's on the other side of the hills. The place is really a country house turned into a hotel and I'm told it's pretty good. We could have a nice quiet dinner and a chat—and nobody would be any the wiser."

Charlotte hesitated. It seemed silly to refuse. Outside school hours her time was her own and she could do as she pleased. The prospect of getting away from all her worries and bothers for a few hours was very attractive.

"Do come," said Mr. Swayne urgently. "It will do us both good to get away from spotty faces for a bit."

"All right, I will," nodded Charlotte. "I'll meet you at Borley Manor to-morrow evening at half-past seven."

"Cheers, loud and prolonged!" exclaimed Mr. Swayne.

Charlotte was early at the rendezvous but Mr. Swayne was

there before her; he came down the steps of the hotel to meet her as she drove up to the door. He was wearing a dinner-jacket and a soft white pleated shirt and he looked extremely well in the conventional evening dress. Charlotte, also, had dressed up for the occasion so they made a modish couple and Mr. Swayne commented upon the fact in his usual forthright manner.

"I say, we do look nice, don't we?" he said pausing before a long mirror in the hall. "I was hoping you'd do me proud—and you have."

"I thought of putting on my Board-Meeting hat," declared Charlotte with mock solemnity.

"Don't joke about it," begged Mr. Swayne with a shudder. "That hat isn't a subject for jest."

"I wouldn't dream of joking about it," Charlotte told him. "That hat got me my job."

"Oh, no!" he exclaimed . . . and then suddenly he chuckled. "Oh—I see. Yes, perhaps it did. I'm rather dim, aren't I?"

"Only in some ways," replied Charlotte kindly.

They were both in a festive mood—it was a reaction from measles—the dinner was good and a bottle of claret completed their enjoyment. They joked and laughed and chatted companionably.

"Look here, Miss Fairlie," said Mr. Swayne. (He always prefixed any important remark in this unnecessary fashion; but perhaps it *was* necessary at Bells Hill). "Look here, Miss Fairlie, I'm not going to call you Miss Fairlie any longer; I'm going to call you Charlotte. My name is Lawrence in case you don't know it already."

"I've seen it on the list of members of the Board of Governors," said Charlotte gravely.

"You don't mind, do you?"

"Mind? Why should I mind what name you were given at your baptism?"

"I mean—Oh, you know perfectly well what I mean," declared Lawrence Swayne. "Anyhow I'm going to call you Charlotte; you can call me anything you like."

" 'He would answer to hie, or to any loud cry,' " suggested Charlotte in a thoughtful voice.

Lawrence chuckled. "That's the fellow who left his luggage behind on the beach! Gorgeous rubbish, isn't it? My little brutes love it. I read it to them over and over again and they never seem to get tired of it—neither do I for that matter—I suppose your young ladies are too sophisticated for nonsense rhymes?"

Charlotte did not know the answer to that question. She found herself envying Lawrence (she would have to call him Lawrence she supposed) for being in such close touch with his "little brutes". It was pleasant to think of him sitting reading *The Hunting of the Snark* surrounded by little boys, listening with all their ears and sniggering delightedly. Her job was different, it was less human and more administrative; one could not be in close touch with three hundred girls. She explained this to her companion.

"Yes, that's true enough," he agreed thoughtfully. "Your job is much more difficult; I couldn't do it to save my life. Your job needs tact and I've no tact at all—but I'm quite useful at the human side of schoolmastering. Between you and me and the gate-post I like my little brutes except when they're being particularly brutish. It's their parents that get me down . . . but I told you that before."

"You ought to get married," declared Charlotte laughing at him.

"Oh, I know," he agreed. "That would be the answer. A wife would be a tremendous help in all sorts of ways. Not only would she deal with the parents and pour out tea, she would protect me from Miss Sorley, the kindergarten mistress, and sew buttons on my pyjamas."

This sort of talk—half sense and half nonsense—whiled away the time very pleasantly and Charlotte was sorry when it was time to go.

* 10 *

SOME WEEKS after the dinner-party at Borley Manor Hotel Miss Pinkerton asked for an interview with Miss Fairlie and was granted the request. Miss Post ushered her into the headmistress's sitting-room and retired to the office. She retired most reluctantly for she would have given a week's salary to have heard what the two ladies said to one another. Everybody in Saint Elizabeth's knew that there was no love lost between them; everybody in Saint Elizabeth's knew there had been " a row " and that Miss Pinkerton had sent in her resignation. How this news had got about is one of those mysteries which will probably remain a mystery for all time; but somehow or other it had spread all over the school like wild-fire and not a single person had expressed regret upon hearing it. Miss Pinkerton's was an unlovable personality.

When Miss Post had retired, and shut the door behind her, Miss Pinkerton re-opened it to see if she were listening at the keyhole. Fortunately for her she was not.

"A most inquisitive woman," explained Miss Pinkerton. "I don't know why you keep her."

"I have no secrets," replied Charlotte, not quite truthfully.

"Haven't you?" asked Miss Pinkerton significantly. She added in dramatic tones, "I know everything! "

"You know everything?" echoed Charlotte in bewilderment.

"Yes, everything. It has taken some time to collect all the facts, but I was determined to get to the bottom of the mystery."

"What mystery?"

"You needn't look so innocent! I tell you I know everything—all about your scheming and the way you carried on with that girl—and about the lies you told."

"You must be mad!" exclaimed Charlotte.

"Oh no, I'm not!" cried Miss Pinkerton. "I can say what I like. It doesn't matter what I say because I'm leaving Saint Elizabeth's anyhow."

Charlotte looked at her in disgust. Her face was very red and her eyes were shining fiercely behind her spectacles.

"Well, haven't you anything to say?" asked Miss Pinkerton.

"I should like to hear what you have to say first," replied Charlotte very quietly. "What are you accusing me of doing?"

"Lying," declared Miss Pinkerton. "I know all about it now. I know everything . . . " she gasped and continued, "You took that MacRynne girl for a drive in your car and pretended she was ill—pretended she was sickening for measles. You were *seen* with the girl. The wife of the man at the Thornbush Inn saw you coming out of the wood together so it's no use denying it. What were you doing in the wood, I wonder! She saw you both—and she saw your car standing in the road with all its lights on. There's no mistake about it because she spoke to you and you said you were in a hurry and must get back to school! Then you came back here and took the girl to your private sitting-room. One of the maids saw you; she thought nothing of it at the time, but when I asked her about it she remembered. Then you came to me and said the girl was ill and you had sent her to the sick-room. It wasn't true! I don't care what you do with the girls—though it seems very strange—but I *do* mind your lying to *me*. The girl wasn't ill at all, but you had to cover your tracks so you put her in the sick-room and kept her there. Sister Ferguson stood in with you of course —I went to her and asked her about it but she evaded all my questions—I could get no satisfaction out of her. She said they thought the girl was sickening for measles; you had told her to say that. Is it likely that Sister Ferguson would have borrowed a book of poems for her out of the School Library if she thought the girl was sickening for measles? Is it likely she would have kept the girl in the sick-room? She would have sent her straight to the San. to be isolated—that's what she would have done."

Miss Pinkerton paused for a moment to gasp, and then continued, "The girl was in it too. The girl lied to me when I asked her about it—and she was very impertinent. That's the worst of all. That's much the worst part of it. How can I maintain my authority if the girls are taught to lie to me and encouraged to be impertinent? I don't know what you were doing with the girl—taking her out in your car when she should have been in class and entertaining her in your private sitting-room. One of the unwritten laws of Saint Elizabeth's is that there should be no favouritism—Miss Bain was very particular that all the girls should be treated alike—but if that isn't favouritism I don't know what is! To take the girl out in your car, to entertain her in your own room—isn't that favouritism? However of course that's your affair and I wouldn't have interfered if it hadn't been for the way the girl behaved—the lies and impertinence and showing off and making the other girls laugh—that's what annoyed me. Naturally the girl was above herself, having received all that attention from you. She thought she could do as she pleased! At the best of times she isn't at all a *nice* girl. She's too full of herself. She's the type that should be put in her place and kept there. I find her impossible to teach—impossible. She's extremely backward and she doesn't even try. She's a bad influence—a disruptive influence——" Miss Pinkerton stopped. She was out of breath—and no wonder.

Charlotte was silent. She was thinking quickly. The affair had taken on an ugly aspect; it was horrible. To Charlotte it seemed that the most horrible part of the affair was Miss Pinkerton's vindictive nature which had prompted her detective work. Charlotte shuddered at the idea of Miss Pinkerton ferretting about; poking into everything with her thin pink nose; asking this person and that; talking to Mrs. Spurling at the Thornbush Inn; interrogating the servants and piecing the story together. It was appalling to think that any woman could behave like that. But it was no good dwelling upon Miss Pinkerton's behaviour, Charlotte realised that she must pull herself together and decide how she was to tackle the matter. Unfortunately she could not deny Miss Pinkerton's accusations for they were founded on fact. Unless she told Miss Pinkerton the exact truth she could deny nothing . . . and she did not want to tell Miss Pinkerton the truth about Tessa's affairs. Miss Pinkerton could not be trusted.

"What are you going to do?" asked Charlotte at last.

"You mean you admit it?" asked Miss Pinkerton incredulously.

"No," replied Charlotte quietly. "I don't admit anything and I don't deny anything. There is no need for me to justify my actions to you. If you have a complaint to make about Tessa MacRynne's behaviour that's different. You can send her to me and I'll speak to her."

Miss Pinkerton was so taken aback that she was speechless. She opened her mouth twice and gasped—rather like a cod—and shut it again without saying a word. She had expected Miss Fairlie to be very angry indeed and to deny everything . . . or else to admit everything and beg for mercy. Miss Fairlie did neither the one nor the other. She was perfectly calm and collected—at least she appeared so to Miss Pinkerton.

"You know the rules," continued Miss Fairlie, pressing home her advantage. "If you have a complaint to make about a girl's behaviour you have only to say so. I shall certainly send for her and speak to her about it."

"But that's only—secondary," gasped Miss Pinkerton. "Of course she is—impertinent and—and difficult, but that's only—secondary."

"Secondary?" asked Miss Fairlie, frowning in perplexity.

"Yes, it's you—your behaviour. I mean you aren't fit to be—to be in your position."

Miss Fairlie remained calm and silent.

"Miss Bain thinks so too!" exclaimed Miss Pinkerton, stung into indiscretion and thereby divulging the fact that she had been to see Miss Bain and had talked the whole thing over with that lady.

Miss Fairlie still said nothing.

"Oh, you think it doesn't matter!" cried Miss Pinkerton. "You think Miss Bain has nothing to do with the school! But you'll find you're mistaken. Miss Bain still has a good deal of influence with some members of the Board of Governors."

"I'm afraid I have some letters to write," said Miss Fairlie quite pleasantly. "I want them to catch the afternoon post; so unless there's anything else you want to tell me . . ."

Apparently there was not. The interview was over.

Charlotte was by no means as calm as she had seemed; in fact she was absolutely furious; but it was a cold sort of rage which left her brain as clear as crystal. Of course the whole thing was a storm in a tea-cup but if Miss Bain and Miss Pinkerton took their story to Mr. Allnut they might cause a good deal of trouble.

Charlotte considered the matter for a few moments and then she went to her telephone and asked for the number of Sir Joseph Spinner's house. Sir Joseph was at home and signified his willingness to see Miss Fairlie in about half-an-hour, if that would suit her. It suited her admirably. She dressed and got her car and drove into Larchester at an unusually rapid pace.

The Spinner Mansion was on the outskirts of the town; it was a large place standing in a park with fine old trees. Everything was beautifully kept; the gates were properly painted; the drive was smooth and weedless; the gardens were in perfect trim. Miss Fairlie was expected and was ushered into Sir Joseph's study without delay; he was sitting at his knee-hole desk which was covered with important looking documents.

Miss Fairlie apologised for bothering Sir Joseph.

"Not at all, not at all," said Sir Joseph. "You know my interest—my deep interest in the affairs of Saint Elizabeth's. Please sit down, Miss Fairlie; you will find that chair quite comfortable, I think." As he spoke he looked at his visitor and was somewhat surprised; he had always thought Miss Fairlie a good-looking woman, but to-day he suddenly realised that she was very pretty indeed—in fact beautiful— and she looked years younger than usual. Her grey eyes were shining and her cheeks were pink and several little curls of very pretty hair had escaped from under her hat. Sir Joseph did not know much about women's clothes but he knew a well-dressed woman when he saw one and he realised that he was seeing one now.

"I'm in rather a fix," said Miss Fairlie, smiling at him in a very charming manner. "I expect it will sound very petty to you; but I don't know what to do; so I've come to ask your advice."

Sir Joseph almost purred. "My dear young lady—of course! Any help I can give you—any advice—either—er—private—or—or about school affairs."

"A school affair," said Miss Fairlie.

Sir Joseph looked a shade disappointed.

"But very confidential," added Miss Fairlie.

This sounded more interesting and Sir Joseph pushed his papers to one side and prepared himself to listen.

"I'm afraid it's a very long story," Miss Fairlie warned him. "But it's no use asking your advice unless I tell you everything."

"No use at all," agreed Sir Joseph smiling encouragingly. "Begin at the beginning and tell me the whole thing."

Charlotte hesitated for a moment (it was merely to collect her thoughts and to put them in order) and then she began at the beginning as Sir Joseph had suggested and told him everything. She began by telling him about her talk with Mrs. MacRynne (for that was really the beginning of it) and she went on to describe her drive back from Larchester after the Board Meeting and her capture of the runaway near the Thornbush Inn. She told Sir Joseph about Tessa's grief and despair and how she had smuggled the child into her sitting-room, and managed to cover up her escapade; she told him about her letter to Colonel MacRynne and the Colonel's reply . . . finally she told him about Miss Pinkerton's ferreting and the stormy interview which had taken place that very afternoon. She told her story clearly and in detail: it was the truth, the whole truth and nothing but the truth. When she had finished she sat back in her chair and waited for the verdict.

"Dear me," said Sir Joseph. "That's bad news about the MacRynnes."

This reaction to her tale was not quite what Miss Fairlie had expected but in a way it was quite satisfactory. "You know the MacRynnes?" she inquired.

"Of course I know Rory MacRynne! He has some of the best salmon fishing in Scotland."

"At Targ?" suggested Miss Fairlie.

"Oh, he's a big landowner. He owns a good slice of the mainland as well as the island . . . I don't know how many thousands of acres. The salmon fishing is on the mainland. I mean in the river, of course."

"Of course," nodded Miss Fairlie. They seemed to be getting a long way from her particular problem but no doubt they would return to it in time.

"I never met Mrs. MacRynne," continued Sir Joseph. "She was away from home—in Italy I think—when I stayed at Targ, but I believe she's a beautiful woman, isn't she?"

"Very beautiful."

"Dangerous," said Sir Joseph shaking his head sadly. "Targ is a lovely spot—absolutely unique—but I don't wonder she found it dull. I shouldn't like to stay there all the year round myself. Rory is perfectly happy there, but he is used to it. Do you think he is very much upset by this deplorable affair?"

Miss Fairlie had brought Colonel MacRynne's letter with her; she handed it to Sir Joseph and waited while he read it.

"Yes," said Sir Joseph thoughtfully as he folded it up and handed it back. "Yes—a very good letter. One wonders what he really feels about it. Somehow, when I was there, I had a feeling that things were a little strained and that he avoided speaking of his wife. He is devoted to the child, of course."

"Did you see Tessa?"

"Yes, a most attractive child with delightful manners. One evening Rory tackled me and said he was thinking of sending her to school: what did I think about it? So of course I told him he couldn't do better than send her to Saint Elizabeth's. He took my advice and put down her name then and there. As a matter of fact," said Sir Joseph with a little smile, "As a matter of fact—since we seem to be having such a very confidential and truthful conversation—I may tell you that I managed to create a vacancy for Tessa MacRynne. As you know the school is full, and there is a waiting list, but Rory was so anxious that she could come to Saint Elizabeth's this term that I managed to—er—create a vacancy."

"Yes, I see," nodded Miss Fairlie. She hesitated for a moment and then said, "But, Sir Joseph, what am I to do?"

"What are you to do?" echoed Sir Joseph in surprise. "You've done all you could—nobody could have done more. You've been the soul of tact and discretion. You prevented the child from running away; you comforted her and covered her tracks and sent her back to school. What more could anybody have done?"

"You think I did right?"

"Most certainly," said Sir Joseph with conviction. "It is entirely due to your—er—resource that the child has been able to settle down happily at school. If she had carried out her plan of going home without official leave it would have been exceedingly bad for the prestige of Saint Elizabeth's and—in addition—the school would have lost a very valuable connection. Rory MacRynne knows everyone worth knowing in the West of Scotland and I am hoping we may get quite a number of girls—and girls of the right type—with the help of his influence. No doubt Rory will recommend the school to his friends. Oh yes, it will be a very valuable connection."

Miss Fairlie looked somewhat taken aback; she said

quickly, "I didn't think of all that—I didn't know—I mean it was Tessa herself—it was for her sake that I——"

"But of course," agreed Sir Joseph interrupting her. "I understand your feelings perfectly. You have made them abundantly clear. Naturally you are more concerned with the human side of the problem, but pray do not think me inhuman because my first concern is the prestige of the school. The girl is your chief responsibility; Saint Elizabeth's is mine. We approach the matter from a slightly different angle but we arrive at the same conclusion."

Miss Fairlie felt she ought to clap—somebody should clap—but, although she was amused at Sir Joseph's way of putting it, she saw that what he said was perfectly true and she acquitted him of inhumanity.

"But what about Miss Pinkerton?" she inquired, bringing him back to the point.

"A most obnoxious female," declared Sir Joseph, roundly.

"Yes," agreed Miss Fairlie, who thought the adjective exceedingly well-chosen. "Yes, she is . . . but I can't help being sorry for her. In fact I feel a little guilty about Miss Pinkerton. If I hadn't been appointed headmistress of Saint Elizabeth's Miss Pinkerton would have got the post."

"The Board of Governors would not have selected Miss Pinkerton," said Sir Joseph with conviction.

Miss Fairlie was silent. She was wondering how Sir Joseph would have prevented the Board from selecting Miss Pinkerton; she had no doubt whatever but that he *would* have prevented it.

"Let me see now," said Sir Joseph. "You say that Miss Pinkerton has talked it over with Miss Bain and they intend to take their story to Mr. Allnut?"

Miss Fairlie nodded.

"Let them do their worst," said Sir Joseph cheerfully.

This seemed to be the end of the interview so Miss Fairlie rose. "I won't take up any more of your time," she said. "I'm afraid I've been very long-winded, but I wanted to explain everything——"

"Yes, yes—quite right—but don't run away. My wife would like to meet you. She said she would have tea ready for us about five—it must be five now." He glanced at his clock as he spoke. It was exactly five. Sir Joseph had said it must be, so of course it was. Miss Fairlie realised that even time—which is said to wait for no man—was influenced by Sir Joseph's wishes.

"Don't worry about it any more," said Sir Joseph as he led the way to the drawing room. "Just leave it to me. I may have to—er—have a little chat with one or two members of the Board before the next meeting, but depend upon it I shall be discreet. Leave it to me, Miss Fairlie."

Miss Fairlie assured him that she would leave the matter in his hands with absolute confidence.

Lady Spinner was small and frail; somehow she seemed older than Sir Joseph but perhaps this was because she was delicate and he was robust. He was very gentle with her and Charlotte saw the fire-eating Sir Joseph in quite a new light that afternoon. He handed tea, filled the tea-pot with boiling water from the silver kettle and hurried to find his wife's spectacles.

Lady Spinner asked Charlotte where she was going for Christmas and Charlotte replied that she was going to stay with her aunt who had a flat in Kensington. As a matter of fact she was not looking forward to it at all for she found the Christmas festivities, in which Aunt Lydia expected her to take part, false and artificial. Charlotte was a lonely person, and at Christmas lonely people are more lonely than usual; they are apt to look back to happier times with longing, or to look forward to the future with apprehension. Where shall I be next Christmas, wondered Charlotte. Where shall I be ten years hence—or twenty years hence?

"Talking of holidays," said Sir Joseph. "I am wondering whether you have made any plans for the Easter holidays, Miss Fairlie. There is to be an international educational conference at Copenhagen——"

"But my dear!" objected Lady Spinner. "Perhaps Miss Fairlie would rather have a real holiday after her hard work at Saint Elizabeth's during the term. If Miss Fairlie went to the conference it would not be a holiday at all."

"There would be compensations," replied Sir Joseph smiling quite humanly. "If Miss Fairlie wished to attend the conference she would go as a representative of Saint Elizabeth's and it would be only proper for the Board of Governors to defray the expenses of her trip. The conference lasts for three or four days and the rest of the time would be her own. I think Miss Fairlie would find it interesting—but there is no need to decide here and now."

Charlotte was attracted by the plan. It certainly would be interesting to attend the conference, to meet delegates from other countries and to hear their views about educational matters . . . and she was not averse to having all her expenses paid.

"Leave it for the meantime," said Sir Joseph. "Think it over at your leisure and let me know. I feel sure the Board will agree with me in the matter."

Charlotte felt sure of it, too.

* 11 *

MISS PINKERTON had complained of Tessa MacRynne's behaviour in class so it behoved Miss Fairlie to send for Tessa and reprimand her for her sins, but when Tessa appeared, wearing her usual friendly smile, it was not easy to be stern.

"Miss Pinkerton has complained to me about you," said Charlotte, doing her best.

The friendly smile faded. "Oh dear, has she?" said Tessa regretfully. "I'm sorry Miss Fairlie, but she really is most awfully unreasonable."

Charlotte sympathised inwardly, but continued to do her duty. "She said you were impertinent, Tessa."

"But I wasn't—or at least I didn't mean to be. She hates me like poison because I'm so bad at algebra. That's the trouble, really. I suppose I couldn't stop having algebra, could I?"

"No, you couldn't," replied her headmistress firmly.

"It's such a waste of time," mourned Tessa. "I'm miles behind the others and I couldn't possibly catch up however hard I tried."

"So you don't try?"

"Well—no, I don't really. Miss Pinkerton is never satisfied so what's the good of bothering? You see, Miss Fairlie, my brain isn't that sort of brain."

"Everyone has to learn algebra," declared Miss Fairlie.

"I couldn't possibly make an exception of you, so you must just grapple with it and do your best—even if you don't like it."

"It's Miss Pinkerton I don't like," said Tessa frankly.

"You must do your best with her too," declared Charlotte, hiding a smile.

"I suppose I must," said Tessa reluctantly. "I'm quite polite to her you know. Honestly I'm not impertinent. It's just sometimes I—well, I say something that makes the other girls laugh—if you see what what I mean."

Charlotte saw exactly what she meant.

"What about asking Daddy if I need learn algebra?" suggested Tessa with a sudden gleam of hope. "I believe he would say I needn't. I asked him before, when I had Miss Sloan, and he agreed at once. He said cut it out and read Shakespeare instead, because algebra would never be any use to me and Shakespeare would."

Charlotte tried to think of an occasion when algebra had been of use to her, but unfortunately she failed. "But it might be useful," she said without much conviction. "It depends upon what you're going to do when you're grown-up."

"Oh, that's decided," declared Tessa. "There's no difficulty about *that*. Daddy has no son, so of course I shall help him with Targ—and it's a whole-time job I can tell you. There are the farms to look after and the tenants and all the people on the island. They belong to us, you see, and if anything goes wrong they come to Daddy and he tells them what to do. They come to Daddy when they're ill, or if they've quarrelled with their neighbours and he arranges everything. Of course they help us too—it isn't a bit one sided—they think there's nobody in the world like Daddy; he's—he's a sort of king," said Tessa trying to explain. "He's a sort of king, but much *nearer* than a king. I know it seems silly *here*," said Tessa, looking round the cosy room with its cretonne-covered chairs and its air of conventionality, " but it doesn't seem silly *there*. It seems quite ordinary and right."

Charlotte nodded. It was interesting to discover that the Feudal System still existed in this year of grace and apparently functioned admirably with benefit to all concerned.

"Daddy lets me help him," continued Tessa, who enjoyed nothing better than to talk about Targ. "I help him in all sorts of ways. There was one night—it was New Year's Eve —when he came and woke me and we took a girl across to the mainland in the yacht. She was frightfully ill and Daddy thought it was appendicitis so of course he wanted to get her to hospital as soon as possible. There's an early morning plane from Invergoily to Glasgow and we had to get her there in time. Of course Euan usually goes with Daddy in the yacht but they were having a *Ho-ro-gheallaidh* and Euan wasn't fit to go."

"What were they having?" asked Charlotte.

"It's a party," explained Tessa with a little smile. "An absolutely terrific party that goes on all night—sometimes it goes on all the next day as well, it depends upon how much whisky there is. They always have a *Ho-ro-gheallaidh* at Hogmanay. That's THE night, of course. Well, none of the men were fit to go with Daddy and of course he couldn't manage the yacht and look after Morag all by himself; that's why he took me. It was cold and windy but the moonlight was gorgeous and I would have loved it if I hadn't been frightened. Morag was so ill, you see. I had to keep her covered up with blankets. It was difficult because every time I got her comfortably settled she turned and twisted and threw them off. I thought she was going to die any minute. Daddy was too busy steering the yacht and managing the engine to help me, but he kept on calling out to me and saying it would be all right and to hang on to Morag and we would soon be there. Well, we got her there in plenty of time for the plane so I needn't have worried . . . and coming back it was lovely. It really was simply lovely, just Daddy and me together, and the feeling that I really had been useful."

Tessa paused. Her eyes were shining like stars at the memory of how lovely it had been.

Charlotte had listened absorbed to the little story. It had been told so simply and yet so graphically that it was like a window, opening upon another world . . . and what a strange world! thought Charlotte. What a simple natural world! What a good sort of world!

"Did Morag get better?" she inquired.

"Oh yes," nodded Tessa. "They operated on Morag the moment she got to the hospital and she recovered quite soon. Mummy was angry about it—about Daddy waking me up and taking me—but Daddy said it was good for me to learn to do things for other people. Of course Euan was terribly upset and ashamed—but, as a matter of fact, it did him good because I don't think he has ever got drunk again—not even at Hogmanay."

There was a silence when Tessa had finished her story. Charlotte felt a little uncomfortable, for this interview seemed to have got off the lines. She had summoned Tessa with every intention of scolding her for her behaviour but she had not managed to do so and now she felt even less inclined for the task. Still, it must be performed and, although she would fain have heard more about Targ and about Tessa's father (who had now become an almost legendary figure, a cross between The Forsaken Merman and The Lord of the Isles), she was obliged to do her duty.

"Tessa," she began.

"Oh, Miss Fairlie, what a darling, ugly, beautiful creature!" exclaimed Tessa rapturously. "Why didn't I notice him before? I suppose I was too miserable or something. Do tell me who he is."

It was the Buddha of course. There he sat upon the mantelpiece in his night-blue robes, smiling his enigmatic smile. Charlotte should have resisted this red herring, but she could not resist it. Tessa so obviously appreciated the beautiful ugliness of her treasure.

"I'm afraid I don't know very much about him," said Charlotte regretfully. "I call him my Buddha but he's really The Buddhist Priest in Contemplation. I bought him in a little junk-shop in London because I liked him so much." She hesitated.

"Tell me . . . *please*," cried Tessa, scenting a story.

Charlotte had never told the story to anybody—except the young policeman—but there was no harm in telling Tessa about it so she related it in detail then and there, and Tessa listened to every word with flattering attention.

"Oh, I *do* think it's nice," declared Tessa when she had finished. "Of course he's magic, you know—that's the explanation. He was tired of sitting on the shelf, all dusty and dirty with nobody to admire him, so he made the shower come on at the right moment . . . and he magicked the young man into thinking the price was five pounds, because he knew you wouldn't pay more for him . . . and when you went back to look for the shop you couldn't find it because he had magicked it away."

Charlotte was enchanted with this solution of the mystery and by the serious manner in which Tessa had offered it. The solution harmonised so beautifully with her own feelings about the Buddha that Charlotte—almost—believed it.

Charlotte felt quite ridiculously grateful. Tessa had given her something worth having . . . for the truth was that until now there had been an uneasy feeling at the back of

Charlotte's mind (she could not enjoy the companionship of the Buddha without a feeling of guilt) but Tessa's little story about his magical propensities had cleared away the shadow completely. No ordinary human could do anything to counteract the powers of magic, so she need not feel guilty any longer.

It was now more than ever difficult to re-open the subject of algebra and the obnoxious Miss Pinkerton; in fact Charlotte found it impossible, so she left it alone.

"May I tell Daddy about the Buddha?" asked Tessa as she said good-bye. "I won't tell anybody *here*, because that would be swank, but Daddy would understand."

"Yes, of course you can tell him."

"He'll like it," declared Tessa. "And you see I want to have lots of interesting things to tell him—to cheer him up." She hesitated and then added joyfully. "It's only a week until the Christmas holidays! Oh dear, I can hardly believe it! It feels like a hundred years since I saw Daddy—and Targ."

* 12 *

CHRISTMAS CAME. Charlotte spent the holidays with Aunt Lydia as had been arranged and found herself even more out of tune with the festivities than usual. She had nothing in common with Aunt Lydia's friends and it did not amuse her to see a group of middle-aged people pulling crackers and wearing paper hats and kissing coyly beneath the mistletoe. In fact she found it revolting and although she did her best to disguise her feelings she was not altogether successful.

"You should try to join in the fun more whole-heartedly," said Aunt Lydia. "It's the Christmas Spirit, Charlotte."

Charlotte said nothing in reply but she thought about it seriously: was there any connection between Aunt Lydia's parties and the "Christmas Spirit?" Was it priggish to be unable to join in the "fun?" She thought of the noise and the laughter and the feasting . . . and then she thought of the birth of a little baby in a quiet stable; the singing of the angels and the coming of the shepherds to worship their Heavenly King. The more Charlotte thought about it the more she became convinced that the orgies of Aunt Lydia and her friends were not Christian at all, but pagan.

When the holidays were over Charlotte returned to her comfortable quarters at Saint Elizabeth's with a sense of relief; this little suite of rooms was her home—or at least she felt more at home in it than anywhere else. Here she

had privacy and her own treasures round her, and although
her days were busy her evenings could be spent in peace.
She decided that she would not go to Aunt Lydia's for the
Easter holidays, she would take Sir Joseph's advice and go
to Copenhagen instead . . . so she made all her arrangements and began to look forward to her trip. She was to go
by air and the Board of Governors agreed unanimously
that her expenses were to be paid.

The term was somewhat dull. It was all the more so
because there was scarlet fever in the town and various
precautions were taken to prevent it from invading Saint
Elizabeth's. Larchester was put "out of bounds" and as
little communication as possible was held with the outside
world. There were several cases at Bells Hill which meant
that Lawrence Swayne was in quarantine and there were
no more dinners at Borley Manor Hotel. It also meant that
Donny Eastwood could not go home and spend Sunday
afternoons with her brothers. In fact the outbreak of scarlet
fever caused a great deal of inconvenience to the pupils and
staff of Saint Elizabeth's. Fortunately the precautions were
successful and Saint Elizabeth's escaped.

The day before school broke up there was a discreet tap
upon the door of Charlotte's sitting-room and Miss Post
appeared.

"It's Tessa MacRynne," she said. "Tessa is leaving to-day
instead of to-morrow with the others so she has come to
say good-bye. She says you gave her permission to leave
to-day—perhaps you don't remember—she lives in some
outlandish place in Scotland."

Charlotte nodded.

"She's all dressed up," added Miss Post in disapproving
tones.

Tessa was dressed up in the sense that she had discarded
her school unifrom, but there was no need to be disapproving

for girls were allowed to travel home in clothes of their own choice. Besides, the clothes of her choice were suitable and becoming: Charlotte thoroughly approved of the brownish-green tweed coat and skirt which matched Tessa's hazel eyes, and the small felt hat turned up at the side with a black-cock's feather.

"How nice you look, Tessa!" exclaimed Charlotte impulsively.

"Oh, I'm glad," said Tessa. "I mean I'm glad you think so, Miss Fairlie. It doesn't feel right to come and see you in these clothes but the taxi is coming for me in half an hour so I had to have everything packed. That was why."

"Yes, of course," said Charlotte.

There was a slight constraint between them. They had been very close to one another—they shared a secret—but they had not spoken to one another for weeks. It was because their little world was full of inquisitive eyes. If Miss Fairlie were seen to speak to one girl more than another everybody noticed it and discussed it. They both understood the situation perfectly but that did not make them feel any easier nor banish the constraint.

There was a short but somewhat uncomfortable silence and then Tessa's eyes fell upon the Buddha. "He's still there!" she exclaimed.

"Still working his magic," agreed Charlotte.

They smiled at one another and the constraint was gone.

"Miss Fairlie," said Tessa. "I want to tell you something. I had a letter from Daddy this morning: Mummy is going to marry somebody else. I just wanted to tell you about it, that's all. You needn't be sorry for me, because I don't mind a bit and I think Daddy is glad. He knows it's finished now."

It was a strangely adult speech for a girl of fourteen; all the more strange because in some ways Tessa seemed younger than her contemporaries. Charlotte had been forbidden to

C.F.   H offer sympathy and, this being so, she did not know what to say.

"Oh, I know you think I'm hard!" exclaimed Tessa. "But it makes you hard when somebody you love goes away and forgets all about you. I mean you've either got to be hard or soft—there's no medium. I can forgive her for leaving me but I can never, never forgive her for leaving Daddy."

"Yes—well—I should forget about it if you can." Charlotte hesitated and then went on: "It's a very bad thing to harbour resentment, Tessa. Do you understand what I mean? It won't do your mother any harm if you think unkindly about her, but it will do harm to yourself—to your own character. We should forgive people who have hurt us not only for *their* sake but because if our hearts are full of unkind feelings it puts us wrong with God."

"I know," admitted Tessa rather uncomfortably. "You mean that bit in the Bible where it says you must leave your gift on the altar and go and make it up with your brother and then come back and offer your gift. You read it at Prayers one morning and of course I saw it meant me. But I can't make it up with her, can I?"

Charlotte was surprised for she had always thought that particular passage applied to herself and her own problems; not only to her relationship with her father but also, more recently, to her relationship with Miss Pinkerton. In both cases she had harboured resentment and in both cases she had used the same remedy and had found it worked.

"You can't make it up with her," agreed Charlotte. "But you can forgive her. I think you'll find you can forgive her if you pray for her. Pray for her to be happy in her new life."

Tessa looked doubtful. "I don't think I could," she said. "I could say the words of course but it would be difficult to mean them."

"Try," said Charlotte. "Say the words. Perhaps it won't be as difficult as you expect," She hesitated and then added, "The cure for not being able to pray is—just to pray."

Tessa was silent for a few moments and then she nodded. "All right, I will," she said. "I'll do it for you—because you want me to. Will that be all right?"

Charlotte was somewhat startled. She said "yes" without thinking, and then wondered if she ought to have said "no." It was a difficult problem and she would have liked to have time for consideration before giving an answer . . . but this was not a "pi-jaw", it was one human being giving a piece of advice to another human being, and Charlotte knew that it was awfully easy to say *too much* and to dim the clear gem of wisdom with a cloud of words. So she said no more.

"There's another thing—quite a different thing—that has been bothering me," said Tessa. "It's about Donny Eastwood. You said you wondered why she didn't do better at lessons but it had nothing to do with me. But you see, I know what's the matter with Donny."

"You know?"

"It's because of her father. He's fantastic, Miss Fairlie."

Charlotte gazed at her in amazement. Anyone less fantastic than the staid and pompous professor it was difficult to imagine.

"Absolutely fantastic," repeated Tessa nodding solemnly. "He frightens them out of their wits—not only Donny but the boys as well. In fact it's worse for the boys because they live at home and Donny only goes home on Sundays."

"Do you mean they're really frightened?"

"Yes, really and truly—especially Barney. Barney is a perfect darling, and very amusing indeed. He makes up nonsense rhymes—he made up a very funny one about me—that's clever isn't it, Miss Fairlie?"

Charlotte thought it was.

"Yes, Barney is quite clever," said Tessa. "But the moment his father appears he seems to—to flop. The moment his father appears he stammers and stutters and says the silliest things—anybody would think he was half-witted. It's horrible, Miss Fairlie. Honestly it is. That dreadful man is making them stupid. That's what he's doing."

"But what does he do to them, Tessa?"

"I don't know exactly," replied Tessa in perplexity. "I don't know why they're so frightened of him. He doesn't seem frightening to me. As a matter of fact I think he's a silly little man—not clever a bit—his collar is always dirty and his trousers are baggy at the knees."

Charlotte laughed—she could not help it—but she was worried all the same. If this were true (and she did not doubt Tessa's word for a moment) it could be the reason for Donny's backwardness . . . and Lawrence Swayne had said the two boys were "nit-wits"! Of course Tessa was quite wrong about the professor; he might wear a dirty collar but he was by no means silly. In fact Charlotte happened to know that he was extremely clever in his own way and had written a book upon economics (so extremely complicated that only an expert upon the subject could make head or tail of it) and this work had brought him recognition and renown.

"Well, I've told you," said Tessa heaving a sigh of relief, for now that Miss Fairlie knew about it she felt that all was was very nearly well. Tessa had abundant faith in Miss Fairlie's power and resource. "You'll make it all right, won't you, Miss Fairlie? You'll go and see Professor Eastwood and——"

"Go and see him!" exclaimed Charlotte in horrified tones. "Oh, but I couldn't possibly—besides I'm going abroad."

"Oh, I know," agreed Tessa. "You're going to Copenhagen, aren't you?"

"How did you know?"

"Everybody knows. Everybody in Saint Elizabeth's always knows everything about you. It's just—well, you're News, you see—like the Queen."

"Oh, I see," said Charlotte vaguely. She was thinking back to the days when she had been a girl at Saint Elizabeth's and trying to remember whether Miss Bain had been News. She thought not. In fact she could not remember taking the slightest interest in how or where Miss Bain spent her well-earned holidays.

"Everybody knows you're going to Copenhagen," repeated Tessa. "There's been a frightful run on a book in the school library about Denmark. It's awfully interesting (about Hans Andersen and the little mermaid and the Vikings and Elsinore Castle) but you won't be staying in Denmark *all* the holidays, will you? So you can go and see the Eastwoods when you come back."

Charlotte tried to think of some reason for refusing the request, but she could think of none.

"Do say you will, Miss Fairlie," pleaded Tessa.

Charlotte heard herself saying she would—which was odd, because she had had every intention of saying she would not.

"Good," said Tessa smiling.

It was now time for Tessa to go—the taxi would be waiting—Charlotte pointed this out to her, but still she lingered and it was obvious that there was something else on her mind.

"I was wondering about the Summer holidays," said Tessa in a mumbling sort of voice, very different from her usual forthright manner. "I mean I don't suppose you possibly could—you probably wouldn't want to—but it doesn't take long if you fly—four hours from London Airport, that's all. You have to change at Renfrew, of course —but you probably wouldn't want to——"

"Oh!" exclaimed Charlotte who had suddenly realised that she was being invited to stay at Targ. "Oh, Tessa, how nice of you! But I don't think——"

"I knew you wouldn't," said Tessa hastily. "I never expected it really, so I'm not disappointed—at least not very."

Charlotte had to smile but she was pleased and touched all the same. It was sweet of Tessa to want her.

"It was just that I *did* want you to see Targ," added Tessa. "It is *so* beautiful; I know you'd love it."

"Yes, I'm sure I should," said Charlotte. She hesitated. She had heard so much about Targ. Why shouldn't I go? she thought.

"Oh, Miss Fairlie, you're thinking about it!" cried Tessa. "Oh, Miss Fairlie, please come—even just for a fortnight."

"But are you sure you want me? And what about your father?"

"You'll come!" cried her prospective hostess joyously. "Oh, Miss Fairlie, how absolutely gorgeous!"

"But your father may not want me——"

"Of course he will. He said I could ask a friend."

"I expect he meant a girl," said Charlotte, alarmed at the prospect of being foisted upon the Lord of the Isles against his wishes. "In fact I'm sure he meant a girl——"

"Oh yes," agreed Tessa. "And as a matter of fact I've asked the Eastwoods. They don't think their father will let them come, but I expect I'll be able to persuade him."

"Will you?" asked Charlotte doubtfully for her experience of Professor Eastwood was of a man difficult to persuade.

"I shall try, anyway," declared Tessa. "It would do them good to come to Targ . . . but that won't affect you, Miss Fairlie. You must come when it suits you and I can have the

SAINT ELIZABETH'S   119

Eastwoods either before or after. It's for you to choose."

"But we shall have to see what your father says. I can't come unless he asks me."

"I'll make him write," Tessa assured her. "I'll make him send you a proper invitation."

Charlotte tried to explain that this was not what she meant and that it would be better if Tessa could find out tactfully whether or not Colonel MacRynne would welcome a woman guest, but Tessa did not seem to understand.

"Of course he'll welcome you," she declared. "I'll make him write to you straight off the moment I get home."

13

THE WAITING-ROOM at the airfield was crowded with people; some were sitting quietly with their travelling bag beside them, others were moving about, talking to one another excitedly. Charlotte had come early and was having a cup of coffee and watching the scene with interest. She was in a holiday mood; all her worries were behind her and for three whole weeks she could be herself instead of the staid and dignified Miss Fairlie. Charlotte liked looking on and seeing the game and it amused her to fit out her fellow travellers with personal histories. It was a joy to see all these people—so wrapped up in their own affairs—and to feel interested in them but without responsibility.

Yes, that was the joy—she was not responsible for them. At Saint Elizabeth's she was responsible for everybody: for instance if one of her staff had looked as ill and miserable as that woman in the green hat Charlotte would have had to find out what on earth was the matter with her (whether it was anaemia or love or possibly liver) but the woman in the green hat was not Charlotte's concern. Charlotte was sorry for her, and could not help wondering whether a course of iron tablets would help her, but as it was impossible to do anything about it she need not worry. She heaved a sigh of relief and her eyes moved to the next table where two young girls were sitting. They were behaving very stupidly indeed, giggling and trying to smoke cigarettes and ogling the young man who was leaning against the bookstall. If they had been her own girls . . . but of course they were not, so that did not matter either.

"Hallo, Charlotte! " said a voice at her side.

She looked up, a little startled, and saw Lawrence Swayne smiling down at her. "Goodness, what are you doing here! " she exclaimed.

"The same as you, I expect," replied Lawrence. "Going over to this blinking educational conference."

Charlotte was not particularly pleased to see Lawrence; just at the moment she was perfectly satisfied with her own company; but Lawrence was so friendly and so obviously delighted to see her that her heart was melted. Lawrence reminded her of a very large black Labrador belonging to her Uncle Tom which used to follow her everywhere. On Sundays when she went to church she always tied him up in the yard, but one Sunday morning he escaped his bonds and following at a gallop overtook her at the church door and greeted her with ecstatic barks and tail-waggings. It was impossible to be cross with Sultan (though it meant she had to give up the idea of attending the service and take him home) and it was equally impossible to be cross with Lawrence.

"This is jolly," declared Lawrence (wagging an invisible tail). "I had no idea you were going to Copenhagen. To tell you the truth I haven't been looking forward to it much—conferences are always as dull as cold boiled mutton —but it will make all the difference going with you. We can laugh together at all the funny people, can't we? Where are you going to stay? "

They discovered that they had booked rooms at the same hotel.

Lawrence was a very pleasant travelling companion; he was the sort of person who receives good service without raising his voice or exerting himself in any way whatever and he made it his business to look after Charlotte's comfort.

The day was fine and sunny but there was a good deal of cloud in the sky. The plane circled round before it set out on its course and gave its passengers a marvellous view of London, tilted up like a tray. There were the green spaces of the parks and the Thames (meandering like a carelessly flung down ribbon between the buildings) and there were windows flashing in the rays of the sun. Then the land was left behind and below was the sea, slightly corrugated with waves.

The passengers had lunch in the air and by tea-time the plane was approaching Copenhagen—the Venice of the North. It was not difficult to see the reason for this proud title for the city looked perfectly beautiful from the air with its snow white buildings beside the blue sea and its blue canals and waterways . . . and there were a great many churches most of which had pale green spires or domes. Charlotte was entranced by her first sight of Copenhagen, it was a city straight out of a fairytale, nor was she disappointed when she landed and drove through the wide streets and saw the well-proportioned buildings close at hand. Everything looked so clean and tidy and the people all looked happy and well-fed.

The conference was to begin the following morning so Lawrence suggested that they should go out to dinner that evening and after a long discussion with the head-porter they ordered a taxi and went to the Wilbex Restaurant. They discovered it to be a very smart place with bright lights and a first class orchestra. Lawrence, with his usual *savoir faire*, had engaged a table upon the veranda which overlooks the Tivoli Gardens and they sat down to a real Danish meal. There was lobster with mayonnaise sauce, chicken cooked with plums, mushrooms in cream and then vanilla ice with hot chocolate sauce. The waiter was a little anxious in case they had not had enough to eat; they had had no meat, nothing solid, declared the waiter (who spoke English with an American accent) but Charlotte and Lawrence assured him that his fears were groundless; they could not have eaten another mouthful to save their lives.

After dinner they went down some steps into the Tivoli Gardens and walked round, looking at everything and enjoying themselves tremendously. It was dark by this time but there were lights everywhere and a huge fountain with rainbow illumination was playing in the middle of a garden of flowers. There were bands and scenic railways and merry-go-rounds; there were shooting galleries and coconut shies and peep-shows . . . and there were hundreds of people strolling about and amusing themselves or sitting upon chairs and listening to the music.

"Does anything particular strike you about these people?" asked Lawrence at last.

"They're very well dressed, aren't they?" replied Charlotte. "They're very quiet and well-behaved. I suppose that notice says, ' Keep off the grass ', or something of that sort, and nobody is walking on it—not even the children."

"Exactly what I was thinking," agreed Lawrence. "And there's no litter. Even the children are putting their ice-cream papers into those litter-bins. I suppose it's a good thing in a way to be so law-abiding."

"Of course it's a good thing."

"In a way," said Lawrence doubtfully. "It's a good thing from the point of view of keeping things tidy . . . but I'm thinking of my little brutes. It isn't the frightfully law-abiding ones that grow up into the finest men."

Charlotte was silent. She found the idea deeply interesting. The next few days were full of meetings; some were carefully arranged, with long speeches by delegates from various different countries, and others were free and easy debates. Delegates raised their points and explained them, others agreed or disagreed politely. Charlotte found her knowledge of French and German useful, for the conference room was like a modern Tower of Babel. She enjoyed the meetings but even more she enjoyed chatting to the delegates in the restaurant over a cup of coffee and a Danish "sandwich" (which consisted of a large slice of bread and butter with almost anything you liked to think of piled on the top). The delegates crowded into the restaurant after the meetings and sat down to talk to anybody who happened to be there.

Charlotte talked to a very smart Frenchwoman who kept a girls' school in Paris and listened to her views upon how young ladies should be polished elegantly to take their place in a drawing-room, and she talked (or rather listened) to an earnest schoolmaster from Munich, whose ideas were very different indeed. Everybody talked to everybody else . . . or to anybody who was willing to listen and could understand. Quite often Charlotte found herself playing the part of interpreter and very soon her powers became known and people would call for "Mees Fairlee" to come and unravel some misunderstanding which had arisen. Her most difficult assignment was interpreting the conversation of a Frenchman and a German who were exceedingly anxious to compare notes on the education of the young and had no knowledge whatever of one another's language. Here there was not only a difference of language but a difference of mind and it was almost impossible to explain to each gentleman what the other meant.

Sometimes Charlotte saw Lawrence for a moment amongst the crowd but she was too busy to speak to him. He looked bewildered, but quite a number of the delegates looked bewildered and anyhow she could do nothing about it.

After four days of lectures and talks and meetings the conference broke up and the delegates went home to try out all sorts of new ideas upon their pupils. Charlotte stayed on; now that she was here in Copenhagen she had no intention of leaving until she had seen some of its sights . . . and as Lawrence had the same idea they joined forces and went about together.

Amongst other things they visited Hans Christian Andersen's little mermaid who sits upon a rock in a very dejected attitude watching the ships pass by; and they visited the State Museum of Art and the National Museum and several beautiful churches. They strolled round the docks and lunched at Davidsen's Restaurant and they went to the Meat Market; they hired a car for a whole day and drove to Kronberg Castle—which is Hamlet's Elsinore—and, standing upon the ramparts, looked out across the strait to the far off coast of Sweden.

It was not exactly a restful holiday but it was a very interesting one and Charlotte enjoyed it.

The day of departure arrived. Lawrence was going over to Sweden and Charlotte was flying home. She had packed her case the night before and went down to breakfast and took her seat at the small table in the window which looked out into a large and spacious square. Presently Lawrence appeared and sat down opposite to her as usual.

" This has been extraordinarily pleasant," declared Lawrence. " I'm sorry it's over—but there you are! All good things come to an end."

Charlotte agreed. " But I'm tired," she told him. " I feel I've seen enough for the time being. I feel as if I had had a large meal of Denmark and I shall have to digest it quietly."

The waiter appeared with Lawrence's usual breakfast of

bacon and eggs and coffee and arranged the table carefully.

"Why do you always have bacon and eggs?" asked Charlotte.

"To keep up the tradition," replied Lawrence promptly. "Englishmen are supposed to breakfast upon bacon and eggs; ask any foreigner you like and he'll tell you the same story. I can't do it at home—or at least only on Sundays—but it would be a pity to destroy the illusion. I'm sorry you're tired, Charlotte."

"Not too tired," said Charlotte quickly.

"You don't look tired. In fact you're looking very nice this morning—if you don't mind my saying so. You always look nice, of course, but the fact always strikes me afresh every time I see you."

"Thank you, Lawrence," said Charlotte laughing. "I don't mind your saying so in the least."

"You really are a very pleasant companion," he added.

"So are you, Lawrence."

"Good," said Lawrence, taking up his knife and fork and beginning to eat his bacon and eggs with obvious enjoyment. "That's very good news. It opens the way, if you see what I mean. Look here, Charlotte, will you marry me?"

"Marry you!" exclaimed Charlotte in amazement. The idea of marrying Lawrence had never entered her mind for a moment. They were friends. They were good companions —nothing more.

Lawrence smiled. "This is so sudden, Mr. Swayne," he said teasingly.

"Well, it is," declared Charlotte, She smiled back at him and added, "I suppose it's a joke."

"No, it isn't a joke—it would be in very bad taste if it were—I mean it seriously. I've thought of it for some time. In fact I've thought about it ever since that night at Borley Manor when we were talking about the sort of wife I ought to have."

"You thought I'd fill the bill," said Charlotte in amusement.

"Look here, I really mean it," said Lawrence earnestly. "Just listen to me for a minute. It would be no use saying I love you deliriously because you'd know it wasn't true, but I like you immensely and your company gives me the greatest pleasure. We're good companions—you've just said so yourself—we like the same things and we laugh at the same jokes. I think we could be very happy together."

Charlotte looked at him. It was true of course.

"Think of it like this," continued Lawrence. "We're both lonely. There we sit, miles apart (you at Saint Elizabeth's, I at Bells Hill) what's the good of that? We can't even meet and chat without a horde of nosey parkers talking about it. If we were married——"

"But Lawrence——"

"Listen, Charlotte. You're fed up with all those tiresome females at Saint Elizabeth's. It's getting you down—you know it is. Well, why not marry me and come to Bells Hill? I need you. Together you and I could make a dashed good job of the school. It's quite a good school, you know. I'm working it up like anything. I've got twelve more boys this term and I'm having to take another house. The place is booming. If I had you to help me . . . "

"I don't think——" began Charlotte uncertainly.

"It's sensible," declared Lawrence, tucking in to his bacon and eggs.

But that was just the trouble, thought Charlotte. It was sensible . . . and somehow she did not want it to be sensible. She wanted . . . well, what did she want? Was she yearning for moonlight and kisses? (Idiot! said Charlotte to herself as she watched Lawrence eating bacon and eggs. Idiot, what do you want? You know you'd hate moonlight and kisses. You're not seventeen, you're nearly thirty. Lawrence is a dear. You're very fond of him and he would be a very satisfactory husband).

"Don't answer straight off," said Lawrence pouring out his coffee and sugaring it liberally. "I'd rather you thought it over. You see I've been thinking about this for ages. I can see it's a new idea to you."

"Completely new," agreed Charlotte rather breathlessly. "You aren't—I mean there isn't anyone else?"

"No," said Charlotte.

"Well that's all right. We know where we are, don't we?"

Charlotte was not sure that they did. "Have you ever been in love?" she asked a trifle diffidently.

"Lord, yes!" he replied. "Several times. It's like measles and chickenpox; you have it when you're very young and get immunised. There was never anything very serious— if that's what you mean."

It was exactly what she meant but Lawrence's cheerfully candid confession did not help Charlotte, for she had never suffered from love-chickenpox. She had seen other people knocked off their balance by the curious complaint and had wondered. I suppose I must be different, she had thought. It was true that her life had been somewhat cloistered and she had had few opportunities of meeting attractive men ... but here was Lawrence who was definitely very attractive— and pleasant—and eligible—and, although she saw all that quite clearly, she was not in love with him.

"Don't worry," said Lawrence as he spread lashings of the best Danish butter upon a hot roll. "Don't worry about it whatever you do. Just think about it off and on until you get used to the idea. I'm pretty certain you'll see what an absolutely clinking idea it is." He grinned at her and took a large bite out of the roll. When he was able to speak again he continued cheerfully. "This isn't going to spoil our friendship, you know. If you say yes I'll be as pleased as a dog with two tails to wag, and if you say no we'll go on just as we are."

Lawrence was very sensible. There was no doubt of that.

"I think it will be no," said Charlotte uncertainly.

"But you haven't thought about it," Lawrence pointed out. "You haven't weighed the pros and cons. Naturally your first reaction is no. That's what I expected. Just do as I said and think it over, there's no hurry at all . . . but there is hurry about your plane," added Lawrence, glancing at his watch. "Yes, we'll have to leave here in about ten minutes. I'm coming to the airfield to see you off."

* 14 *

ON HER return from Denmark Charlotte went straight back to Saint Elizabeth's. The term had not begun and the school was in process of being thoroughly cleaned and re-painted, so it was not very comfortable, but she did not mind. She was free to do as she pleased; that was the main thing. She had said to Lawrence that she wanted to be quiet and digest all that she had heard and seen; first there were her notes upon the conference and second her impression of Denmark. But she could not settle down comfortably to these pleasant and interesting tasks until she had performed another task which she felt sure would be unpleasant. She had promised Tessa that she would visit the Eastwoods. It could do no good, of course; she could not possibly speak to the professor about his behaviour to his children and "make it all right" but a promise was a promise.

Charlotte dropped in at teatime (she had decided that she would have a better chance of seeing what was what if her visit were unexpected). She was uneasy about it, for it was not her habit to invade the houses of her pupils without invitation, and it did not help matters when she saw Donny's amazement and dismay at the unheralded appearance of her headmistress.

The boys were startled too. In fact the three Eastwoods—who as usual were having tea together in the dining-room—

were as terrified as three little rabbits at the sudden appearance of a stoat.

"Oh!" exclaimed Donny, springing to her feet and dropping the breadknife with a clatter. "Oh dear! Oh, Miss Fairlie—er—er——"

The boys sat open-mouthed and staring.

Miss Hurdstone, who had opened the door to Miss Fairlie and ushered her in, was horrified at this reception of an important guest. "Boys, where are your manners?" exclaimed Miss Hurdstone. "Get up at once. Harold, fetch a chair for Miss Fairlie! Barney, run and get another cup!"

The Eastwoods did as they were told and Charlotte sat down. She accepted a cup of tea from the trembling hand of her hostess and began to talk about her visit to Denmark . . . but the Eastwoods scarcely listened and she could see they were all wondering why she had come and arriving at the most alarming conclusions. Barney's eyes were fixed upon her with the wild expression of a cornered rabbit and the other two were gazing at their plates.

"Aren't you going on with your tea?" asked Charlotte helping herself to a sandwich (she had not been offered food).

"Oh yes—of course——" stammered Donny, taking a large bite of cake and trying to eat it. She discovered that she could not. Her mouth was so dry that the cake would not melt; it was like having a mouthful of sawdust. (I'm going to be expelled, thought Donny. That's what she's come for. She's come to see Father and tell him I'm too stupid).

The advent of the professor did not help to ease the tension. (Miss Hurdstone had told him of Miss Fairlie's arrival and he had changed his collar and brushed his hair before coming downstairs to greet the guest).

"Ah, Miss Fairlie!" he said, shaking hands. "This is an

unexpected pleasure. You see us *en famille*. You take us unawares."

He sat down and Donny poured out a cup of tea for him.

"I must apologise for intruding upon you like this," said Charlotte.

"But we are charmed," declared the professor. "We are honoured by a visit from such an important lady. Isn't that so, Dione?"

"Er—yes——" said Donny miserably.

"I'm on my way back from Larchester," explained Charlotte. "So I thought I would look in for a few minutes and see you."

"An excellent idea," declared Professor Eastwood. He added, "Harold, you are not looking after our guest. Miss Fairlie has nothing to eat."

"Oh, sorry!" exclaimed Harold in alarm. "I wasn't—thinking——"

"It was only too obvious that you were not thinking," said his father with a playful air. "You find thinking somewhat fatiguing, I am afraid."

Harold was silent. He offered Charlotte a piece of seed-cake and, although she disliked seed-cake, she felt obliged to accept it.

"There is something I wanted to speak to you about, Professor Eastwood," said Charlotte. "I thought it would be better to see you about it than to write."

"Quite, quite," agreed the professor. "I imagine your visit is on account of Dione's progress—or more correctly her lack of progress—in her studies. You would prefer to speak to me in private, perhaps."

"No, it isn't that," replied Charlotte. "It's quite a simple matter. I wondered if you would allow Donny to have riding-lessons this term. I think it would be good for Donny," she added, smiling at Donny as she spoke.

Donny gazed back at her with an expression of blank amazement. She could hardly believe her ears.

"It's an innovation at Saint Elizabeth's," continued Charlotte. "We haven't been able to offer the girls riding-lessons before, but now we've managed to make a very satisfactory arrangement with a riding-school in Larchester."

"Dear me," said the professor. "I should have thought a busy woman like yourself would have relegated details of this kind to—ah—an underling."

There was a nasty sting in this remark, in fact Charlotte found it impertinent and was somewhat annoyed; she was all the more annoyed because there was a good deal of truth in it. Certainly she had no intention of going round in person to the parents of all the girls in Saint Elizabeth's touting for the Larchester Riding School. The riding-lessons were an excuse for her visit, that was all, and now she realised that they were rather a poor one.

"The riding is my own idea," replied Charlotte, disguising her feelings and speaking pleasantly. "I've been trying to arrange it for some time and now at last I've succeeded. I used to have a pony when I was a child and I enjoyed riding so much that I want as many girls as possible to take advantage of this opportunity."

"There are far too many distractions already," Professor Eastwood replied. "Dancing, drawing, music! The girls should be kept to their studies and instructed in the rudiments of education; at least until they are able to read and write and add a column of figures correctly."

"But I can read and write!" exclaimed Donny impulsively.

"You can read fairy-tales I admit," replied her father smiling in no very pleasant manner. "But your writing is illegible and you are unable to add. The laundry-book is my authority for these facts. I must apologise, Miss Fairlie, for mentioning these domestic affairs in your presence but I do not wish to be considered unreasonable. If Dione were more industrious and showed more interest in her studies I might feel inclined to allow her to have riding lessons as a reward for merit."

"But Professor Eastwood," said Charlotte. "I think Donny's trouble is that she lacks confidence in herself. Professor MacLaggan is very much in favour of riding. His two daughters are at Saint Elizabeth's and he's arranged for them both to ride. He's a psychologist—but you've heard of him I expect."

"Of course I have heard of him," replied Professor Eastwood crossly. "MacLaggan is an eminent man, an expert in his own subject. Psychology is not in my line but I have nothing against it. You say that MacLaggan advocates riding for a girl who lacks confidence in herself?"

"Yes, he does," replied Charlotte. She had begun to feel slightly more hopeful. Here was the chink in Professor Eastwood's armour . . . he was a bit of a snob!

"It would be—er—an expensive extra, I suppose?"

"If I may make a suggestion . . ." began Charlotte and hesitated.

The professor gave her leave to do so.

"I suggest that Donny should discontinue drawing, for which she has no real talent, and have riding instead."

"But riding would cost a great deal more."

"It would come to the same figure," replied Charlotte mendaciously (if necessary she was prepared to pay the difference herself). "You see," she added, "we have been able to make advantageous arrangements with the riding-school because so many of our girls are having lessons." And that's true, anyhow, she thought.

"Ah," said the professor thoughtfully. He turned and asked, "And what does my little daughter think of the idea?"

His little daughter started in alarm. "Me?" she asked incredulously.

"We happen to be discussing your affairs," her father pointed out. "You take no interest in them, I suppose. It is the same to you whether you continue to waste your time over drawing lessons—for which you have no talent —or to try your skill in the art of managing a horse."

"Yes, Father," said Donny, gazing at him with frightened eyes. "I mean no—I mean of course I'd like riding——"

"Good, that's settled then," said Charlotte rising as she spoke.

Professor Eastwood was surprised at Miss Fairlie's assumption; in his opinion the matter was by no means settled; but for once he was at a loss for words to express his views and before he could find words Miss Fairlie had made her *adieux* and gone.

As she got into her car and drove off her feelings were mixed. Her visit had not been entirely fruitless, it had produced good fruit and bad. It was good that Donny was to have riding-lessons (they really might help her to gain a little confidence in herself) it was bad to have had Tessa's story confirmed. The professor had not browbeaten his children in her presence—at least not very seriously—but it was obvious that they were terrified of him. Poor little rabbits, thought Charlotte frowning. What can one do?

The answer was NOTHING. Charlotte did not suppose for a moment that the Eastwood children were misused physically; they were not neglected nor ill-fed and one could not imagine the professor laying on with a cane. His methods were much more subtle.

* 15 *

THE SUMMER TERM began. It was a more interesting period at Saint Elizabeth's than the preceding term, for all sorts of new things were happening. There was riding for instance—the riding-lessons were a tremendous success—there was a new games mistress who was madly keen on cricket and infused the girls of Saint Elizabeth's with her enthusiasm; and, of course, there was the Coronation. It had been decided, after a good deal of argument, to celebrate the Coronation by an Historical Pageant of the Queens of England. This was not a very original idea but nobody produced a better one and those in favour of it urged the claim that it would be educational. Miss Pinkerton was in favour of it; this was her last term at Saint Elizabeth's and she was determined to make her mark before she left. She would show Saint Elizabeth's what they were losing!

Miss Pinkerton regretted her decision to leave the school. She had begun to regret it the moment she had posted her letter and had heard it fall into the pillar-box with a dull thud. Why on earth had she done it? Why had she resigned and left the field clear for Miss Fairlie? She had hoped the Board would refuse to accept her resignation and beg her to stay on—Miss Bain had assured her that they would—but they had not done so. This, of course, was entirely due to Miss Fairlie; all Miss Pinkerton's troubles were due to

Miss Fairlie. Miss Pinkerton lay awake night after night hating Miss Fairlie, boiling with resentment and bitter rage, racked with indigestion. It was so unfair. Miss Pinkerton knew herself to be clever and conscientious, and good (she said her prayers and went to church regularly and spent hours of her spare time making garments for foreign missions); she often wondered why her undeniable virtues had not produced suitable dividends. She knew people did not like her but that must be their fault of course. Like the young Irish recruit on his first route march everyone was out of step except herself.

Miss Pinkerton had done her best to discredit Miss Fairlie; she had found out that disgraceful affair with the MacRynne girl and had taken it hot-foot to Miss Bain, and Miss Bain had been suitably horrified. Together they had composed a long letter to Mr. Allnut and sat back to await results. Strangely enough there were no results; Mr. Allnut had not even answered the letter and when Miss Pinkerton had seen him one afternoon in Larchester he had tried to avoid her by taking refuge in a butcher's shop . . . but by this time Miss Pinkerton was desperate so she followed him in and tackled him boldly. Cornered and without hope of escape Mr. Allnut hummed and hawed and said they did not want a scandal; it was better to let sleeping dogs lie.

"A scandal!" cried Miss Pinkerton. "But it *is* a scandal. It's disgraceful for anyone in Miss Fairlie's position to carry on like that. Miss Bain thinks the whole affair should be exposed at the next meeting of the Board of Governors."

"Oh, I don't think we could do that," said Mr. Allnut uncomfortably. "My feeling is that the less said about it the better. The MacRynne's are—er—influential people— valuable connections. We have to think of the prestige of Saint Elizabeth's. That must be our first consideration. I am sure you agree, Miss Pinkerton. Nobody has the interests of the school more at heart than yourself."

There was no answer to this, or at least none that could be spoken. If she had spoken the truth Miss Pinkerton would have replied that she did not care a rap for the interests of the school; all she cared about was to get her own back on Miss Fairlie. Perhaps she still could, reflected Miss Pinkerton. Mr. Allnut had failed her but if she were to drop a hint here and there amongst the staff of Saint Elizabeth's (there were one or two who were not particularly fond of the head-mistress) she might be able to cause some trouble.

"And it would be better," continued Mr. Allnut, who was no fool. "It would be better for all concerned if this little— er—story remained a secret. There is such a thing as slander, Miss Pinkerton. The Law takes rather a serious view of slander and—er defamation of character. You may have noticed a case in the papers quite recently—a very sad case. Well, I am afraid I must be off. It is always a great pleasure to see you. I hope you are coming to the Sale of Work? Ah, good! We depend upon you, Miss Pinkerton."

Miss Pinkerton went straight back to Saint Elizabeth's and looked up SLANDER in the encyclopædia (there was a copy of it in the school library of course) and after reading what the encyclopædia had to say upon the subject she decided to hold her peace.

Thus baulked, Miss Pinkerton tried to think of some other way of getting even with Miss Fairlie. There was still the pageant of course. She set her hopes upon the pageant.

It had been arranged that each of the senior mistresses should present one scene at the pageant and undertake the production of it (this would promote a spirit of rivalry and would give them all a fair chance of showing what they could do) but before going further it was essential to hold a meeting and to work out the programme of events. Miss

Margetson, whose subject was history, made a strong bid
for the convenership but was overborne by Miss Pinkerton.
(Oh well, let her, thought Miss Margetson. She won't be
here next term.)

Miss Fairlie was a little late for the meeting, she had been
interviewing a prospective parent so it was not her fault,
but she apologised and explained.

"You said you didn't want to be the convener," said Miss
Pinkerton. "So of course the task devolves upon me. I have
been longer at Saint Elizabeth's than anyone else."

Miss Fairlie was of the opinion that Miss Margetson was
the right person to direct a historical pageant but apparently
it had all been arranged. Miss Pinkerton had taken posses-
sion of the chair and it was obvious that unless she were
removed by brute force she would remain there.

"Have you decided upon the date?" asked Miss Fairlie.

"It must be after the Coronation," replied Miss Pinkerton
firmly. "That will give us more time."

"And what about the different scenes? My suggestion is
that we write the names of the Queens on slips of paper and
draw lots for them."

"I'm producing a scene depicting Queen Elizabeth," said
Miss Pinkerton. "I have taken it from *Kenilworth* and
worked out the details very carefully. I have chosen the
girls and they have begun to learn their parts."

There was a moment's silence. Everybody had wanted
Queen Elizabeth—everybody was furious—but nobody had
actually begun work upon her scene.

"Oh, I see," nodded Miss Fairlie, "I had no idea you had
arranged the scenes already or I wouldn't have made the
suggestion. I just thought balloting would be the fairest
way."

"It would have been," murmured Miss Agnew.

"May I be permitted to 'ave Marie Stuart, the Queen of

Scots ? " inquired Mademoiselle Boule. "She was Queen of La France as well so I feel I 'ave some right to the unfortunate lady . . . and my plan is to 'ave some of the talk in French."

The games mistress asked if she might have Queen Boadicea. The other mistresses were silent.

"I expect everyone wants a little time to think it over," said Miss Fairlie with her usual tact. "There's no hurry, of course. I'm sure Miss Margetson will help anyone who wants advice—about costumes and so on. Oh, and that reminds me; the Board of Governors are letting us have a hundred pounds for expenses."

"That isn't nearly enough! " objected Miss Pinkerton.

"Oh, I think so," replied Miss Fairlie. "Some of the dresses can be run up in the sewing-room quite cheaply, others can be hired. As the Pageant is to take place out of doors we shan't need any scenery. I can see you're thinking it all out and I'm not going to interfere. Of course I shall be interested to see the rough draft of the programme when you've settled it."

"Yes, of course, Miss Fairlie," agreed Miss Margetson.

"There's just one stipulation," said Miss Fairlie as she rose. "I'm afraid I must insist that no girl who is sitting for her Higher Certificate is to be given any part in the Pageant."

"What! " cried Miss Pinkerton. "But that's nonsense! It would cut out all the senior girls."

"Most of them, I'm afraid," agreed Miss Fairlie regretfully.

"It's impossible! " cried Miss Pinkerton, turning crimson. "We might as well abandon the project altogether. Surely the girls can spare a few hours to rehearse the scenes . . . my girls are so well grounded that they can easily spare a few hours." She looked round the table as she spoke but none of her colleagues echoed the proud boast, in fact they all looked extremely uncomfortable. There was not a mistress present (except the fortunate Miss Pinkerton) who could lay her hand upon her heart and express complete confidence in her pupils' ability to pass the forthcoming examination with flying colours. (You never *know*, thought Miss Margetson. Sometimes the ones you feel sure of come the most awful croppers. The Old Girl is right, of course. It's a pity, but it can't be helped.)

"But I must 'ave Betty Mollett for Marie Stuart!" cried Mademoiselle Boule in dismay. "Miss Fairlie, I must 'ave Betty! There is no one else with the necessary poise and the pure accent. All the others are gauche—and they say ' miaow,' like little cats."

Miss Fairlie shook her head. " I'm going to be very hard-hearted about it. If I gave you Betty Miss Ricketts would immediately ask me for Susan Lane. I'm sure she had her eye on Susan for Queen Boadicea."

Miss Ricketts blushed. It was only too true. Susan, who was Captain of Cricket, would have made a magnificent Boadicea.

"Well, who!" cried Mademoiselle Boule. "If not Betty who can I 'ave for the unfortunate Marie? Ah, I 'ave it. Yes, yes, it must be the little Tessa."

"Tessa MacRynne!" exclaimed Miss Pinkerton. "What a ridiculous choice! This is only her third term at Saint Elizabeth's. She's stupid and lazy and she has no looks— Mary was beautiful! And besides it would be very bad for that girl to be pushed into the limelight and given such an important part."

"Stupid and lazy?" said Miss Margetson in surprise. "I don't agree at all."

"*Moi non plus!*" declared Mademoiselle Boule. "Tessa is neither stupid nor lazy . . . and she 'as the air of a queen. As for 'er looks: all that is needed is a little make-up and the very becoming dress——"

"Well, I must leave you to decide," said Miss Fairlie and she left them to their task.

As she went back to her sitting-room Charlotte felt very uneasy. She had sensed all the cross-currents (they were cross in more ways than one) and she realised that there might be serious trouble amongst her staff. Miss Pinkerton was selfish and tactless, it was a thousand pities she had managed to get herself into the chair. If Charlotte had thought there was any chance of that she would have presided herself, but she had assumed, not unnaturally, that Miss Margetson would direct the Pageant. In addition to these anxieties Charlotte was aware that she had made a very unpopular ruling (all the members of her staff were annoyed and the girls themselves would be disappointed) but she knew she was right. The Higher Certificate Examination was more important than the Coronation Pageant; it was important for the girl's future careers and she would not have been doing her duty to them or their parents if she had allowed anything to interfere with their work. Miss Pinkerton had spoken of "sparing a few hours " but that was nonsense. If the girls were given parts in the Pageant their minds would be full of it; their work would be completely upset; they would be taken away from their classes and rehearsed at all hours of the day.

Charlotte sighed. She hated to disappoint people . . . but the Queen would agree with me, thought Charlotte. This conclusion comforted her considerably.

* 16 *

NATURALLY TESSA was delighted when she heard that she had been chosen to play the part of Queen Mary in the Pageant. She had hoped for a small part— possibly a page-boy—Queen Mary was beyond her wildest dreams. She was still full of excitement over her good fortune when, the following Sunday, she went to tea with the Eastwoods.

It was some time since Tessa had been to the Eastwoods' to tea (all last term the Saint Elizabeth girls had been prisoners on account of scarlet fever in the town) so this was a great occasion and Miss Hurdstone had baked a special ginger-bread cake.

"Isn't it lovely?" said Donny. "I don't mean the cake; I mean Tessa being Mary, Queen of Scots. She'll do it splendidly," added Donny with generous pride.

"Why have they chosen Tessa?" asked Barney.

"Because she can talk French."

"But she wasn't French, she was Scotch."

"She was brought up in France," explained Donny, who had learnt more history in the last few days than she had ever learnt before. "She married the son of the French King —he was called the dolphin—so of course she often spoke French. Anyhow she's going to speak French in the Pageant and that's why the Bull has chosen Tessa."

"I thought Mary Queen of Scots was supposed to be beautiful," objected Harold in a puzzled tone of voice.

Tessa was undisturbed by the insult. She shared Harold's poor opinion of her looks. "Oh yes," agreed Tessa. "Of course she was beautiful, but the Bull says she can make up my face and people won't be very *near*. The Pageant is outside in a glade and I shall ride in on a pony. I've just escaped from Loch Leven Castle, you see."

They were still lingering over tea and discussing the matter when Professor Eastwood came in. He had been informed by Miss Hurdstone that Tessa had come to tea and although he did not like his daughter's new friend she had a curious fascination for him.

"Ask him now," muttered Barney, giving Tessa a little kick beneath the table.

"What did you say, Barney?" inquired Professor Eastwood. "Your remark was unintelligible; probably because your mouth was full of food. How many times have I told you not to speak with your mouth full?" He fixed Barney with his eye and waited for an answer.

"I don't know," said Barney.

"You don't know what you said?"

"No, I mean—I mean I thought you asked me how many times you told me," mumbled Barney. "I mean how many times you told me not to—not to talk with my mouth full —and of course you've often told me. I don't know—how many times . . . " his voice trailed away into silence.

The professor sighed elaborately. "It is unfortunate that my sons are morons," he said. "Both of them," he added with a swift glance at Harold, who withered beneath it like a hot-house plant in an easterly wind. "Morons," repeated the professor savagely.

There was a short silence.

"Have a chocolate biscuit, Tessa?" said Barney in a

whisper. He gave her another gentle kick beneath the table as he spoke.

Tessa did not like chocolate biscuits so she refused the offer. She knew what the kick meant, of course, but it seemed to Tessa that this was not a propitious moment to make a request to Professor Eastwood. It seemed to Tessa that it would be better to wait and catch the professor in a more genial mood; but she had promised to make the request at the first opportunity and she saw that her three friends were waiting for her to make it.

"Professor Eastwood," said Tessa. "May Donny and Harold and Barney come and stay with me in the Summer holidays?"

"Stay with you!"

"Yes, at my home—at Targ. It would be so lovely if they could. You *will* let them come, won't you?"

"Er—this is a very unexpected proposal."

"It would be so good for them," urged Tessa. "There's bathing and—and we could have picnics on the moor—and——"

"May I ask whether your parents—er——"

"Oh Daddy won't mind a bit. I mean he'll be delighted to have them. He said I could ask a friend to stay and Donny is my greatest friend—and of course I want the boys too."

"No, I think not," replied Professor Eastwood. "It is good of you to think of it, Miss MacRynne, but I intend to engage a tutor for the children. If they cannot—or will not—learn at school they must pursue their studies in holiday times."

"Couldn't they come for part of the holidays?" asked Tessa.

"No, I am afraid we must refuse the invitation."

"Father, couldn't we?" asked Donny in a low voice.

C.F.   K

"We've been talking about it. Tessa says it will be all right. The boys want it too."

"It is much too far to go for a holiday," replied the professor firmly. "I might consider allowing you to go if it were not so far, but——"

"Tessa says it only takes four hours," put in Barney desperately.

"Four hours! It would take several days to journey from here to the West of Scotland. If you would take the trouble to consult a map of the British Isles you would realise——"

"But of course they would fly," said Tessa interrupting him.

"Fly!" exclaimed Professor Eastwood. "Certainly not. I never heard of such a thing."

His hearers were aware that this statement was a *façon de parler* (obviously the professor must have heard of air-travel, it was the idea of his own family taking to the air which was unheard of).

"But everybody flies," declared Tessa in surprise. "Even the aunts think nothing of flying and they're about eighty. Flying is so much easier and more comfortable."

"Certainly not," repeated the professor. "I could not think of it for a moment. You had better put this wild idea out of your heads." He rose from the table as he spoke and went away.

"I told you," said Harold. "I knew he wouldn't let us! I told you!"

"He's a beast!" cried Barney in a shrill trembling voice. "He's a beast and I hate him!"

"Oh Barney!" cried Donny, aghast.

"I do, I do!" screamed Barney. "I hate him—and you hate him too! What's the good of pretending!" Barney burst into tears and blundered out of the room.

The other three sat in silence for quite a long time. It was a very uncomfortable silence.

"Perhaps he'll change his mind," said Tessa at last. "I'll get Daddy to write and ask you properly. We shouldn't have asked him suddenly like that; he wasn't in the right mood."

"He never is," said Harold hopelessly.

17

SINCE PARTING from Lawrence at the air-field Charlotte
had heard no more of him; he had neither written nor
rung her up. In a way she had not really expected to
hear from him for he had said he would not bother her;
she was to think over his proposal and let him know. So
the next move was hers. She thought it over off and on
(when she had time to think) and gradually as the strangeness
of the idea wore off she began to feel that it might be very
pleasant to marry Lawrence. They got on so well together
and enjoyed one another's company . . . and there was the
future to think of. On the one hand was the prospect of a
lonely future, going on year after year until one became too
old for work and retired into even lonelier lodgings, like
Miss Bain; on the other hand was the prospect of Bells
Hill, and Lawrence as a companion . . . and possibly a
family to be a joy and solace in one's old age. Once or twice
Charlotte very nearly rang up Lawrence and even considered
what words she would say. Should she say, "Do you still
want somebody to pour out tea and sew the buttons on your
pyjamas? " or should she treat the matter more seriously?
But somehow it was difficult to ring up in cold blood. If
she could see Lawrence it would be easier.

One evening she felt lonelier than usual. It happened to
be her birthday but nobody was aware of the anniversary
except herself. Even Aunt Lydia, who usually sent her a

box of soap or a tin of talcum powder, seemed to have forgotten the date. It was ridiculous to mind, of course. Charlotte told herself she did not mind a rap—what were birthdays anyhow? They were merely dates in the calendar like other dates. She adjusted her reading-lamp, took out a book of French poems and settled down to read them—but somehow they failed to hold her attention. The thought of Lawrence and Bells Hill came between her and the book. I'll ring him up, thought Charlotte. I'll ask him to come and have dinner at Borley Manor and we can talk it over . . . when I see him I shall know.

Charlotte stretched out her hand to the telephone which stood on a little table by her side and as she did so her eyes fell upon the Buddhist Priest—he was looking at her—and smiling in a slightly sardonic manner! For a moment she was startled and her hand dropped to her side. She rose and gazed at him but now, once more, he was deep in contemplation.

The room was dim, except for the pool of light from the reading-lamp and the flicker of the fire, and Charlotte realised that the odd illusion had been a trick of the firelight. The flicker of the flames, reflected from a mirror which hung upon the opposite wall of the room, had lighted up his fat, peaceful countenance. There was no magic about it at all—none whatever. Charlotte proved this by returning to her chair and watching carefully . . . yes, every time the fire flickered the Buddhist Priest seemed to smile. The whole incident was quite ridiculous of course (it was a mere nothing) but for some obscure reason the urge to ring up Lawrence had vanished. Charlotte decided to wait; there was no hurry about it; perhaps she would meet Lawrence some day in the town.

The day of the Coronation drew near. Some of the girls were being taken by their parents to see the procession and one or two were actually going to the Abbey but most of them were remaining at school. Charlotte was anxious that everybody should view the ceremony to the best advantage and had obtained permission from the Board of Governors to install television sets in several of the classrooms. She intended to view it herself, with the girls, but her plans were changed at the last moment. A few days before the great event she received a letter from Sir Joseph Spinner inviting her to be one of his party on the 2nd of June, to go to London and see the procession.

"This is, I am afraid, a fiddler's invitation," wrote Sir Joseph. "My party was complete, but my wife feels it would be too long a day and too fatiguing for her, so her place is vacant and I shall be very glad if you will forgive the short notice and join us. I have engaged a room in the Superb Hotel which has a good view of the route so we shall be very comfortable. My sister is coming, and two nieces, and several other friends including one or two members of the Board of Governors. I have instructed my secretary to enclose a card with the necessary details. You will notice that we have to catch a very early train from Larchester. If you will meet us at Larchester Station about ten minutes before the train is due to leave for London there will be ample time. Seats in the train have been engaged. Perhaps you will be good enough to instruct your secretary to telephone to my secretary at once and let her know whether or not you can come. You may have made other arrangements for seeing the Coronation Procession. . . . "

Charlotte had not made other arrangements. Of course she would go. It would be marvellous. She would see the procession from the best possible viewpoint and in the greatest comfort. What fun it would be! She was so excited about it that she felt inclined to ring up Sir Joseph's secretary herself . . . but Sir Joseph had told her to instruct her secretary to do so and Sir Joseph must be obeyed. She took the letter and the enclosure (which was a neatly written card with the times of the trains to and from London) and went into the office to Miss Post.

"You had better do this at once," she said, showing Miss Post the letter.

Miss Post read it. "Oh, Miss Fairlie, how lovely! You'll go, won't you?"

"Of course," replied Charlotte laughing. "I'd be a fool to refuse, wouldn't I?"

"Well—yes—" agreed Miss Post and she laughed too. It was not often that the Old Girl unbent like this but of course she was excited . . . and no wonder, thought Miss Post. "I'll phone at once, Miss Fairlie," she said aloud, stretching out her hand for the receiver.

Having settled the matter Charlotte returned to her sitting-room. She wondered if she should write to Sir Joseph and thank him for his kindness but decided not to; he had told her what to do and she had done it. She would thank him on the day. Glancing at the clock she saw it was time for her to take the sixth form in French literature, in fact she would have to hurry, she threw the letter on to her desk and hastened away.

Off and on during her busy morning Charlotte thought with pleasure of the forthcoming expedition. Sir Joseph was a dear. He was a trifle too fond of having his own way perhaps, but why should he not have his own way? When a man had reached Sir Joseph's age and attained his position it was only right that he should have his own way. Sir Joseph was a benevolent autocrat. He would do anything for you if he liked you and you did exactly as he said but he might not be so pleasant if you disobeyed his commands.

It was nearly lunch-time when Charlotte returned to the office to sign some letters. Miss Post was waiting for her.

"Oh Miss Fairlie!" she exclaimed. "Miss Pinkerton wants to see you."

"Oh goodness! Is she . . . "

Miss Post nodded. "In a rage about something—something to do with the Pageant. I put her in your sitting-room; she's been waiting for half an hour."

Charlotte's heart sank. The last thing she wanted was an interview with Miss Pinkerton—especially with Miss Pinkerton in a rage—but it was no good delaying and keeping her waiting any longer, so she opened the door and went in.

"I'm sorry to have kept you waiting," said Charlotte, getting her word in first. She glanced at Miss Pinkerton as she spoke and was somewhat surprised; Miss Pinkerton did not look "in a rage." Charlotte had seen Miss Pinkerton in a rage quite often, so she knew the symptoms well. To-day Miss Pinkerton looked a bit queer, but definitely not enraged. Perhaps she had calmed down while she was waiting—though that did not seem likely. "You wanted to see me about something," added Charlotte aloud.

"Yes," said Miss Pinkerton with one of her well-known gasps. "Yes, I did—but—but it doesn't matter."

"It doesn't matter!"

"I mean—I mean would it be convenient for me to leave now instead of waiting until the end of the term?"

Charlotte gazed at her in amazement. "Now?" she asked incredulously. "You mean before the Pageant?"

"Yes, now—at once. The fact is I'm not feeling well."

"Oh, I'm sorry!"

"I can't sleep," declared Miss Pinkerton with another gasp. "That's the trouble really. Sometimes I feel—I feel a little—dizzy. My doctor says I must have a complete rest."

"Oh, of course if Dr. Enfield says——"

"Not Dr. Enfield," interrupted Miss Pinkerton. "My own doctor—in London. I must leave! I simply *must*—at once—if it's convenient——"

Charlotte had been observing Miss Pinkerton and thinking fast. Miss Pinkerton did not look ill, in fact she looked rather better than usual, but she must feel very ill indeed if she wanted to leave Saint Elizabeth's before the Pageant. Charlotte knew that Miss Pinkerton had been working like a slave at her scene from *Kenilworth*; she had taken the greatest trouble with the costumes and had rehearsed her unfortunate cast until they were almost in hysterics.

"What about your scene from *Kenilworth*?" asked Charlotte in puzzled tones.

"I can't help it. I must go," declared Miss Pinkerton. "Somebody else will have to—to complete the arrangements."

It was very odd—and very inconvenient. Not only would somebody else have to produce the scene in the Pageant but somebody else would have to undertake Miss Pinkerton's work; but, on the other hand, how very pleasant it would be to see the last of Miss Pinkerton!

"If your doctor advises it of course you must go," said Charlotte. She hesitated and then added, " I'm very sorry for you, Miss Pinkerton; it must be a great disappointment to you after all your hard work." This was perfectly true; Charlotte felt very sorry indeed for the woman.

"Yes, but I must go," repeated Miss Pinkerton desperately. "I must go to-morrow morning. There are reasons—several reasons—I couldn't bear another day. I can go to-morrow, I suppose?"

Charlotte agreed. By this time she had decided that although Miss Pinkerton did not look ill there was something very queer about her and would have agreed if she suggested leaving then and there. They arranged one or two matters—Miss Pinkerton wrote down her future address for the forwarding of letters—and then said good-bye. Neither of them was anxious for another meeting; both felt it was better to get it over now. Charlotte said politely and sincerely that she hoped Miss Pinkerton would soon recover and that she would be happy in her new post; Miss Pinkerton replied—not so sincerely—that she hoped all would go well at Saint Elizabeth's. There was nothing more to be said but Miss Pinkerton lingered.

"Are you going to the Coronation with Sir Joseph Spinner's party?" she asked.

"Yes, I am," replied Charlotte smiling. "It's a marvellous chance—far too good to refuse. I didn't intend to go up for the Coronation but . . . " she hesitated. It had suddenly struck her that there was something odd about this. How did Miss Pinkerton know? Saint Elizabeth's was a dreadful place for gossip and things got about very quickly, but this was incredibly quick . . . unless Miss Post had told Miss Pinkerton. Could that be the explanation? No, thought Charlotte, that was unlikely. Miss Post had said that Miss Pinkerton was "in a rage" and had ushered her into the sitting-room and left her there. It was most unlikely that she had told Miss Pinkerton anything . . . besides, if Miss Pinkerton had heard the news from Miss Post she would have known that the invitation had been accepted; she would have said, "I hear you are going to see the Coronation Procession with Sir Joseph Spinner's party"—but that was not what she had said.

"Things *do* get about quickly!" exclaimed Charlotte with a little laugh. "I only had the invitation this morning."

"Someone told me," said Miss Pinkerton hastily.

"Miss Post?" asked Charlotte.

"I can't remember who it was," declared Miss Pinkerton. Her eyes, which had been glancing round the room, rested for a moment upon Charlotte's desk, and then glanced away.

Charlotte looked at the desk too and saw the letter lying upon the blotter. So that was it! Miss Pinkerton had read Sir Joseph's letter. She had seen the letter lying upon the desk and had seized the opportunity to read it—probably she had thought there was something in it about herself. There was nothing, of course; there were no secrets in it . . . so it did not matter. Charlotte was annoyed and disgusted but it was useless to say anything about it (Miss Pinkerton would have denied the charge with her last breath) so she opened the door and Miss Pinkerton hastened away.

When she had gone Charlotte went over to the desk and looked at the letter thoughtfully. She had been in a hurry and had tossed the letter on to her desk in a casual sort of way. Now it lay very neatly in the centre of the blotting-pad. Not enough evidence to hang her, thought Charlotte (who sometimes read detective stories), but still . . .

* 18 *

THE MORNING of the 2nd of June was dull; it was not exactly raining but there were heavy clouds all round. Charlotte had set her alarm for a quarter past four, which would give her ample time to dress and get herself some breakfast and to drive to Larchester. The card, enclosed by Sir Joseph Spinner's secretary, informed her that the train left for London at five-fifty, which meant that she must be at the station at twenty minutes to six. Charlotte was so excited that she could eat nothing but she drank some coffee as she dressed. She had decided to wear a grey frock and had bought a very pretty red hat for the occasion and a red scarf to match. When she was ready and looked at herself in the long mirror she was pleased with what she saw. It crossed her mind that the members of the Board of Governors, who were to be her fellow guests, might be a little surprised. They were used to seeing her in the hat which Lawrence Swayne disliked so much and with such good reason, but that could not be helped. The Coronation was a special occasion and, Governors or no Governors, Charlotte was determined to look her best.

She ran the little car out of the garage and off she went. It was far too early, but that was because she was so excited and because she had had a secret fear that the car might refuse to start or one of the tyres might be flat, but nothing at all happened to delay her and she reached the outskirts of

Larchester at twenty-five minutes past five. She must be at the station in fifteen minutes—no more and no less—it pleased her to obey Sir Joseph's instructions to the letter. This being so she stopped the car, got out and leant upon a gate and waited.

The railway line to London ran quite near and presently Charlotte saw a train leave the station and steam off to London. It was crammed with people; the women were wearing gay hats, the children were leaning out of the windows waving little flags and shouting. They were going to the Coronation too; they were all happy and excited; everyone was happy and excited to-day. Charlotte waved to them and they all waved back.

It was now time for a move so she got into her car and drove the last few hundred yards to the station.

As she parked her car the station-master came out of his office to meet her. Charlotte knew him; in fact he was rather a friend of hers—a pleasant kindly man—but to-day he looked worried.

"Miss Fairlie!" he exclaimed. "The train's gone! What happened to you? The train's gone ten minutes ago!"

"Gone!" she cried incredulously.

"Sir Joseph was looking everywhere for you—he was in a great state! We couldn't think what had happened."

"But I'm not late! It was five-fifty. It said so on the card—the card that was sent to me by Sir Joseph's personal secretary. Five-fifty——"

"No, five-thirty," said Mr. Grimister. He took out his large silver watch and looked at it. "It's five-forty now," he added.

Charlotte could not speak. She found the card in her bag and handed it to Mr. Grimister.

"Yes, that says five-fifty," he agreed. "Sir Joseph's secretary must have made a mistake. It isn't like her to make mistakes—Miss Stewart is a very capable lady—but I'm afraid she's done it this time. The train was due to leave at the half hour, and that's when it left—on the dot. Everything's got to be on the dot to-day."

"But what am I to do!" cried Charlotte.

"You can't do anything," said Mr. Grimister regretfully.

"Do you mean there's no way of getting to London—no other train?"

"No, Miss Fairlie, there isn't. I'm very sorry about it but there's no other train—and even if there was you'd be too late to get through the barriers."

Charlotte was so disappointed and so bewildered that she did not know what to do. She felt she could not go straight back to Saint Elizabeth's. She drove slowly along the High Street—it was utterly deserted at this hour of the morning— and leaving her car climbed up some steps on to the Wall. She walked along until she found a sheltered seat near one of the old towers and sat down.

At first her thoughts ran round like squirrels in a cage; that was the train—the train she had seen on its way to London—she had stood, leaning upon the gate, and watched it go! Sir Joseph was angry; Mr. Grimister had said he was "in a great state". She could imagine the scene! But it was not her fault—she had done exactly as he had told her. It was a mistake—that was all—a silly stupid mistake—so he could not be angry with *her*. He would be angry with her until the matter was explained—in fact he would be furious—but once the matter was explained he would understand.

If Charlotte had not been "in a great state" herself she would have enjoyed the scene which lay unfolded before her eyes. There is something about the very early morning which is entrancing: it is so quiet, so new. The world has been reborn during the hours of darkness; there is a bloom upon it like the bloom upon an untouched grape. The sun was hidden behind clouds so the light had a silvery softness; a haze lay upon the meadows by the river; cows grazed peacefully; the town-clock chimed.

After sitting there for some time Charlotte felt cold and set off to walk round the Wall. She had often taken this walk when she was a child—a pupil at Saint Elizabeth's—but she had not done it since. The town was awakening now and the chimneys had begun to smoke, she could see into the windows of the houses: women bustling about getting breakfast . . . and this reminded her that she was hungry. She found a small old-fashioned inn which was nestling under the shadow of the Wall and ate a good meal.

After that, and a cigarette, she felt a great deal better and was able to view her misfortune more calmly. She had missed seeing the Coronation Procession (missed all the excitement and the fun) and she would regret it all her life, but it was not a major disaster and she was a fool to be so upset about it. The first thing to do was to compose a letter to Sir Joseph; she must put herself right with him . . . and then she thought, why not go and see Lady Spinner and explain the whole thing to her? (Lady Spinner was at home, she knew) perhaps Lady Spinner could throw some light upon the matter.

Charlotte sat in the little inn until a more reasonable hour and then made her way to the Spinners' Mansion.

Lady Spinner opened the door herself and exclaimed in amazement when she saw her visitor: "Miss Fairlie! I thought you had gone to London! I thought you were going with the others."

"There was a mistake," Charlotte said. "I missed the train." She followed her hostess into the drawing-room and told her what had happened.

"Oh dear, that's dreadful," declared Lady Spinner. "Sir

Joseph will be so upset. There's nothing he dislikes more than muddles. Are you sure Miss Stewart put the wrong time on the card? She's always so reliable."

Charlotte was a little tired of hearing about Miss Stewart's efficiency so she said nothing but produced the card.

"How extraordinary!" exclaimed Lady Spinner. "I never knew Miss Stewart make a muddle before. I must ask her about it. She's here now, in Sir Joseph's study, dealing with some correspondence. As a matter of fact Miss Stewart and I are alone in the house—I let the servants go to London. Miss Stewart didn't want to go so we decided to stay at home together and have a cold lunch and watch the Coronation on television. I'll just go and ask her. Sit down, Miss Fairlie, I won't be a minute."

Charlotte sat down. She had taken off her hat and left it in the car, for she had felt silly walking about Larchester at that hour of the morning dressed up like a mannequin, so now she took out her comb and tidied her hair and waited. She had not long to wait before Lady Spinner returned with Sir Joseph's secretary.

Miss Stewart looked the perfect confidential secretary; her calling was written all over her. She was about forty, an admirably discreet age, she wore a white silk shirt with a turned-down collar and a navy-blue skirt. Her hair was neatly waved; her shoes were highly polished; her spectacles shone like crystal.

"This is Miss Stewart, Miss Fairlie," said Lady Spinner. "Miss Stewart has made a most extraordinary discovery."

"The mistake is not mine, Miss Fairlie," said Miss Stewart, going straight to the point.

"Not yours?" exclaimed Charlotte. "But it must be! That was the card you sent me."

"Yes, this is the card but the figure has been altered."

"What do you mean?"

"The time of the train has been altered, Miss Fairlie."
Charlotte gazed at her.

"I knew I hadn't made a mistake," declared Miss Stewart. "Sir Joseph is so very particular—quite rightly of course—that I always check everything most carefully."

"The figure has been altered?" asked Charlotte incredulously.

Miss Stewart nodded. "I wrote five-thirty on the card and someone has altered it to five-fifty. It has been very neatly done."

Charlotte did not believe her. Naturally Miss Stewart was anxious to vindicate herself so she had made up this extraordinary tale.

"Look for yourself," said Miss Stewart, handing Charlotte the card and a magnifying glass. "Please look at it, Miss Fairlie. If you use this glass you will see what I mean. Someone has altered the three of thirty and made it into a five."

Charlotte examined the card closely and saw to her amazement that it was true. There was a slight roughness where the paper had been scraped with a knife and the tiny stroke of the five had been made with ink of a different colour.

"But—it's incredible!" cried Charlotte. "I don't understand! It doesn't make sense!"

"That's exactly what I said," declared Lady Spinner. "It doesn't make sense. Who could possibly have done it—and why?"

"Perhaps someone who wanted Miss Fairlie to miss the train," suggested Miss Stewart.

There was a moment's silence.

"Yes," said Charlotte at last in a low voice. "Yes . . . it must have been."

"Oh no!" cried Lady Spinner in horrified tones. "Surely not! Nobody would do such a thing."

"You would be surprised at what people will do," said Miss Stewart in her matter-of-fact way. "I've knocked about the world and I've come across some very queer people. Sometimes people have a grudge against you—or think they have." She hesitated and looked at Charlotte. It was obvious that Miss Stewart wanted to get to the bottom of the matter and have it cleared up—and you could not blame her.

"Yes," said Charlotte reluctantly. "Yes, that's true. I believe I know who did it—and why—but I've no proof. I think I had better tell you the whole story."

She told them. Lady Spinner listened in horror to the tale; Miss Stewart with interest and close attention. Charlotte had a feeling that nothing would ruffle Miss Stewart's calm, nothing would shock her.

"It's dreadful! " cried Lady Spinner when Charlotte had finished. "I can hardly believe that anyone could be so— so wicked."

"But it all hangs together," said Miss Stewart. "She saw the letter lying on Miss Fairlie's desk and she couldn't resist reading it. Some people are like that, you know; they have a passion for reading other people's letters. Then she saw the card and realised that she could alter the time— it isn't difficult to make a three into a five if you're used to working with figures."

"But she must have known she would be found out," Lady Spinner said.

Miss Stewart nodded. "Yes, that's why she was scared and wanted to get away. That's why she had to leave in a hurry. Oh yes, it all hangs together."

Miss Stewart would have made an excellent detective, thought Charlotte looking at her in respect . . . for of course it must have happened just like that. Miss Pinkerton had done the deed in a moment of fury and then had become frightened and had run away from the consequences.

"Of course we can't do anything about it," added Miss Stewart in a thoughtful tone.

"Sir Joseph will be furious," declared his wife. "I don't know *what* he'll say. He'll be simply furious."

But not with *me*, thought Charlotte thankfully. She glanced at Miss Stewart and was pretty certain that the same comforting thought was in that lady's mind.

Charlotte spent the whole day with Lady Spinner and Miss Stewart; they sat with their eyes glued to the screen of Sir Joseph's magnificent television cabinet; they ate a cold meal with the plates balanced upon their knees so that they should not miss a moment of the procession or the ceremonies. It was so thrilling to watch and so beautifully done that they felt quite dazed when at last it was over and "God Save the Queen" had been played for the last time.

When Charlotte said good-bye and drove home to Saint Elizabeth's she felt quite happy and contented. She had missed seeing the procession but she felt as if she had seen more than the procession, she felt as if she had been in the Abbey and had seen the magnificent ceremony with her own eyes . . . and somehow it seemed a long time ago since the morning, when she had driven into Larchester in all her finery, it seemed like weeks.

In addition to this Charlotte had the satisfaction of knowing that she had made two good friends; they would be advocates in her favour and put things right with Sir Joseph when he returned.

SAINT ELIZABETH'S 163

* 19 *

N OW THAT the Coronation was over everybody in Saint Elizabeth's began to look forward to the Pageant, some with dread and others with eager anticipation. Miss Pinkerton had vanished of course; nobody lamented the fact but everybody wondered. The official explanation of her sudden flight (that she was indisposed and had been ordered a complete rest) was difficult to swallow for her colleagues had noticed no lack of energy in Miss Pinkerton.

"And even if she had felt like death she would have carried on until after the Pageant," said Miss Agnew in bewilderment.

Miss Ricketts, the games mistress, agreed with her. In fact everybody agreed.

"Well, anyhow, she has gone," said Miss Margetson cheerfully. " Miss Fairlie wants me to direct the Pageant; I hope nobody minds."

Nobody minded in the least.

"Perhaps I could have Katherine of France after all," suggested Miss Agnew hopefully. "I'd far rather have her than William and Mary."

There had been a great deal of unpleasantness over this matter. Katherine was the wife of Henry V and Miss Agnew had borrowed her scene from Shakespeare's play and transplanted it from *An Apartment in the French King's Palace* to

A Dell in the French King's Garden. Miss Pinkerton had been extremely nasty about it and had insisted on having it scrapped (on the grounds that Katherine was not a Queen of England in her own right but was merely the wife of a King); she had landed Miss Agnew with William and Mary instead—a poor exchange in Miss Agnew's opinion.

Miss Margetson was only too ready to agree to Miss Agnew's request, not only because Katherine was more romantic than poor unhappy Mary but also because it would be a poke in the eye to the ex-director of the Pageant. As an additional poke in the eye she gave permission for the inclusion of an interview between Anne Boleyn and Henry VIII which had been turned down for the same reason.

These decisions put everybody in a good humour and rehearsals for the Pageant went forward with a will.

It was to be a great day for Saint Elizabeth's. The parents had been invited and many people from Larchester who were interested in the school. Sir Joseph and Lady Spinner were coming—all the members of the Board of Governors were coming and bringing their wives—the Bishop of Larchester was coming with his sister and the Mayor of Larchester and his two daughters.

Fortunately there was an ideal place in the grounds of the school for the staging of the Pageant; it was a green glade which lay at the bottom of a gentle slope. The actors could make their entrances and exits from either side of the glade; the spectators could stand upon the rising ground and see everything to perfection. Given a fine day the Pageant was bound to be a success . . . nobody dared to think what would happen if it were wet.

But it was not wet. It was a beautiful summer day with blue skies and a gentle breeze; just enough breeze to temper the heat of the sun and to flutter the pennants and the gay dresses and cloaks of the performers.

The first item on the programme was tea. The guests were ushered into the School Hall on their arrival and the girls who were not taking part in the Pageant helped to hand round tea and sandwiches and cakes. Soon the large hall was so full of people that it was difficult to move . . . and the noise of conversation was beyond belief.

Charlotte had hoped for a few words with Lawrence Swayne, but although she saw him in the distance, looking very smart in a light grey suit, she was so hemmed in by people who wanted to talk to her that it was impossible to get near him. She did her duty by the Mayor and the Bishop and other important people and she spoke to old Miss Bain (who was so bewildered by the crowd that she did not know Charlotte) and she had a few moments' conversation with Sir Joseph and Lady Spinner.

"That was a most extraordinary affair," declared Sir Joseph. "I could hardly believe my ears! It's a pity the crime cannot be brought home to the culprit . . . but this is neither the time nor the place to discuss the matter."

Charlotte agreed. They had people all round them and any conversation had to be conducted in loud tones. "I was terribly disappointed," she told him.

"So was I," shouted Sir Joseph. "I was looking forward to having you with us."

They smiled at one another and she saw that all was well.

Mr. Walpole came up and introduced his wife, a fat comfortable lady in flowered silk. Mr. Cowper presented his daughter. Mr. Allnut spoke to Charlotte and asked what news she had of Miss Pinkerton and seemed surprised when she replied that she had none.

"She promised to help at the Sale of Work," complained Mr. Allnut. "But she never turned up—nor sent any message—and then my wife heard she had left Saint Elizabeth's on account of ill health. We felt she might have let us know. Her unexpected absence caused us a great deal of inconvenience."

Charlotte was commiserating with him when she saw Lawrence Swayne approaching and turned to greet him.

"Hallo!" said Lawrence cheerfully. "You've got a fine day. We had a stinking day for our sports. Look here, Charlotte, is there any chance——"

"Good afternoon, Miss Fairlie," said Professor Eastwood butting into the conversation. "Can you tell me whether Professor MacLaggan is present? You informed me some time ago that he had two daughters here, so it struck me that he might have come this afternoon."

"Yes, he's here somewhere," said Charlotte vaguely.

"I should like a few words with him," explained Professor Eastwood. "But as I have not—er—the pleasure of his acquaintance perhaps you would be good enough to make the introduction."

Charlotte looked round wildly; to find anybody in this crowd seemed almost impossible; but fortunately she spied Professor MacLaggan not far off and, pushing through the crowd with Professor Eastwood in tow, she was able to make the two gentlemen known to one another.

This done she looked to see where Lawrence had gone but he had vanished and several parents who had been pursuing Miss Fairlie managed to get her ear. Some of them wished to know why their daughters had not been given parts in the Pageant; others were of the opinion that their daughters should have been given better parts.

"Silvia is only a lady-in-waiting," lamented one fond mother. "She has nothing to say at all. Of course I know *all* the girls can't have speaking parts but Silvia has such a pretty voice—I mean it seems such a waste!"

"I know—it is a pity," agreed the headmistress regretfully.

" But, as you say, everyone can't have speaking parts—and Silvia's dress is very becoming; she looks charming."

Silvia's mother smiled, and all was well . . . or at least Charlotte hoped so. She was so bewildered by this time that she could not for the life of her remember what part Silvia was playing in the Pageant . . . but it was pretty safe to say that the attire of a lady-in-waiting was becoming and Silvia's mother was almost certain to think that her daughter looked charming.

Fortunately it was now time for the Pageant; the guests trouped out into the grounds and took up their position upon the slope. It was a gay scene, a kaleidoscope of colour, the ladies in their summer frocks and the gentlemen in light suits of grey or brown. The Larchester Band had arrived some time ago and it now began to play Tchaikovsky's Serenade for Strings with considerable verve, and although Charlotte had a feeling that the music was an unsuitable prelude to Queen Boadicea, who was due to enter in her chariot any moment now, she could do nothing about it. In any case she could think of no other music which would be a more suitable prelude to the scene. She glanced round hastily and saw that all was well with the audience and then hurried off to the dressing-room (a large marquee erected amongst the trees) to see how the actors were faring.

Here all was confusion; or at least it looked like confusion at first glance; at second glance the chaos resolved itself into groups of girls dressing and of mistresses lacing them into cardboard armour and pinning veils into place. There was a buzz of talk interspersed with shrieks of despair. " Where's my helmet? " " Has anybody seen my spear? I had it a moment ago . . . "

Boadicea's entrance had been delayed by a mishap to her chariot; she was on her knees beside it, trying to fix the wheel, and Miss Stewart (who had been sent by Sir Joseph to make herself useful) was helping her. Miss Stewart was almost unrecognisable to-day for she was wearing a very flighty hat beneath which her large crystal-clear spectacles flashed in an incongruous manner.

"That's right now, I think," said Miss Stewart, rising from her knees.

"How kind of you!" exclaimed Charlotte.

"Oh Miss Fairlie, thank goodness you're here!" cried Miss Margetson. "Something terrible has happened. Prudence has got stage fright and says she can't go on first and read out the descriptions of the scenes. It isn't any use forcing her. Perhaps you could do it yourself."

"I suppose I shall have to," said Charlotte reluctantly. No girl could suddenly be saddled with the task and the members of the staff were far too busy.

"If I can be of any help in the matter . . ." suggested Miss Stewart.

Miss Margetson looked at her doubtfully—the hat, which had slipped to the back of her head, gave her a somewhat rakish appearance—but Charlotte knew her sterling worth and accepted the offer gladly, explaining that all she had to do was to walk on to the "stage" and read out a short description of each scene before it took place.

Miss Stewart, having accepted this job, felt she was on duty so she prepared herself for action. She took the script and removing the flighty hat put it upon a chair. Immediately Queen Boadicea sat down upon it, exclaiming that she felt a bit wonky about the knees.

Charlotte gave a cry of dismay but the tumult was such that nobody heard, and as nobody else seemed to have noticed she made no further comment. The hat was done for (Boadicea had been chosen by Miss Ricketts for her well-developed figure) and it would be disastrous to upset everybody at the critical moment.

The band stopped playing and the Pageant began. It had
been arranged in chronological sequence, so the first scene
depicted Queen Boadicea and her attendant warriors march-
ing through the forest towards Camulodunum on their
way to do battle with the Romans. Nobody, not even Miss
Margetson, had been able to discover what their costume
should be, so Miss Ricketts had been given a free hand; she
had adorned her cast with dabs of blue paint—to represent
woad—and the minimum of clothing consistent with
decency and she had armed them with home-made spears
and bows and arrows. Being of an optimistic temperament
Miss Ricketts had not bothered about rehearsals but had told
the actors to shout and yell and run about and wave their
weapons in a ferocious manner and, as they were all of the
sporting type, they carried out their instructions with
energy. Charlotte, watching anxiously from the "wings",
decided that the scene might not be historically correct but
it certainly did not lack spirit.

From Queen Boadicea it was a long jump—in time—to
Henry V and Katherine of France in a dell in the French
King's Garden. This scene was carefully prepared—Miss
Agnew had taken a lot of trouble over it—but it was not
nearly so spectacular nor so suitable for an open air perform-
ance and it fell a little flat. Then came two scenes in quick
succession: Henry VIII and Anne Boleyn, dallying in a
forest glade; and Bloody Mary decked for her wedding
(and accompanied by a large retinue of ladies and gentlemen)
on the way to Winchester to meet Philip of Spain. Charlotte
was glad to see Silvia amongst the retinue and to note that
she looked her best.

There was a long pause after this and the band played
Elizabethan dances while the actors prepared for the famous
scene from *Kenilworth*.

The incident chosen by Miss Pinkerton was the meeting

of Queen Elizabeth and young Walter Raleigh when the latter spread his cloak upon a patch of muddy ground for his Queen to walk upon. By rights this historical event took place at the Palace of Greenwich, when Elizabeth was about to enter the royal barge, but as no "Great Stairs" were available Miss Pinkerton had transplanted it to a country setting: a meadow on the banks of the Thames. The barge was visible (or rather a part of the barge, for the major portion of it seemed to be hidden behind the trees); it had been made by Miss Pinkerton with her own hands and consisted of some packing cases covered with canvas and painted in gay colours. Queen Elizabeth and her court had partaken of an *al fresco* repast and were on their way back to the barge when young Walter Raleigh stepped from amongst the trees and made his world-famous gesture.

The scene was one of the best in the Pageant—even Miss Pinkerton's worst enemies could not deny the fact—it was romantic and polished and it filled the eye. Queen Elizabeth and her court were sumptously attired in the correct fashion for the period; Miss Pinkerton had spared no pains over her scene and as she was the director of the Pageant she had been able to appropriate a lion's share of the money which the Board of Governors had allowed for properties.

After this came Mary Queen of Scots escaping from Loch Leven Castle with Lady Fleming, George Douglas and Abbot Boniface in attendance. Mademoiselle Boule had followed the example of Miss Pinkerton and taken Sir Walter Scott as her guide (a delightfully romantic guide but not always reliable in the hard facts of history). The scene opened with the gathering of a large crowd of loyal supporters armed to the teeth who awaited the coming of their Queen with impatience and anxiety. They had begun to think the plans for her escape must have miscarried when Queen Mary and her companions rode in (on ponies borrowed from the Larchester Riding School) and were received with acclamation.

Tessa was every inch a queen, she was dignified and charming and there was an air of tragedy about her which was extraordinarily pathetic. In the other scenes it was the colourful dresses or the action which had held one's attention but here it was the slight and beautifully poised central figure of Queen Mary. Charlotte felt this strongly and the audience must have felt it too; there was a moment's silence when the scene was over before the usual torrent of applause.

Charlotte wished that this was the end of the entertainment for it had taken longer than was expected (as most amateur performances do) and she was aware that the last two items on the programme would be an anti-climax. They were neither spectacular nor romantic and the costumes were dull in comparison with the earlier and more colourful fashions.

There was a scene in which Queen Anne and Lady Marlborough were walking through the woods together chatting amiably and addressing one another as Mrs. Morley and Mrs. Freeman; and an imaginary incident in the life of Queen Victoria where she was discovered picnicking near Balmoral Castle with Prince Albert and some members of her court. Apart from John Brown (portrayed by a girl from Hawick whose Scots accent occasioned a good deal of amusement) the last scene was a dead loss and Charlotte heaved a sigh of relief when it was over.

The band played "God Save the Queen"; the guests departed and the inhabitants of Saint Elizabeth's ate their supper and talked about the events of the day. It was agreed that on the whole the production had gone off as well a could be expected—some scenes had been thoroughly satisfactory, others a trifle disappointing—Miss Ricketts was congratulated upon Boadicea and Mademoiselle Boule upon Queen Mary. Miss Pinkerton was absent of course so she could not be congratulated upon Queen Elizabeth which in some ways had been the high-light of the production.

It was not until Charlotte was getting into bed that she remembered Miss Stewart's hat and wondered what had happened to the mangled remains of the confection. Had Miss Stewart found it—and recognised it—and taken it home, or had it been swept away with the bits of cardboard armour and feathered caps into Saint Elizabeth's capacious dustbin?

PART TWO

Blow the Wind Southerly

* 20 *

I T WAS a perfect day for flying. Charlotte looked out of
the window of the little plane and saw the radiant sunshine, and the puffy clouds floating serenely in the pale
blue sky. Below, spread out like a map, was the wild rugged
country of moor and loch and mountain.

Only a few hours ago Charlotte had been in London,
surrounded by crowds of busy people and deafened by the
noise of traffic. She had flown from London Airport to
Renfrew, had changed planes as instructed and was now
approaching Invergoily. All the way they had had the wind
behind them which had made for a smooth passage, and
the air-hostess had told her that they would arrive before
the scheduled time. The last lap of Charlotte's journey
would be by boat from Invergoily to the island of Targ.

Charlotte was always interested and excited when travelling; there were so many things to see—not only new places
but new people—but to-day she was more excited than usual
and her excitement was tinged with a shade of apprehension
for although Colonel MacRynne had written two very kind
letters, one at Easter and the other quite recently, inviting
her to come and stay at Targ she knew that the invitation
had been prompted by his daughter. Supposing she did not
like him—or worse, supposing he did not like her! But of
course Tessa would be there . . . the thought of seeing
Tessa gave Charlotte a warm feeling in her heart.

The plane was banking now; it slid down towards the sea and alighted upon the narrow airstrip with a scarcely perceptible bounce.

As she came down the ladder Charlotte saw Tessa, waving excitedly, and behind Tessa was a tall broad-shouldered man wearing a shabby kilt and a brown homespun jacket. This must be her host, thought Charlotte, and she experienced a slight feeling of disappointment; for although this man was handsome and, by ordinary standards, "a fine figure of a man" he had not quite the kingly bearing she had expected.

Tessa flung herself into Charlotte's arms and hugged her rapturously. "Oh it *is* lovely to see you! " she cried. "I can hardly believe you're really and truly here. It's simply too marvellous for words! Did you have a good trip? I hope you're not frightfully tired."

"Not tired a bit," declared Charlotte smiling. "In fact I enjoyed every moment."

Tessa turned and introduced her companion. "This is Euan, Miss Fairlie. He'll bring your suitcase and everything. We've got a little way to walk to the harbour. Daddy would have come to meet you himself, but the Eastwoods are here, so——"

"The Eastwoods! " exclaimed Charlotte. "I thought their father refused to let them come."

Tessa laughed. "Yes, but he changed his mind. Daddy wrote to Sir Joseph Spinner and he rang up Professor Eastwood and persuaded him. You see Daddy knows Sir Joseph—he came and stayed at Targ last year—he's a funny old gentleman with white hair and pink cheeks and very blue eyes. He's a nice, clean, polite old gentleman," added Tessa approvingly.

Charlotte was so amazed at hearing the great Sir Joseph thus described that she was speechless.

"Of course I don't know what Sir Joseph said to Professor Eastwood," continued Tessa. "But he's a Governor of Saint Elizabeth's so I suppose he's rather important. At any rate he managed to persuade the professor to let them come for a whole month. Wasn't it splendid? Of course I really wanted them to come later—I mean I wanted to have you here alone—but Daddy said we had better have the Eastwoods straight off before the professor's heart hardened (like Pharaoh and the Children of Israel, you know) so they came, and they're enjoying themselves frightfully. I hope you don't mind them being here, Miss Fairlie."

Charlotte assured her hostess that she did not mind at all and was only too delighted to hear the Eastwoods were having a holiday. Now that she knew of Sir Joseph's parcipation in their affairs she was not surprised that all had been settled satisfactorily.

By this time Euan had collected Charlotte's suitcase and other belongings and they set out to walk through the little village to the harbour. It was bright and breezy. The sea was very blue with crisp white caps upon the waves; the sky was a paler blue and cloudless. The land was green, the beach was of pure white sand with piles of bright yellow seaweed. Far in the distance there were purple hills, their outlines softened by haze. All the colours were clean—like the colours in a brand new paintbox—and the sunshine was so strong that the very air seemed to glitter. Charlotte took deep breaths of air and smelt the faint tang of the seaweed drying in the sunshine—that unforgettable smell which is so characteristic of the Western Isles.

"There's Targ!" cried Tessa, seizing Charlotte's arm and pointing out to sea. "There—look! You can see the black cliffs! That's Targ, Miss Fairlie!"

Miss Fairlie did not reply, but Tessa—glancing at her face—was not disappointed. There was a look of enchantment upon the face of her idol which was better than a spate of admiring words.

They made their way along a rough stone jetty where a sturdy little yacht was lying moored.

"I have the stores shipped, Miss Tessa," said Euan. "I called for the mail and the papers. There is nothing more to get. Will I start the engine?"

"No, Euan, we'll sail."

"But Miss Tessa, we will have to tack and it will be more seemly to go straight across to the island with your guest."

"Nonsense, Euan. You know I hate your smelly old engine. We used it coming over because we were late; there's plenty of time now."

While they were talking Charlotte had been handed into the yacht, told where to sit and provided with a mackintosh.

"But Miss Tessa," objected Euan, continuing the argument in his deep, slow, musical voice. "But Miss Tessa, I cannot manage the sails and steer at the same time and you are wearing your good clothes."

But Tessa had already flung off her hat and jacket and was now removing her shoes and stockings. In another moment she stood up, clad in her white silk shirt and tweed skirt. She rolled her sleeves above the elbows and shook back her dark curls. "You take the tiller, Euan," she said with calm authority.

Euan did so. It was obvious that although he disapproved of the arrangement he had no thought of questioning it further.

Charlotte knew nothing about sailing but she knew efficiency when she saw it and she watched with pleasure while Tessa did what was necessary. The mooring ropes were loosened and coiled, the yacht fended off from the pier, and the sails were run up in a few moments. A few moments more and the white sails filled and the little boat heeled over and moved away from the mainland . . . slowly at first but soon with a bounding motion which was most exhilarating.

"Much nicer than Euan's smelly old engine," said Tessa grinning mischievously.

Charlotte smiled. She had a sudden feeling that she had arrived in another world—thousands of miles away from the ordinary everyday world of work and duty—and the fact that she had arrived by air heightened the illusion, for surely that was the right way to travel to another world.

Their first tack was in a south-westerly direction, close hauled to the breeze. The yacht danced merrily over the bright blue water. It was delightful to listen to the waves slapping the sides of the little boat and to the whistle of the wind in the rigging. Every now and then there was a scatter of spray from a broken wave; a tiny shower of crystal drops, salt upon the lips. Presently Euan made a sign with his hand and the boom swung over; the yacht hesitated for a moment like a reined horse and then bounded off on the new course.

It was more peaceful now with the wind on their port beam and Charlotte heard a new sound; a haunting little tune whistled in a clear true pipe like the song of the thrush. She looked at Euan, but the sound was not coming from him, and then she looked at Tessa. Tessa was sitting on the edge of the boat with her feet upon the seat and her lithe body bending to every motion of the waves . . . and she was whistling merrily.

"It is not lucky for a woman to whistle," said Euan in disapproving tones.

"Oh Euan, you are an old spoil-sport!" cried Tessa. "You know I love whistling—you know I always whistle when I'm happy."

"It is not lucky," he repeated. "You are getting too old

for whistling. Why do you not sing the tune if you are happy, Miss Tessa?"

"All right I will," she replied; she sang it in a sweet clear voice and the words were as well suited to the occasion as the melody:—

> *Blow the wind southerly, southerly, southerly*
> *Blow the wind south o'er the bonny blue sea;*
> *Softly and safely o'er the wide ocean*
> *Blow home the bark of my true love to me.*
> *Blow the south wind,*
> *Blow the south wind,*
> *Southerly, southerly o'er the blue sea.*

The south wind was blowing—it had been blowing softly all day—it was upon the wings of the south wind that Charlotte had been wafted to Targ.

Soon the island took shape before Charlotte's eyes; she saw the rocky shore; she saw black crags and green slopes and hills. There was a gap in the cliffs where a burn ran into the sea and formed a sheltered bay. This natural harbour was guarded on the north by a reef of rocks jutting out from the island, on the south there was a landing place with stone steps. As they neared their destination the sails came down with a rattle and the little boat glided gently to her moorings. The crew made fast; Euan jumped ashore and held out his hand to the passenger . . . and as Charlotte set foot upon the water-worn steps he said in his slow serious voice, "Welcome to Targ, Miss Fairlie! I am hoping you will enjoy your stay upon the island."

"Thank you, Euan," replied Miss Fairlie with equal gravity.

There was a little cottage near the harbour; Tessa pointed to it and said that Euan's mother lived there—and Euan too, except when he stayed in the castle—and she explained that the village was on the other side of the cliff where there was another larger harbour for the fishing-boats.

"Just leave everything, Miss Tessa," said Euan. "I will bring it all up to the castle in the wee cart. Miss Fairlie will be wanting a cup of tea."

"Yes, we'll walk on," agreed Tessa. "But don't be long, Euan, because Mrs. Fraser wants the gigot for to-night's dinner."

"What is a gigot?" asked Charlotte as they began to ascend the path.

"A gigot?" asked Tessa in surprise. "It's—well it's a leg of lamb. Don't you call it that in England? How funny!"

"They call it that in France," said Charlotte smiling. "I suppose you must have borrowed the word from your ancient allies."

The narrow road ran up the gully by the side of the burn. There was heather here, not yet in bloom, and tiny wild flowers and clusters of tall green bracken. A black-faced sheep with curly horns was cropping the grass which grew at the side of the road but when it saw them coming it sprang away and disappeared up the steep hill with goat-like agility.

"You couldn't drive a car up this road," said Charlotte.

"There are no cars on the island," replied Tessa. "We have a pony cart—that's all—Daddy keeps his car at the garage in Invergoily. Some of the children in the village have never seen a motor car and lots of them have never seen a train but they've often seen aeroplanes of course . . ."

Tessa continued to talk about the people and the place. She was thoroughly enjoying herself. It was so wonderful to have Miss Fairlie here and to be able to chat to her in comfort. Somehow Miss Fairlie seemed so much younger—quite a different person from the great Miss Fairlie of Saint

Elizabeth's—and she looked younger too. She had taken off her hat and her hair was loosened (instead of being smoothed back into a knob at the back of her head), it curled on her forehead and round her ears and there were glints of gold in it. Tessa had always thought her beautiful, but to-day she was more beautiful than ever . . . and she was gay and happy and charming.

"Do you like being headmistress of Saint Elizabeth's?" Tessa inquired.

Charlotte turned her head and looked at her companion in amusement for she knew exactly what Tessa was thinking.

"Don't answer if you don't want to," said Tessa hastily. "I shouldn't have asked, really."

"It's difficult to answer," said Charlotte. "When I'm there I like it, but when I come away I like to forget about it and just be myself."

"You can be yourself all the time you're here, can't you?" said Tessa joyfully.

They had climbed up the steep stony road for about a quarter of a mile when it suddenly twisted sharply between two piles of boulders and emerged into a sheltered valley . . . and there, before their eyes, was the Castle of Targ. It was a strangely-shaped building, partly old and partly new. The old part consisted of a squat tower with immensely thick walls and crow-stepped gables; the newer part was square and solid with mullioned windows. It was built of the same grey stone but the stones instead of being rough—like those of the tower—were smooth and even. The Castle was by no means beautiful, in fact it was rather ugly, but it certainly was unique and it fitted perfectly with its surroundings. It had the appearance of being deeply rooted into the soil; as if it had been there from time immemorial and would stand there till the Day of Judgment. The burn ran through the valley, prattling amongst rocks; there were a few fine old oak trees and beyond them a garden enclosed with high stone walls.

The odd mixture of old and new characterised the inside as well as the outside of Targ Castle. The front door of oak, studded with huge iron nails, was in the tower and opened into a large square hall paved with grey stone. Weapons hung upon its walls, and it was furnished with old wooden chests and oak chairs which looked as if they might have come out of a museum. There was a feeling of age in this part of the castle, the very light seemed old as though it had been in the rooms for centuries (not newly minted by the sun when it rose in the morning) and there was a feeling of history as though the place were a book in which one could read of life and death, of gay feastings and of tragedies.

In the newer part of the castle there was quite a different atmosphere; a door on the right led through a five-foot-thick wall into a large comfortable room with a fitted carpet on the floor and deep leather chairs. There were bookcases on the walls and a few good pictures and a log fire burned cheerfully in an open grate. The mullioned windows looked out onto a walled garden where *fuchsias* grew round a square of green turf and there was a solid oaken seat beneath an apple tree.

"This is Daddy's study," said Tessa as she showed it to her guest. "At least we call it the study, but we use it to sit in all the time except when we have a party. It's so much cosier than the drawing-room and it gets all the sun. If Daddy wants to be quiet and write letters he sits in the office. I'll take you up to your room and then we'll have tea."

Charlotte's room was in the newer part of the castle, it was large and comfortably furnished in modern style. The windows looked out upon the same little garden that she had seen from the study and beyond was the glen with trees and a sweep of moorland hills.

"How lovely!" Charlotte exclaimed.

"Yes, isn't it?" agreed Tessa. "And look, Miss Fairlie, this is your bathroom. There's always lots of hot water so have a bath whenever you like."

The dressing-room next door had been converted into a bathroom, with pale-green paint and a pale-green porcelain bath. Charlotte was delighted with it; she was a little surprised to find such up-to-date arrangements in such out-of-the-way surroundings . . . but then she remembered that the castle had had an American lady as its chatelaine and the mystery was explained.

"Daddy will be in to tea," said Tessa. "The Eastwoods have gone for a picnic, but Daddy will be back." She hesitated and then added, "He would have been here to welcome you when you arrived, but I think he knew that I wanted awfully much to show you Targ myself."

* 21 *

WHEN CHARLOTTE came downstairs to tea she realised that her host had arrived for she heard Tessa's voice talking eagerly. They were in the study together—Tessa and her father—and Charlotte paused for a moment before opening the door. She was a trifle apprehensive for, as has been said before, she was aware that Colonel MacRynne had been forced by his daughter to invite her to his home. For a moment she wished she had not come. But it was no use standing outside the door wishing herself elsewhere so she opened the door and went in. They were standing at the window laughing over some joke but they turned as she went in and Tessa made the introduction with her usual aplomb.

Charlotte saw a tall man with a brown face and hazel eyes—his eyes were like Tessa's—his hair was the colour of old mahogany, dark reddish brown, with copper tints where the sun had caught it, and, although it was closely cut and smoothly brushed, it was slightly wavy. He was younger than Charlotte had expected—or at least he looked younger—and he was full of life and vigour. There was nothing of The Forsaken Merman about this man, she thought, and she could see no sign of the arrogance which characterised the Lord of the Isles.

"Miss Fairlie!" he exclaimed, smiling at her with his eyes, which crinkled at the corners. "This is very nice of you! Tessa says she has explained why I didn't come to meet you; but apparently Euan did the honours on your arrival. It must have amused you."

"I didn't think it—funny," replied Charlotte. (She saw the little scene at the jetty as she spoke and heard again Euan's grave voice saying, ' Welcome to Targ, Miss Fairlie. I am hoping you will enjoy your stay upon the island ') "I thought it sounded—right," said Charlotte trying to explain. "He was welcoming a stranger to his home."

"Yes, of course," agreed her host. "That's exactly what he was doing—and feeling. He was doing it because I wasn't there to do it myself. Euan couldn't understand why I wasn't there, you see. But I thought it might have seemed a little odd to somebody who's not used to our ways . . . and Tessa thought so too. Tessa tells me that the janitor at Saint Elizabeth's never makes pretty speeches to visitors."

Charlotte smiled. It certainly was difficult to imagine the crabbed old janitor, who had been at Saint Elizabeth's for about twenty years, welcoming visitors with pretty speeches.

"Oh, if you could *see* him, Daddy! " cried Tessa, throwing herself into a chair and shaking with mirth. "If you could *see* him! Do you know what he said when I arrived? He looked at me as if I were a beetle and said, ' Ere's another of 'em! "

"But that's dreadful! " cried Charlotte aghast. "Why did nobody tell me he was rude? "

Her host and hostess were laughing so heartily that Charlotte was forced to laugh too. "But it *is* dreadful," she repeated. "I shall have to speak to Jakes . . . "

The ice had now been thoroughly broken and tea was a cheerful meal. Charlotte learnt a lot about Targ during tea. Some of the information was given her by her host and some by her hostess, occasionally they both spoke at once. It was pleasant to see them together, teasing one another and laughing, but with deep understanding and love and mutual admiration underlying all the fun.

Charlotte learnt that the island was twelve miles long and about five miles broad at its widest point; there were two farms on the island; one was a sheep farm and lay to the west; the other was the Home Farm which supplied the castle and the village with milk and butter and eggs and other produce. The village, as Charlotte already knew, lay to the southward of the castle. The men worked on the land, helped on the farms and fished; many of the women had looms and made homespun tweeds and scarves or knitted shawls and stockings. There were about two hundred people living on Targ island ("Counting the babies," said Tessa) and they were all busy and happy. There was a school of course and a tiny cottage hospital but when anybody was seriously ill they were taken to the mainland and despatched to Glasgow by plane. There was no doctor at Targ; he lived at Invergoily and was sent for when necessary which was not really very often. Charlotte gathered that a great many improvements had been made by Colonel MacRynne. He had managed to get the telephone put in for one thing.

"It was rather expensive," explained Tessa, "but it really *was* necessary, especially in winter when we're storm bound for days on end. For instance if anybody was ill . . . and of course it was Daddy who got an engineer from Glasgow to dam the burn and make electric light . . . and it was Daddy who started the hospital and got Nurse Anderson to live there, and he started the Home Industries and found a shop that would sell the work. And I must tell you——"

"Peace, child!" cried Colonel MacRynne. "Miss Fairlie has heard quite enough about my interfering ways."

Tessa chuckled and said, "You *are* rather an interfering

sort of person, but as a matter of fact I was only going to tell her about the aunts. She'll have to go and see the aunts to-night after dinner so she had better be told about them, hadn't she? They're your aunts, Daddy, so you can tell her."

Colonel MacRynne smiled and said there was not much to tell. They were his father's sisters and they had a suite of rooms in the east wing of the castle. Sometimes they came downstairs to dinner and enjoyed a game of whist afterwards, but for the most part they lived and moved and had their being in their own comfortable quarters.

"Daddy," said Tessa suddenly. "Need you go to Inverness to-morrow? Is it terribly important?"

Colonel MacRynne looked thoughtful. "I ought to go," he said. "But I wonder—perhaps I could skip that tiresome meeting."

"Of course you could," declared Tessa. "Just say you can't come. Go and telephone this minute."

"I believe I will," he said smiling at her. "But what excuse shall I give?"

"Tell them," began Tessa. "Let me see now . . . tell them the castle is full of children and you must be here to keep an eye on them. It's true, you know."

He laughed. "Miss Fairlie could keep an eye on you."

"Oh, but she's a guest!" cried Tessa. "You can't ask a guest to look after a whole lot of children. Go at once, Daddy, and don't tease."

Colonel MacRynne rose and went out chuckling to himself, and Charlotte could not help wondering whether he would really give the somewhat strange excuse for his inability to attend the meeting or concoct one more suitable.

Soon after that the Eastwoods returned from their picnic; they were full of all they had done and seen and obviously had enjoyed themselves enormously. Charlotte was amazed to see what a fortnight at Targ had done to the Eastwood children; not only were they as brown as berries, with bright eyes and ruddy cheeks, but they were actually noisy. It was difficult to recognise them as the three little rabbits on whose account she had felt so distressed.

* 22 *

AFTER DINNER Charlotte was taken upstairs to pay a call upon the aunts, Miss Mary and Miss Anne MacRynne.. Tessa conducted her to their sitting-room and left her there, saying she was sure they would like to have Miss Fairlie to themselves, and obviously Tessa was right for they settled down one on each side of Charlotte with smiles of pleasure. They were very old ladies and resembled one another so closely that they might easily have been twins: small and frail with silvery hair and very dark eyes.

"It *is* so delightful to meet somebody from the Outside World," said Miss Mary. "We don't see many people, you know."

"But we are very happy here," said Miss Anne.

Charlotte could not help gazing round their sitting-room for it was a perfect mid-Victorian period piece and would have graced any museum of historical furnishings. There was a patterned carpet and curiously shaped chairs, with carved wooden backs and upholstered seats; there were small inlaid tables, laden with photographs in plush frames and with silver boxes and knick-knacks. There were water-colours and painted plates upon the walls and over the mantelpiece was a large gilt-framed mirror—it might easily have been the mirror which melted and gave Alice access to Looking Glass House. The mantelpiece itself was draped with old-gold plush and crammed with ornaments of all shapes and sizes. Last but not least the curtains which hung at the windows, and also over the door, were of old-gold plush trimmed with bobbles.

Miss Mary noticed Charlotte's interest in their belongings. She said: "It is a *little* too crowded, I'm afraid, but my sister and I like all our treasures round us."

"When our nephew married," said Miss Anne, "there were a great many alterations and he gave us this comfortable suite of rooms so that we might still live in the castle without being a trouble to anybody. And when Esther—Tessa's mother—refurnished the drawing-room she told us to take everything we wanted."

"We collected all our treasures and brought them up here," added Miss Mary.

Charlotte could see them hurrying round like two little mice (or perhaps two little squirrels was a better simile) collecting all their treasures before they were thrown onto the dust-heap.

"Esther was very particular about decorating and furniture," continued Miss Mary. "She said mid-Victorian furniture was an anachronism in a 14th century castle—and I'm sure she was right."

"14th century furniture wouldn't be very comfortable," suggested Charlotte, thinking involuntarily of the chromium-plated taps (which had winked at her so gaily when she was having her bath before dinner) and trying to hide a smile.

"Oh!" exclaimed Miss Mary. "I never thought of that. Esther should have had rushes on the floor and wooden stools to sit on."

The two old ladies looked at each other and chuckled.

"And they didn't have any bathrooms at all," said Miss Anne. "No bathrooms, no running water and no electric light! That wouldn't have suited Esther."

"But she was very kind to us," said Miss Mary hastily. "So very kind."

There was a momentary silence and then Miss Anne said, "Of course you know all about it, don't you, Miss Fairlie?"

"Yes—at least I know a good deal," admitted Charlotte. "It must have been a great shock to you, I'm afraid."

"Oh no, dear, it was not a shock at all," replied Miss Anne comfortably. "My sister and I had been expecting it for years, hadn't we, Mary? Poor Esther was not suited to Targ from the very beginning and instead of settling down as she grew older she became more and more unsettled and went away for longer and longer periods. Of course she had money of her own and she spent it as she liked."

"Travelling abroad," said Miss Mary nodding.

"There was no reason why she shouldn't," Miss Anne declared.

"N'no," said Miss Mary doubtfully.

"People can do what they please with their own money," said Miss Anne firmly. "And in Esther's case it was just as well. She would never have been happy at Targ—never—so it was just as well she could go away when she liked. It was just as well for us and for Rory and for everybody concerned because we all got used to doing without her and when she went away she left nothing behind."

"Rory was upset," put in Miss Mary. "Poor Rory was very upset indeed."

"He was not so much upset as annoyed," said her sister in a reflective tone. "For one thing Rory is proud, so he felt insulted, and for another he does not like things to get spoilt or broken."

It was a curious statement to make—so Charlotte thought —and at first she felt inclined to smile but afterwards she decided that Miss Anne knew exactly what she was talking about.

"But Esther was always very kind," said Miss Mary, who seemed determined that Charlotte should not forget this. "She was never cross nor unpleasant. Some people might not have liked to have two old ladies living at Targ but it was Esther's idea that the east wing should be made into a little flat for us to live in—and we were very glad to accept. It would have been sad if we had had to go and live in a strange place."

"We used to go away every year for a holiday," said Miss Anne.

"But you don't now?" asked Charlotte.

The two old ladies looked at one another.

"I think Miss Fairlie would like to hear about it," said Miss Anne.

"She would think us very silly," objected Miss Mary.

Charlotte persuaded them to tell her the story.

"Oh well," said Miss Mary smiling. "Miss Fairlie is bound to find out sooner or later how silly we are, so it may as well be sooner. You see, my dear, we used to go away every year for a fortnight. I hated leaving Targ but I never said so because of my sister. I could see she enjoyed our annual holiday so of course I pretended to enjoy it too. Every year we went to a different place and stayed at an hotel. It was a dreadful ordeal; there were so many people —and not the sort of people we were used to. Anne seemed to be able to chat to them but I found it very difficult . . . and I knew they laughed at us behind our backs. They thought we were queer. Two queer old ladies, that was what they thought! I didn't like the food either, and I didn't like the noise. It's so peaceful at Targ. Have you noticed how peaceful it is, Miss Fairlie?"

Charlotte said it was one of the first things she had noticed.

"Three years ago we arranged to go to Crieff for our

holiday," continued Miss Mary. "It was all settled. The night before we were leaving, Tessa came up to see us and say good-bye. I was in my bedroom, packing, when the dear child came in and—I am afraid you will think this very silly, Miss Fairlie—I was crying. You see I was so miserable at the thought of leaving Targ even for a fortnight. Tessa is a very sympathetic little girl and she asked me what was the matter and why I was crying—so I told her the truth. She looked at me in surprise and said, ' But why do you go if you don't like it, Aunt Mary?' ' Aunt Anne enjoys it,' I said. ' It's a little dull for Aunt Anne at Targ.' ' But Aunt Anne is crying too,' said Tessa."

"Of course I was," declared Miss Anne chuckling. "I hated leaving Targ every bit as much as Mary. I thought she enjoyed our holiday, you see."

"Wasn't it silly?" said Miss Mary. "Don't you think we are two very silly old ladies, Miss Fairlie?"

Charlotte thought they were two very delightful old ladies but she was too shy to say so.

"We thought we would have to go to Crieff," continued Miss Mary. "We had booked our room, you see—but Tessa said there was no need and when we asked Rory he laughed and laughed until the tears ran down his cheeks and he went to the telephone and cancelled our rooms and our seats on the plane."

"So we never went," said Miss Anne smiling happily. "And we have never had a holiday since."

"It was Tessa's doing," said Miss Mary reflectively. "Tessa is so *sensible*. If it had not been for Tessa we would still be taking a holiday every year."

Miss Anne shuddered. "Do you really think we would?"

"I am sure of it, Anne," replied her sister firmly.

There was a short silence. At last Miss Anne said, "We think Tessa a most remarkable child."

"She certainly is unusual and very attractive," agreed Charlotte.

"We wondered if it could be her heredity," said Miss Mary eagerly. "There is so much in heredity, isn't there? Tessa is a mixture of the Old World and the New World. The MacRynnes are such an old family that they are apt to live in the past and Esther was always pressing forward to the future. Tessa is a child of the present; she is so balanced and sensible and not afraid of anything."

"Yes, she's a whole person," said Charlotte thoughtfully. It was an interesting theory and although Charlotte was aware that heredity is not quite such a simple straight-forward matter as Miss Mary seemed to imagine (not like mixing blue and red to obtain purple) she was ready to admit there might be a good deal in it.

After that the conversation turned to Charlotte's affairs. The two old ladies were anxious to know all about their guest and she was touched and flattered by their interest. She realised that to them she was as interesting and exciting as somebody who had just arrived from Mars and she was prepared to satisfy their curiosity. Of course she had no intention of relating the whole history of her life to Miss Mary and Miss Anne, her intention was to tell them some of the odd things that had happened to her—incidents which they might find amusing—but this was not their idea at all. They wanted to know everything; they wanted to know about her childhood: where she had been born and brought up, where she had been to school, and they plied her with such searching questions that by the time they had done with her there was not much of her history that they did not know. It was a curious experience, Charlotte found, and by no means an unpleasant one, to be urged on to talk about oneself and to be listened to with sympathy and intelligence.

"Goodness, how late it is!" exclaimed Charlotte, glancing at the clock and rising hastily.

"But you haven't told us about when you went to Saint Elizabeth's," objected Miss Anne. "It was lovely for you to go back to your old school as headmistress. It was your dream come true."

"Yes, it was my dream come true," agreed Charlotte.

"And is it as wonderful as you expected," Miss Mary wanted to know.

Charlotte hesitated. Tessa had asked her the same question in slightly different words, but the reply she had given Tessa was not suitable for Miss Mary. In fact she could think of no suitable answer for Miss Mary. In some ways her position at Saint Elizabeth's was satisfying, for she felt she was doing useful work, but she had not expected all the difficulties she had encountered: the strain of dealing with vagaries of the staff and of being tactful with the parents . . . and she had not expected to be so lonely.

"Things are never *quite* what we expect," said Miss Anne, answering the question for her.

"No," agreed Charlotte gratefully. "And now I really must go. I'm sure you've had enough of me for to-night."

"Well, perhaps it *is* a little late," said Miss Anne reluctantly.

"Come back another time and tell us more," said Miss Mary. "It has been so interesting—just like a story book."

"Your world is so different from ours," added Miss Anne.

Charlotte had never thought her history very interesting but she realised it must sound strange to the Misses Mac-Rynne. Their world was so safe and sheltered. There had always been somebody to do things for them and make decisions for them; they had never had to fend for themselves.

"Good-night, Miss Fairlie," said Miss Mary.

"Good-night, Miss Fairlie," said Miss Anne. "We both

hope you will have a very happy and peaceful holiday at Targ."

Charlotte hesitated and then she said: "Do you think you could call me Charlotte. You know so much about me now, don't you?"

"I think we would like to," said Miss Anne nodding. "It's a very pretty name and it suits you, my dear."

They both kissed her and said: "Good-night, Charlotte," and she came away.

* 23 *

THERE WAS no shortage of food in Targ, so much was obvious from the assortment of porridge and bacon and eggs, of oat cakes and scones, of honey and marmalade, which made its appearance at breakfast. Charlotte was contented with an egg and some oatcakes and honey, but the other members of the house-party waded through every dish with relish.

"Targ *does* make you hungry," said Barney at last, leaning back with a sigh of satisfaction. He had been up early and had gone out to see Tessa's pony and to give him a carrot so perhaps he had more excuse for his appetite than those who had stayed in bed.

"What does everybody want to do this morning?" asked Colonel MacRynne.

"Oh Daddy, you *know*," declared Tessa. "I told you I *must* take Miss Fairlie to see Euan's mother. She'll be hurt if we don't go. I thought the others could come with us, and——"

"I'd like to fish if nobody minds," interrupted Harold, who had been introduced to this peaceful sport and found it suited to his temperament.

Colonel MacRynne nodded. "All right," he said. "Take the small trout rod—the one you had before—I've got to go up to the farm and see Macdonald."

"Oh Daddy, do take your gun and get some rabbits," said Tessa.

"Could I come, Colonel MacRynne?" asked Barney. "You might want somebody to carry the rabbits, mightn't you?"

Colonel MacRynne said he certainly would—if he managed to shoot any—and as everybody knew that the hill was teeming with rabbits and the Colonel a first-class shot the qualification was not considered seriously.

"That's settled then," said Tessa. "Donny can come with us. I'll just see Mrs. Fraser about food and then we can start."

It was a misty day, warm and sultry, banks of mist lay upon the hills drifting slowly with the faint breeze, but there was a sort of radiance in the sky which showed where the sun was shining. Charlotte and the two girls walked down the narrow road to the little harbour.

"It's going to clear up," Tessa assured her companions. "It will be beautiful this afternoon."

"It's beautiful now," said Donny. "I like this sort of day almost better than a sunny one—everything is so soft and quiet—like dreams. But I wouldn't mind if it rained all the time, I'd like to stay here for ever."

There was nothing much that could be said after this, so they walked on in silence and soon approached the cottage.

"Perhaps I had better tell you a little about her," said Tessa, pausing before they went in. "She's old, of course, because she's Euan's mother. Daddy and Euan are the same age. Her husband was drowned before Euan was born. He was out in his boat, fishing, and a storm came on very suddenly . . . so after Euan was born she came and lived at the castle with her baby and looked after Daddy too. That's why she's rather special, you see."

Charlotte said she understood.

"We'll go to the village another day," said Tessa. "I want *all* the people to see you, but Mrs. Euan is first."

"Mrs. Euan?" asked Charlotte. "I thought she was Euan's mother."

"Euan's father was called Euan too. She's really Mrs. Euan MacRynne," explained Tessa. "A lot of the people here are MacRynnes. They belong to Clan MacRynne—it doesn't mean they're our relations. Those who are not MacRynnes are mostly Macdonalds. I know it must be muddling for you," added Tessa kindly.

Mrs. Euan was doing her washing when they arrived. Tessa shouted to her and she came out from the back of the cottage attired like a scarecrow in a torn and faded tartan skirt and a ragged blouse. Her bare feet were thrust into wooden clogs, and a faded red-cotton handkerchief was tied over her head and knotted beneath her chin. Charlotte thought she had a wild look about her and could have played the part of Meg Merrilies to perfection.

"Perhaps we should come back some other day when Mrs. Euan isn't so busy——" began Charlotte but neither Tessa nor Mrs. Euan listened. They were greeting one another affectionately and when this little ceremony was over Mrs. Euan wiped her hands upon her tartan skirt and shook hands with her new acquaintances.

"It is a great pleasure to meet Miss Fairlie and Miss Eastwood," said Mrs. Euan gravely. "I have been hearing a great deal about them from Euan and the others."

They went into the cottage and sat down: the two girls upon three-legged stools and Charlotte upon an oak settle. Their hostess stirred up the fire and put on the kettle and fetched cups and saucers and plates of scones and a large dish of butter. She moved quietly and with a natural grace, and as she performed the little domestic duties she continued to talk in a slow soft voice, asking for Miss Fairlie's health and if she had had a pleasant trip and inquiring how Miss Eastswood was liking her holiday in Targ. When she moved and spoke one forgot her ragged clothes—it was obvious that she herself was unconscious of them.

Charlotte had sometimes visited cottages in Larchester and been greeted with shyness and embarrassment and with all sorts of excuses for not being "dressed," and of course she had had to take the lead in any conversation . . . here in Targ it was very different. These people were fundamentally different from any people she had ever seen before. Their beautiful manners and their dignity of bearing were not "put on" for the occasion but were perfectly natural. Mrs. Euan looked like a scarecrow but she behaved like a queen.

Presently the kettle boiled and Mrs. Euan made tea. Charlotte had just partaken of an unusually solid breakfast but she realised that she must not refuse the meal so she drank the tea and ate a scone with butter and honey. She wondered whether all the other people she was to call upon —the people in the village—would produce a meal and expect her to eat it. If so it might be difficult to avoid putting on weight.

"I was telling Miss Fairlie and Donny how you looked after Daddy when he was little," Tessa said.

The old woman smiled—her smile lighted up her grave face like a sunbeam—"Och, he was a fine wee boy!" she exclaimed. "He grew so fast and thrived so well it was a pleasure to see him—and he was always in mischief, that one, with Euan following close behind."

"You must have had a busy time with them," suggested Charlotte.

"But there was no harm in him—no wickedness—it was his nature to be bold. How should it be otherwise since he is the Red MacRynne?"

"Miss Fairlie and Donny don't know what that means," said Tessa, helping herself to another scone and spreading butter upon it with a lavish hand.

"It is an old prophecy," said Mrs. Euan, rising to the bait. "It is an old story that was made up long ago—so long ago that nobody knows who made it nor how it came to be made. There was no writing, Miss Fairlie. It was told by the old people as they sat round the fire in the winter evenings; and the young people listened and told it again when they grew old. There are many stories and songs which have been told from one to another in this fashion."

Charlotte nodded. That was the way folk-lore had survived.

"The MacRynnes have all been dark," said Tessa. "Daddy is the first MacRynne to have red hair, so of course the old prophecy is all about him. Everybody in Targ thinks so . . . besides some of the prophecy has come true already, hasn't it, Mrs. Euan?"

"It has indeed," declared the old woman gravely. "The story begins by saying that some day there will be a Red MacRynne and that he will be bold and free and splendid and beloved by all his clan . . . it is in the Gaelic of course, Miss Fairlie."

Charlotte had guessed that. She had realised that the story was being translated into English for her benefit.

"And then," continued Mrs. Euan. "And then it goes on to say how he will be known: that he will be born of his mother in the bed of another woman." She paused and looked at Tessa for help.

"And Daddy *was*," declared Tessa. "It was a funny thing to happen wasn't it? You see Grandmama and Mrs. Euan were both going to have babies. Mrs. Euan had hers first— it was Euan of course—and Grandmama came to the cottage to see how she was . . . and while she was here, in this very cottage, she began to feel ill. Grandmama was very ill—much too ill to be moved—so they put her into Mrs. Euan's bed and Daddy was born the next morning. Go on, Mrs. Euan," nodded Tessa.

"But you are telling it better than me," said the old woman smiling.

"You know the story," said Tessa. "It's such ages since I heard it."

"There is a lot more," Mrs. Euan declared. "It says that the Red MacRynne will fly above the clouds, that he will kill his enemies with fire and will harness the water to be his servant. It was all made up hundreds of years ago and it has come true."

"But that's not all," said Tessa. "There's *lots* more. I've forgotten how it goes on."

"And me too," said Mrs. Euan. "I have forgotten how it goes on. A great deal of it is rubbish and not worth remembering."

"But I'm *sure* you remember it *all*!" cried Tessa in surprise. "Say it in Gaelic, Mrs. Euan, and we'll translate it for Miss Fairlie and Donny as we go along."

"I have forgotten it," said the old woman firmly. "Yes, it has gone from my memory entirely. When you get old, like me, it is funny how you forget."

She was looking down at her work-worn hands as she spoke and her eyes were veiled by her eyelashes. Charlotte felt certain she had not forgotten a word of the prophecy about the Red MacRynne . . . there was something horrible in the prophecy . . . some dreadful fate . . . and Tessa must not be told. Of course it was all nonsense (just sheer ignorant superstition, thought Charlotte, trying to pull herself together) but all the same she felt a sudden chill.

* 24 *

THE DAYS passed quickly. There was a sort of enchantment about Targ; the unsettled weather conditions of
the Western Highlands (which some people deplore)
seemed to Charlotte a part of the enchantment. There were
days of calm and mist; days of sunshine and breezes; days
when clouds swept in from the sea in dark masses and
torrents of rain fell. There were never two days alike, and
the sea changed colour and character to match the changing
skies; sometimes blue and smiling, sometimes dark green
like the glass of a dark green bottle with veins of white in
the curling billows which flung themselves against the rocks
in anger. There were no big storms—they would come in
winter—but it could be stormy enough to make sailing a
dangerous sport . . . and you could see the gulls and
gannets wheeling about the cliff like shreds of torn up paper
and hear their sad cries.

Charlotte's favourite walk was to a grassy knoll which
was as round as an old-fashioned beehive and covered with
short green turf. Tessa said it was a fairy hill—fairies like
their dwelling places to be round and symmetrical—and
somehow it was easy to believe. The Eastwoods loved this
place too, for below the hill there were rocks and a little
cave and a sandy bay which was perfect for paddling.

The first day that Charlotte saw the fairy hill was very
bright and peaceful. For once the restless sea was calm and

206

lapped gently against the rocks and whispered upon the sandy shore. Charlotte sat upon the dry grass and presently Tessa came and sat down beside her.

"Targ is like the island in *The Tempest*," said Charlotte, looking at Tessa and smiling.

"Oh no! It's not an enchanted isle—honestly. It's good and solid and full of good solid people. Daddy isn't a bit like Prospero and I'm not beautiful like Miranda."

"Perhaps you will be beautiful some day."

Tessa took this seriously. "I don't want to be," she declared. "Beautiful people make such a lot of trouble."

It was obvious that she was thinking of her mother (she never spoke of her mother, but perhaps she thought of her mother more often than one imagined).

"I don't want to be ugly of course," continued Tessa in a reflective manner. "At one time I was sure I would always be ugly, but I looked all right in the Pageant when the Bull had done my face."

"You looked perfect," Charlotte told her; and this was true, for Mademoiselle Boule was clever and by the discreet use of cosmetics had transformed the not-very-pretty schoolgirl into a lovely woman.

"Yes—well—it was queer," said Tessa slowly. "I *was* Mary, you know. I wasn't just pretending to be. It was queer and a little frightening. I knew what she was thinking and everything. The Bull wanted me to be terribly happy and excited because I had just escaped from prison; she was rather annoyed with me when I wouldn't be. Of course all the others were happy and excited but Mary wasn't a bit. She sort of knew what was going to happen."

"Your way was right."

"Oh yes, and the Bull saw it in the end. You know, Miss Fairlie, if you're sure about things and want them frightfully you usually get them in the end."

Charlotte could not help smiling at Tessa's philosophy. "You managed to get the Eastwoods here," she admitted. "I never thought you'd manage that."

"The Eastwoods? Oh yes," nodded Tessa.

It was obvious that she had not been thinking of her success over the Eastwoods' holiday. What had she been thinking of, Charlotte wondered. What *was* she thinking of? She was sitting with her arms round her knees gazing out over the sea and there was a little secret smile curling up the corners of her mouth. Charlotte would have liked to know what it was that Tessa wanted so frightfully and was hoping to obtain in the end.

The other children came and sat down.

"This is an awfully peaceful place," said Donny in her usual dreamy fashion.

"But it's not always peaceful," replied Tessa, waking from her reverie. "It's one of the most exposed places in the whole island. I've seen spray from the waves tossed right over the top of this hill—where we're sitting now—and only last winter a fishing-boat was wrecked on the point; you can still see its remains."

Tessa pointed and they saw the bones of the fishing-boat wedged in the teeth of the rocks. It looked like the skeleton of a huge sea monster.

Colonel MacRynne had not come with them this afternoon. Sometimes he accompanied them on their expeditions but more often he was busy going round his farms and attending sales of livestock and occupying himself with all the hundred and one duties which his large property demanded. He might be a "Lord of the Isles" but he worked as hard as any labouring man. Tessa had told Charlotte that it was a "whole time job" being MacRynne of Targ and she saw for herself that this was true.

The household at Targ castle ran smoothly and pleasantly;

it was an odd sort of household, for it was made up of people who were not related to one another and yet it seemed like a family party. To Charlotte, who had never had any real home life, it seemed very strange indeed and somehow rather amusing. The six members of this synthetic family sat down to meals together four times a day (except when they were out for a picnic). They consumed large quantities of plain but excellent food and they talked and laughed and teased one another as if they had known each other all their lives. All four children were good and sensible but occasionally if they became a little too boisterous their host would put his fingers to his ears and call for order—and order was established forthwith. He saw to it that the boys looked after the other members of the party: a significant glance from Colonel MacRynne and Harold and Barney would spring up to hand the vegetables or to perform some other little service.

All sorts of questions were asked and answered as they sat round the big shining table.

"What does Targ mean?" asked Donny.

"I know that!" cried Harold. "I'm learning a bit out of *The Lady of the Lake* for a holiday task. Mr. Swayne said we could each learn a piece of poetry—anything we liked— so I'm learning about Fitz James's fight with Roderick Dhu. It's frightfully exciting and very easy to learn because of the rhymes. Roderick Dhu has a targ—or targe—it's the same thing, isn't it?"

"Let's hear it," said Colonel MacRynne encouragingly.

Harold immediately sprang to his feet and declaimed:

Ill fared it then with Roderick Dhu
That on the field his targe he threw,
Whose brazen studs and tough bull-hide
Had death so often dashed aside;

For, trained abroad his arms to wield,
Fitz James's blade was sword and shield.

"Why did he?" asked Barney. "I mean throw his targe away?"

"Because he was a gentleman," replied Harold. "Fitz James hadn't got a targe so Roderick Dhu didn't want one either. He nearly beat him too," added Harold whose sympathies were obviously with the Highlander.

"So Targ means a sort of shield," said Donny.

"With knobs on," agreed Colonel MacRynne laughing.

"I wonder what pieces of poetry the other boys will choose," said Donny.

"One person is learning a poem about a love-sick swain," said Harold giggling. "I bet him tuppence he wouldn't have the lip to say it to Mr. Swayne when the time comes."

"Is he love-sick?" asked Tesssa eagerly.

"Good gracious, no," replied Harold. "He's frightfully hard-boiled. The kids' mistress and the matron run after him like anything but he takes no notice. You couldn't imagine old Swayne in love with anyone."

Charlotte, listening with interest, decided that Harold was right. Lawrence Swayne was too sensible to fall in love. It was funny to think of Lawrence; she had not thought of him once since she had arrived at Targ; she had not seen Lawrence for months except for that brief moment at the Pageant. His offer to take her into partnership (for that was what his proposal of marriage had really meant) was still open, she supposed, but somehow the idea of it seemed less attractive.

Colonel MacRynne was an easy-going host and left his guests at liberty to do as they pleased. If they wanted to go out in the yacht and he was unable to take them he sent them out with Euan or Fergus or one of the other men.

Sometimes they all went out together and sailed in the yacht or picnicked on the shore and bathed; at other times they split up and went their separate ways.

One morning Colonel MacRynne took his guest up to the dam, which was the pride of his heart, and explained how the water-power was used to make electricity. This was not exactly in Charlotte's line, but she had a clear brain and was interested so she was able to show a reasonable amount of intelligence in the plant.

"It's frightfully clever," she said thoughtfully.

"And frightfully cheap," agreed its owner smiling. "Of course the initial cost was pretty steep but now we can light and heat the castle and the farm without bothering about paraffin. And I supply the village as well. Paraffin used to be one of our most troublesome imports—I don't know how many hundreds of gallons had to be brought over from the mainland in one year."

Another day Tessa took Charlotte to the village which was even more interesting in its own way. It was not like an ordinary village with houses in a straight row. Each house seemed to have found its own place and settled down comfortably. (It reminded Charlotte of a group of people who settle down to have a picnic together and after a few movements discover a position to suit them. This one likes the sun in his face, that one must have a view, another finds a rock to lean his back upon.) The cottages were all solidly built of grey stone and no two were alike. Some of them had tiny gardens with low walls and borders of bright flowers: snapdragons and nasturtiums and old-fashioned roses: others were set down firmly in turf. There was a tiny shop which sold all manner of goods from needles and buttons to mole-traps and cartridges. You could buy tea or onions or toys or books at Mrs. Macdonald's shop and, although it was not a post office, you could buy stamps;

outside the door there was a red pillar-box where you could post a letter. Charlotte asked how often the box was cleared and Tessa smiled and replied that it was cleared three times a week unless it was too rough for the postie to come over from the mainland . . . or unless he had something else to do.

"But supposing it was an important letter!" exclaimed Charlotte.

"I don't think people mind," replied Tessa thoughtfully. "I mean they don't write many letters but when they've written one they just put it in the box—and they don't think about it any more. If it was *very* important they might bring it to the castle . . . yes, I expect that's what they would do."

Charlotte and Tessa walked on. They called at several cottages and were welcomed with warmth and dignity and were regaled with scones and honey and tea. It was curious to see the old-fashioned furniture (the old wooden settles and chests and stools) and then to look up and note the electric light bulb hanging from the old wooden beam in the ceiling; it was curious to see a modern electric cooking-stove in the corner of a room which otherwise would have made a perfect setting for a play about Prince Charlie.

Some of the cottages had hand-looms and the women were weaving Targ tweed or head-squares and scarves, others had knitting-machines and were making stockings. Charlotte received the impression that everybody was busy . . . but there was no haste about their business. There was plenty of time to receive visitors and entertain them, plenty of time to talk, to ask intelligent questions and listen with attention to the answers.

"What do you think of them?" asked Tessa anxiously as they walked back to the castle.

It was difficult to reply, but after a few moments' thought

Charlotte found an answer. "They're mysterious," she said. "They seem to me such a queer mixture of old and new."

"But you like them?"

"Nobody could help liking them!" exclaimed Charlotte impulsively.

Tessa nodded happily. "And they liked you," she declared. "Oh yes, they liked you. I know them, you see, and I can tell you they're not friendly to people they don't like. In fact they can be rather terrifying."

Charlotte did not altogether believe her.

The children had done some rock-climbing before Charlotte's arrival. Barney had not forgotten Tessa's prowess in climbing the Old Wall at Larchester and her promise that when he came to Targ he would learn how to emulate her remarkable feat. He was anxious to go on with the lessons so they all went down to the bay one morning and did some easy climbs. Tessa scaled the rocks like a monkey and Barney, under the Colonel's tuition, was progressing rapidly but the other two were less adventurous and soon grew tired of the sport.

To Charlotte the climbing looked horribly dangerous. She could hardly bear to watch them crawling like flies up the steep cliff-face. She could hardly bear to watch them—yet she could not keep her eyes away.

By contrast she thoroughly enjoyed the walk up the hill in the afternoon. Colonel MacRynne was obliged to go across to the mainland to see about some improvements which were being carried out at one of his other farms, so Charlotte and the four children set out together. It was a lovely day, there was a lightness in the air, a sort of buoyancy so that one felt one could walk for miles. Tessa led the way up a steep path and through a grove of birch-trees;

their leaves fluttered gently in the breeze and the golden sunshine flickered on the path.

"Fairy trees," said Tessa. "This is a fairy grove, you know. It's name in Gaelic means the place where the fairies dance."

"Fairies with wings?" asked Donny.

"Goodness, no!" said Tessa. "Fairies with wings are just nonsense out of children's fairy-books. Our fairies are just like you and me only much smaller. They live inside the hills and have little houses and they spin and weave and sing. Some of them are kind and good, but others are mischievous and if you offend them they play all sorts of tricks with their magic spells."

"You don't believe in them, do you?" asked Harold in surprise.

But Tessa did not answer. "Catch me if you can!" she cried and skipped away up the path as if she were a fairy, herself.

The path grew steeper as they mounted; the last hundred feet was a scramble over rocks and boulders, and Charlotte was breathless when she got to the top; but the view was worth it for this was the highest point of the island and one could see for miles in all directions. The island lay spread beneath their feet, like a coloured medallion set in the silvery sea. Westwards there was nothing but sea, stretching to the hazy horizon, but to the east lay the mainland with its tiny crofts and towering mountains and a glint of silver ribbon where the river flowed.

The children ran about, looking for white heather, but Charlotte was content to sit and dream. She was thinking about Saint Elizabeth's, and wondering what it would feel like to be back in her narrow groove after this freedom of body and soul, when a shadow fell upon the rock in front of her. The shadow was Euan's. He stood and looked down at her and asked with his usual careful politeness if he might speak to her.

"Why of course, Euan," she said, smiling at him.

"It is nothing much," he told her, sitting down at a convenient distance. "It is just that Miss Tessa was telling me you are very clever at Modern languages. I am clever at German," he added, not boastfully but merely stating a fact.

Charlotte was amused; she did not question his statement but began to speak to him in German—and found to her amazement that he spoke it with fluency and ease. He explained that he had begun to learn the language in 1935 when he realised that the Germans were re-arming and that there might be another war. Euan had been too young to take part in the First World War but he had heard a great deal about it from the older men and it had seemed to him that if there were to be another war against the Germans it would be useful to understand their language. There are long dark winter evenings at Targ and it is good to have something to do, so Euan bought books and studied industriously.

"Miss Tessa is interested in languages," added Euan, still speaking in German. "She intends to go to Oxford like you did, Miss Fairlie."

"I thought she intended to help her father to look after Targ?"

"But she could do both. To study languages is good, whether or not it is a help in one's chosen career; it is an education in itself and education is always good even if one were to spend all one's life in a desert. Perhaps in that case it would be even more necesssry," said Euan thoughtfully. He hesitated and then added in English, "But I am teaching my grandmother to suck eggs."

Charlotte laughed. She could not help it.

"It is just a saying," said Euan hastily. "It has nothing to do with age, Miss Fairlie—for I am older than you—it just means that you are so much cleverer about education than me."

"But no wiser," said Charlotte humbly. "Of course you're right, Euan. But tell me how you managed to learn to speak German from books. Your accent is perfect."

He looked pleased. "Och, it was not difficult, Miss Fairlie. The pronunciation is not unlike the Gaelic and in the War I missed no opportunity of listening and talking. They wanted me to be an interpreter but I could not do that."

"Why not?"

Euan looked at her in surprise. "I could not leave MacRynne!" he exclaimed. "It would have meant going away to another place."

Charlotte realised she had asked a foolish question. She asked some more questions—less foolish—and learned that they had both served in a territorial battalion which had been sent to France at the beginning of the war; they had taken part in the retreat at Dunkirk and been rescued from capture by a fishing-boat. Euan told the story in a matter-of-fact way in his slow musical voice. "We were together all the time," he said. "When we got back from Dunkirk MacRynne was transferred to the Air Force, for he had flown before and had a taste for it and they needed pilots badly, and he managed it so that I was transferred too. We were in Bomber Command, Miss Fairlie. I did not like it so much as the regiment, for in the regiment I was beside my own people, but it was exciting enough at times."

Charlotte glanced at him. He was quite serious in making this amazing understatement. "Were you never frightened?" she asked; she really wanted to know whether this curious being was capable of feeling fear.

"Yes indeed," he replied, smiling at her. "There were

times when my heart was in my mouth, for I was one of the crew in MacRynne's bomber and there was nothing he would not attempt, but that was just at first. After a while I came to believe in his star—he was the Red MacRynne and nothing could hurt him. That was how I felt. Och, I could tell you some stories about the things we did! I have thought sometimes it would be a fine thing to make a poem about it like they did about battles in the old days."

"Why don't you?" Charlotte asked.

"It is not in me to make a poem," replied Euan regretfully. "It seems that we have lost the art. Men are as brave now as they were in the old days but there are no bards to weave songs and poems about their deeds . . . so people forget."

"Why are there no bards, I wonder."

"That is a big question," said Euan, turning his head and smiling at her. "I have often wondered that. Maybe it is because people can read the newspapers and listen to the radio. Long ago it was the bards who brought the news (made into songs so that it could be remembered more easily); they went from place to place and were welcomed wherever they went."

The children had now become tired of their fruitless search and had gathered round, flinging themselves down upon the springy heather in attitudes of exhaustion.

"I wouldn't welcome the bards," declared Barney.

"You wouldn't welcome them!" exclaimed Tessa in surprise.

"News is dull," Barney told her. "If you turn on the radio it just says somebody has flown somewhere and had a talk with somebody else."

"But that wasn't the kind of news the bards brought," said Harold.

"No indeed," declared Euan. "They brought news of

battles and of brave deeds and sang about them as they sat round the fire."

"Oh, that's different of course," admitted Barney. "War is always exciting . . . " and he sat up and began to question Euan about his experiences as a fighting man.

* 25 *

THAT EVENING at dinner Barney nerved himself to make an important request; he asked leave to call his host MacRynne, "like Euan does," said Barney.

His brother and sister were somewhat scandalised at what they thought showed a lack of respect for the Colonel's age and position.

"But it isn't cheeky," said Barney, getting very red in the face. "It's a frightfully important title. It's far more important to be MacRynne, than to be a colonel—or even a general—that's what Euan says. It means he's Chief of the Clan, and if you belong to the clan you *ought* to call him MacRynne—Euan says so."

"But you don't belong to the clan," Harold pointed out.

Barney was silent.

"It's like this," said the Chief of the MacRynnes gravely (but Charlotte thought there was a twinkle in his eyes). "The rule is—my rule, I mean—that anybody living upon Targ is a member of the Clan MacRynne."

"Then I am!" exclaimed Barney rapturously.

"Undoubtedly," replied his chief.

"And what about me?" asked Charlotte smiling. "Am I to call you MacRynne?"

"Ladies are in a different category," he replied. "You ought to call me Rory."

Charlotte had not expected that reply and was somewhat taken aback; it would be very difficult to call him Rory—

nobody called him Rory—and to tell the truth Charlotte had lived so long in the rarified atmosphere of Saint Elizabeth's that she had got out of the way of calling her contemporaries by their Christian names (there was Lawrence of course but somehow Lawrence was different). Of course Colonel MacRynne had said it as a joke, thought Charlotte, but since he had said it with outward gravity in the presence of four observant witnesses she would have to comply with his request. She realised it was her own fault—she had asked for it—but that would not make it any easier.

The following evening Miss Mary and Miss Anne came downstairs to dinner and the traditional game of whist. The two old ladies were attired in black moiré silk dresses which crackled when they moved, and they each had a fichu of fine lace pinned with diamond brooches. Charlotte had been warned that evening dress would be suitable for the occasion and had put on a black lace frock with straps over the shoulders and while she was dressing Barney had knocked at her door and handed her two glorious red roses which he informed her were from MacRynne. They were to wear, of course, and when she had pinned them in her bosom she saw they were exactly what she wanted.

If the ladies were somewhat sombrely garbed their host most certainly was not and the sight of him, standing on the hearth-rug before the drawing-room fire, was positively breathtaking. He was in full rig to-night, with kilt and silver buttoned doublet and lace falls at neck and wrists . . . and he wore his finery with the same unconscious ease as the old faded kilt and patched tweed jacket which he wore upon the hill.

The children were somewhat subdued at dinner but afterwards when the two card-tables were produced they began their usual chatter. They had decided to play Monopoly which they all knew, while their elders played whist.

Charlotte had warned her companions that she had never played whist, and now she repeated the warning. She had played contract bridge when she was at Oxford but . . .

"Oh, it's just the same," said Miss Mary cheerfully. "Only whist is much easier, and you are so clever, Charlotte dear."

"Exactly the same," repeated Miss Anne pouncing upon the cards with shining eyes. "It's the same, isn't it Rory?"

"Well—more or less," he replied with a little chuckle. He was very polite to his aunts, very punctilious, but it was obvious that they amused him considerably.

"Cut!" said Miss Anne, who was anxious not to waste a moment.

"Are we having any money on it?" asked Rory.

"Oh no, dear," said Miss Mary. "Unless you particularly want it. Whist is quite exciting enough without."

They cut. Charlotte found herself partnered with her host. They all took their seats at the table.

"It's *much* easier than bridge," said Miss Mary as she dealt the cards with a practised hand. "We have never played bridge of course but we have seen people playing when we stayed at hotels and we saw how *very* difficult it was. The poor things looked quite worried."

"But what *is* the difference?" asked Charlotte taking up her hand.

As neither of the two ladies had ever played bridge they could not explain the difference, but fortunately their nephew had played both games so he was able to come to the rescue.

"No calling, no dummy, no conventions," he said gravely. "You play by the light of reason. You make tricks as quickly as you can. If you can get away with a revoke so much the better—at least that's how the game is played at Targ Castle."

"Oh Rory!" cried his aunts in horrified accents.

Put like that the game sounded easy and it might have been easy—or at least easier—for the novice if her companions had not been so expert; if they had not played so quickly and had not chatted all the time in a dégagé fashion. For instance Charlotte was just wondering what to lead (and wondering how you could possibly know what to lead when you had no more idea than the man in the moon how the cards lay) when Miss Mary said, "What lovely roses, Charlotte! I have been admiring them all the evening. Rory, why don't we have some like that in the garden? It is you to play, Charlotte."

Charlotte played hastily. She played the ten of clubs and remembered too late that her partner had led a diamond at the beginning of the hand and might possibly want his lead returned.

"But we have, Aunt Mary," declared, Rory trumping the trick with the knave of hearts and beginning to lead out diamonds himself. "Those that Charlotte is wearing are out of the garden. I picked them myself. It's a new rose. I saw it at the Rose Show in Inverness last year and ordered a few bushes."

They had all followed suit and he swept up the trick and played another diamond—a small one this time.

Miss Anne played the queen. She said, "How wise of you, Rory! I am particularly fond of a deep crimson rose. But you ought to have picked three of them for Charlotte."

"There were only two perfect ones," he told her. "The others were slightly blemished——"

"What is the rose called?" asked Miss Mary with interest.

"Charlotte," said Rory.

"Charlotte! But how delightful!" cried Miss Anne.

"I was reminding Charlotte it was her turn to play." explained Rory. "That isn't the name of the rose."

"Oh, sorry Rory!" exclaimed Charlotte . . . and then suddenly realised that she had done it! She had called her host by his Christian name—and without thinking. It was because his name had been bandied about by his aunts all the evening. That was the reason of course . . . but they were all waiting for her to play. She played hastily, trumping Miss Anne's queen with a small heart.

Miss Anne gave an involuntary exclamation of dismay.

"What *is* the name of the rose?" asked Miss Mary.

"I don't think I should tell you," Rory replied, looking at the trick for a moment before gathering it up. "Or perhaps I *will* tell you—Shakespeare said a rose by any other name would smell as sweet—it's called Miss Hogg."

"Charlotte is much prettier," said Miss Mary. "It's your lead Charlotte."

By this time Charlotte had lost her head completely and had no idea who had played what. She reviewed her hand and, discovering the eight of diamonds, played it.

"Oh!" exclaimed Miss Anne. "But you should have played that last time. I mean you trumped my queen——"

"Goodness!" exclaimed Charlotte aghast. "I'm terribly sorry——"

Miss Anne (in whom the loss of her queen rankled severely) found the trick and displayed it. "Look, Charlotte, Rory led a diamond——"

"I know," declared the culprit. "I'm terribly sorry. I wasn't thinking——"

"It was a mistake," said Miss Mary.

"Rory didn't you notice——" began Miss Anne.

"Of course I noticed," said Rory beginning to laugh. "But it wasn't for me to draw attention to my partner's crime. In fact—I was hoping—we'd get away with it—ha, ha, ha!" cried Rory, leaning back in his chair and abandoning himself to mirth.

"She made a mistake," declared Miss Mary. "Charlotte has never played whist before, so of course——"

"It was *terribly* stupid," Charlotte declared.

They were all talking at once except Rory who was laughing too heartily to be capable of speech.

"What a noise you're making!" said Tessa's voice from the other table. "I suppose somebody has revoked or something."

"It was Charlotte," said Miss Mary. "It was a mistake——"

"If it was *her*—it *was*," declared Tessa significantly and returned to the important business of amassing property and building hotels.

In spite of Charlotte's lapse the evening was a great success. It was after eleven when the party broke up; the children were chivvied off to bed and Rory went up with his aunts to escort them to their own quarters. When he returned to the drawing-room he found Charlotte tidying it, putting away the card-tables and re-arranging the chairs.

"What on earth are you doing?" he inquired.

"I promised Mrs. Fraser I would beat up the cushions," explained Charlotte. "They get so crumpled if they lie all night." She seized a cushion and beat it up as she spoke.

Rory watched her with a little smile; he did not offer to help with the cushions but he emptied the ashtray and put the guard on the fire.

"Your aunts are darlings, Rory," added Charlotte.

"Yes," he agreed. "They are darlings and they are extremely amusing. There's only one thing that worries me about the aunts: what on earth shall I do when one of them dies?"

Charlotte looked at him and saw him staring into the fire.

"They have never been parted," continued Rory. "I don't remember them being parted for a single day—and now

Aunt Mary is eighty and Aunt Anne seventy-nine. They can't live for ever, can they? What will happen to the one who is left? What shall I do with her?"

"It's no use worrying——" began Charlotte.

"I know—but I do, sometimes." He smiled suddenly and added, "The kindest thing would be to put her down painlessly like a faithful old dog."

As they came out into the hall on their way to bed Rory switched on the lights in the hall and on the staircase (the effect was quite dazzling). "I wish I had a candle to give you," he said regretfully.

"A candle!" exclaimed Charlotte in amazement.

"Yes, a candle. When I was a boy there were rows of candles in silver candlesticks standing on that table. My father used to light them and give them to his guests; it was a charming little ceremony."

"That's life, isn't it?" said Charlotte. "When you progress with the times you always have to give up something in return." She smiled at him and added, " If you harness the water to be your servant you have to give up candles." Then she turned and ran upstairs to bed.

Somehow the little talk with Rory had upset Charlotte and made her feel restless—and this was strange because up to now she had felt so peaceful and happy at Targ. She made her preparations for bed and drew back the curtains and opened the window wide. Already the view had become familiar to her—as if she had been here all her life—the sweep of the hills was etched upon her mind, the little patch of dark wood, the gleam of the burn. There was no moon, but the stars were glittering brightly, it was a warm gentle comforting sort of night and Charlotte leaned out of the window for a long time and allowed the peacefulness to comfort her.

C.F.   P

26

I T WAS a thoroughly wet day. Targ was enveloped in a thick curtain of rain and mist with no glimmer of sunshine to give promise of better things to come. The children mooned round the house peering out of the windows and wondering aloud if it were going to clear up soon.

"Couldn't we put on our waterproofs and go out?" asked Barney. "I mean rain doesn't matter; we could change when we come in."

"Rain doesn't matter but mist matters a lot," replied Rory. "You would get lost—that's what would happen—and I should have to go and look for you . . . and I'm going to be much too busy to do any such thing. This is the sort of day when I write letters and do accounts. I've got enough to do to keep me busy until teatime."

"We'll go and play in the attic," said Tessa. "You haven't seen the attic have you? It's a huge place and there are all sorts of queer things stored away in it—come on, everybody."

Charlotte had letters to write so she got her writing-case and sat down by the fire; it was very quiet, very peaceful and pleasant. There was a feeling of leisure at Targ; life moved slowly and gave one time for thought. The letters did not get written because Charlotte had so much to think of and presently she decided that she was being very lazy and if she could not fix her mind upon tiresome letters she could at least do some needlework. She went upstairs and looked out a piece of tapestry which she was embroidering and brought it down to the study.

The tapestry was a large oblong piece of work intended for an old-fashioned firestool; Charlotte had had it for years, working at it off and on when she had time. She had very little time at Saint Elizabeth's for in the evening she usually read French or German—it was essential to keep up her languages—or else read travel books to take her mind off the worries of her work. Occasionally she set aside an evening for mending, but that was a necessary evil. This being so the tapestry did not get on very fast—and now, when she looked at it, she could not help smiling for in a way it had become a part of her life. That little flower in the corner had been completed last Christmas when she was staying with Aunt Lydia, and the queer heraldic beast reminded her of a visit to Cornwall. Her stay in Denmark had produced one green leaf—no more and no less.

Life was like a piece of tapestry . . . or perhaps one should say a piece of tapestry was like life . . . for there was the background, which was rather dull, and the coloured bits, which were fun. And it was not until you had got to the end and the whole thing was complete that you could see the pattern properly. Charlotte decided that if the tapestry continued to progress at its present snail's pace she would not see the pattern properly until she was very old indeed . . . but she would make an effort while she was here at Targ. She would try to get a whole corner completed. It would be rather nice—afterwards—to look at the corner and remember Targ. She sorted out the wools and set to work.

At lunch time the mist was thicker than ever, but after tea it cleared a little and Rory suggested that the whole party should walk down to the harbour and back for a little fresh air and exercise. The idea seemed good and they all set off clad in waterproofs and sou'westers. The children had been told not to stray from the road so they walked along together, seeing nothing all round them but a blanket of mist.

"I think it's weird," declared Barney. "I don't understand it. Why isn't there mist here, between you and me I mean?"

"There is mist between you and me, you ass," replied his elder brother. "You can't see it, that's all——"

"I can see it all round us, but there's none *here*."

Oddly enough Charlotte had sometimes wondered the same thing when she was out in a London fog. Why could you see only so far and no farther? She wondered whether Rory would explain the phenomenon and put an end to the argument—it was his practice to allow the children to argue things out and then explain them—but to-day he was silent, in fact he did not seem to hear, and the argument continued in a rude but friendly manner until the contestants grew tired of it. They walked to the harbour and played about on the yacht, which was firmly moored to the jetty, and then walked back to the castle.

Afterwards when Charlotte had left Targ and gone back to Saint Elizabeth's she remembered every detail of that walk and yet it was completely uneventful.

Last night they had dined in state and spent the evening in the drawing-room but to-night they returned to their usual routine. It was a very pleasant routine and Charlotte enjoyed it. In fact although the days were delightful—the happiest she had ever spent—she sometimes found herself looking forward to the evenings. It was good to feel a little tired and full of fine fresh air and to relax in the comfortable leather chair in Rory's study. There was always a log fire burning in the grate, for even in the summer the evenings were apt to be chilly.

At half-past eight the children went off to bed and after that it was very peaceful; Charlotte worked at her tapestry and Rory sat at the table, cleaning his gun and tying flies. They talked about their childhood, and about all they had done in their lives—small things and big things.

On this particular evening Rory began to talk about Esther, quite naturally and without any bitterness, and Charlotte decided that he was talking about her as if she were dead. In fact she was more dead to Rory than if she had died (for a dead person is remembered and leaves behind memories happy and sad). Esther had gone of her own free will, she had chosen to live elsewhere rather than at Targ with her husband and child. It seemed incredible that any woman could have made such a choice—could have gone away and left these two; Rory and Tessa. But that was what she had done; she had packed up and gone and left nothing behind her—just as Miss Anne had said.

During the night a stiff westerly breeze blew all the clouds and mist away and the next morning was as fine and bright as anybody could ask for.

"I'm walking across the island to-day," said Rory at breakfast. "Who would like to come? What about you, Charlotte? It's a longish walk; perhaps it would be too far for you."

"Not a bit too far. I'd love to go," replied Charlotte quickly.

The children seemed uncertain of their plans but at ten o'clock when Charlotte and Rory set off for their walk they found Tessa and Barney waiting for them.

"We're coming," said Tessa. "The others are going to bathe."

Rory hesitated. "Wouldn't you rather bathe? It's a long way, you know."

"We'd rather come—if you don't mind," said Barney.

The two ran on up the steep path together and Charlotte

and Rory followed. Charlotte had a feeling that there was something mysterious in the air, not only because Tessa and Barney adored bathing but also because there was an odd sort of excitement in their manner . . . and apparently Rory had the same feeling.

"What are they up to?" Rory said. He laughed and added. "Well, it doesn't matter. They can't come to much harm."

It was a lovely walk. The first part was a steep climb beside the burn, which was coming down in spate after the previous day's rain, but when they had passed over the watershed the moors went rolling away before them in gentle slopes to the westward shore of the island. The sun was golden, the skies were blue, the breeze was cool and pleasant; in sheltered places the heather was in flower and hummed with inummerable bees. Here and there Charlotte saw clefts in the ground which showed the peaty subsoil, rich brown like chocolate cake.

There were cushions of pale green moss growing in the bogs; Rory picked a handful and showed her how soft and delicate it was and how, when you squeezed the water out of it, the moss was as fluffy as cotton wool.

"It's sphagnum," said Rory. "They used it for surgical dressings during the war, but they don't seem to want it now. I had a plan to start a Home Industry and I offered to supply sphagnum dressings to some of the big hospitals—but they weren't interested."

"Why not?"

"Goodness knows," said Rory with a sigh. "Sphagnum has definite curative properties; it's more absorbent than cotton-wool—and cheaper. It grows here on our own moors and cotton-wool has to be imported. You would think it had all the advantages, wouldn't you?"

He went on talking about sphagnum, telling Charlotte

that it had been used for centuries by Highland women to cure the wounds of their men-folk—wounds resulting from the fierce battles which raged between the clans—"In those days," said Rory, "The sphagnum was taken straight from the bog, they knew nothing about sterilization, but in nine cases out of ten it worked wonders. As a matter of fact only last winter one of the shepherds was out with his gun and shot himself badly in the leg. The weather was so stormy that it was nearly a week before Doctor Mackintosh could come over from the mainland and he discovered to his horror that the shepherd's wife had been dressing the wound with unsterilized sphagnum moss. She had gathered the moss from the bog at her door and squeezed it and clapped it on . . . but the wound was perfectly clean and healing beautifully." Rory laughed and added, "Mack's face was a study. There he was with his little bag full of nice clean sterilized dressings and the old shepherd absolutely refused to let him put them on."

"I don't wonder, really," said Charlotte thoughtfully.

"No, my sympathies were with the shepherd," Rory agreed. "But of course there is a danger unless it's sterilized. There might possibly be a source of contamination in the bog. There might be a dead animal lying about."

The path wound across the moor and presently they came to a little hill which was crowned with wind-blown birch-trees. At the foot of the hill was an outcrop of black boulders and Tessa and Barney were sitting here waiting.

"We're not coming any farther," Tessa said. "We'll wait here until you come back. That will be all right, won't it?"

Rory paused and looked at them doubtfully. "Why not come down to the shore?" he suggested. "It isn't much farther. I want to have a look at the jetty and see if it needs any repairs."

"I know," agreed Tessa. "Barney and I will be here waiting for you when you come back."

Charlotte saw that Rory disapproved of this arrangement. He took his responsibilities seriously and the children were never allowed to stray about the island alone. Tessa was all right by herself but the Eastwoods were town-bred and unused to the dangers of bogs and cliffs . . . and Barney was of an adventurous disposition. Knowing this Charlotte offered to remain behind with the children and after some discussion the plan was adopted; Rory went on to the jetty alone and Charlotte sat down and leant her back against the sun-warmed rock.

It was a delightful spot, so sheltered and peaceful; the only sound was the rustle of the breeze through the heather. For a little while Barney and Tessa sat beside her, without speaking, and then they got up and strolled away.

"Where are you going?" asked Charlotte, rousing herself . . . she had almost fallen asleep.

"Not very far," Tessa replied. "There's a little well half way up the hill. Mrs. Euan told us about it and we thought we would try to find it. You don't want to come, do you, Miss Fairlie?"

Charlotte certainly did not. She was warm and comfortable where she was, so she lay back and closed her eyes. But after a few minutes her conscience began to bother her (Rory had left the children in her charge) so she rose and followed the little path which zig-zagged up the hill.

By this time the two had disappeared from view, and she could not hear their voices. She began to feel a trifle uneasy about them and hastened her steps. Presently she reached the grove of birch-trees; the path she was following took a turn round the shoulder of the hill . . . and here she stopped. Before her lay a little dell, a dimple in the ground carpeted with soft green turf, and in the middle of the dell was a pool. Tessa was standing a few yards away and Barney was kneeling beside the pool gazing into it.

Charlotte's first impulse was to call to the children but something prevented her. There was a queer hushed feeling about this place and the children were so absorbed in what they were doing that it seemed wrong to disturb them. It was some sort of game, she supposed. At any rate it was a harmless game and she need not have worried about them. She decided to go away and leave them to their own devices when Barney rose from his knees and the two children came towards her and saw her standing on the path.

"Oh Miss Fairlie!" exclaimed Tessa in dismay. "Oh, I didn't know——" She hesitated and blushed.

Barney said nothing, but seemed equally embarrassed. In fact the two of them looked exactly as if they had been caught stealing jam.

"What's the matter?" asked Charlotte in surprise.

Tessa hesitated again and then said, "We were having wishes."

"Having wishes?"

"Yes, as a matter of fact it's a wishing-well . . . I expect you think it's silly."

"So that's why you came!" exclaimed Charlotte smiling. She was relieved at having the mystery explained so simply.

"Please don't tell Daddy," said Tessa. "You won't, will you Miss Fairlie?" and she raised her eyes to Charlotte's face beseechingly.

Charlotte was amused and promised to keep the secret. It seemed a very harmless secret and she supposed that Tessa did not want to be teased about it.

"We had better go back, hadn't we?" Tessa said.

"There's no hurry," replied Charlotte. Now that she was here she wanted to have a look round. There was a piece of ruined wall beyond the pool, a heap of rough blocks of stone covered with ivy, and it occurred to her that long ago this place might have been inhabited by a hermit. There are dozens of springs and little fountains all over the country where holy men have lived in seclusion . . . saintly men to whom people in the district would come to be blessed and healed. What peace there was in this tiny deserted spot! What a beautiful place it was! All round were the bleak moors, rolling away to far horizons, making one feel as small and insignificant as a fly, but here there was shelter of rock and tree and a man could feel at home . . . and somehow it seemed as if the spirit of the good man still lingered in the hazy sunshine, undisturbed for hundreds of years.

The pool which lay in the middle of the glade was not Charlotte's idea of a well, for it was merely a hole in the ground—a round basin about four feet in diameter. The water was clear and sparkling, it welled up from the gravelly bottom and overflowed into a tiny rivulet which trickled down the hillside. Charlotte leaned over and looked into the pool and she saw something shining amongst the little stones.

"Come on, Miss Fairlie," said Tessa pleadingly. "Please come. Daddy may be waiting——"

"Can't I have a wish?" asked Charlotte, turning and smiling at her impatience.

"Please don't!" cried Tessa. "You don't believe in it."

"You haven't got a sixpence," added Barney.

"A sixpence?"

"It's a silver wishing-well," explained Tessa reluctantly. "You've got to drop a piece of silver into the well and then wish. But it isn't the sort of well to have fun with—it's real magic."

Tessa was so anxious to be gone that Charlotte allowed herself to be dragged away but as they walked down the hill together she tried to convince her two young companions that there could not be "real magic" in the silver wishing-well. She told them her idea about the holy man (which she was sure was true) and explained that the place where he lived would be regarded with awe by the people in the district and that, when he had died or gone away, a whole crop of superstitions would grow up and flourish.

"Oh yes, I expect you're right," said Tessa nodding. "But all the same it is a wishing-well. I mean people get their wishes if they do it properly. Mrs. Euan says so."

"Euan said so too," declared Barney. "Euan got his wish. He told us how to find the place. It's so well-hidden that if you didn't know exactly where it was you might spend days looking for it."

"But didn't Tessa know about it before?" asked Charlotte in surprise.

"Vaguely," said Tessa. "I'd heard rumours about it—but you see people don't like talking about it openly. It's safer not to. Magic is a dangerous sort of thing."

"But Tessa——"

"Oh, I know you don't believe in it, but Daddy does. Daddy always says people shouldn't dabble in magic . . . and I wouldn't have done it if I hadn't wanted my wish so very, very much." She paused and then added earnestly, "I can't tell you what it is, but it isn't a wrong sort of wish—honestly—no harm can come of it."

Nor any good either, thought Charlotte, but she kept the thought to herself for obviously nothing that she could say would shake Tessa's faith in the magic well.

By this time Charlotte had begun to regret her promise that she would not tell Rory about the children's escapade. She had promised because she had thought it unimportant, but now she realised that to Tessa it was very important indeed—not just a childish game of which she was ashamed. She regretted it even more when Rory appeared, having carried out his inspection of the jetty, and they all set off home across the moor. Charlotte had got into the habit of telling Rory what she was thinking and the silly little secret made her feel like a conspirator. Fortunately Rory had plenty to say and did not notice any constraint. Soon the bright sunshine and the blue skies and the breeze—which was now behind them, blowing them along—took their effect and Charlotte's discomfort vanished. When they reached the castle, a little late for lunch, she decided she had been making a mountain out of a mole-hill and was able to laugh at herself for being so foolish.

* 27 *

WHEN ONE is happy the time goes too fast—so the Eastwoods discovered. They were dismayed when the end of their holiday drew near.

"We can't possibly have been here a month," declared Harold. "It feels like a week."

Donny agreed with him but Barney said nothing. Barney had become very silent.

Their last day at Targ was warm and still with a thundery feeling in the air, but although there were heavy thunder clouds over the mountains of the mainland there were clear blue skies above Targ and it was decided to have a picnic. Rory had taken the day off and in the afternoon the whole party went down to a small bay where there was a sandy shore for bathing. It was warm here, for the bay was sheltered from the north by high black cliffs. Southward from the bay were sand-dunes clothed with coarse tufty grass which glittered like the spears of a Lilliputian army in the sun.

The children were in the water splashing about happily; Charlotte and Rory were sitting on the dry white sand, watching them and talking.

"It's a pity they have to go back to-morrow," Rory said. "I wrote to their father and asked if they could stay on to the end of their holidays but the answer was no. He says he has arranged for them to have a tutor because they're so backward. They're fine children—especially Barney. One could make something pretty good of Barney if one had the chance."

"You've helped him a lot," said Charlotte.

"I've done very little. I've let him trot about after me, that's all."

This was such a good description of what happened that Charlotte could not help smiling. Barney trotted after his hero most of the day. It was all Barney wanted: just to be near MacRynne, just to be able to see him . . . and never, never to go away from Targ and leave him.

"Well, whatever you've done—or not done—Barney is a different boy."

"I know," agreed Rory. "When he first came here he used to nearly jump out of his skin if you spoke to him; it made me feel quite sick. Does he get beaten at home?"

"Not with a stick," said Charlotte thoughtfully. "They get beaten with words. People say, 'Hard words break no bones'. Well, I suppose they don't break bones but they can break other things."

Rory lay down on his back and gazed at the sky. "Can't we do anything about it?" he asked.

"I don't see what we can do——"

"Have we got to sit back and see the child ruined? Honestly, Charlotte, he was like a dog that's been kicked round the house . . . you can break a dog's spirit like that, and he's no good for anything any more. I had a keeper once who did that to one of my shooting dogs; it was the winter we spent in Edinburgh and I had left the dog with him. When I came home and saw what he had done to that poor brute—well, I went a bit mad."

"I suppose you sacked him on the spot."

"No, my dear, I beat him up," said Rory, turning his head and looking at Charlotte with a rueful smile. "I gave him a damn' good thrashing. Fortunately Euan was there and saw fit to interfere when he thought the fellow had had enough—but Euan's idea of enough was more than sufficient. His own mother wouldn't have known him."

"Goodness! " exclaimed Charlotte. "I didn't know people could do that nowadays—even you."

"People can't," replied Rory with an involuntary chuckle. "Even I—as you put it—can't do that nowadays. He had me up for assault so I stood up in court and told them the truth, the whole truth and nothing but the truth. As a matter of fact it was rather fun. I didn't care what happened; they could have sent me to prison if they had wanted. But the sheriff had a pet spaniel so I got off lightly—fined and bound over for two years."

"Bound over? " asked Charlotte.

"Bound Over to Keep the Peace," explained Rory. "It means you have to promise not to repeat the offence for two years . . . it's nearly three years ago now."

"So you're thinking of beating up Professor Eastwood," said Charlotte lightly.

"By jove, I'd like to! " Rory exclaimed. He rolled over and began to scrape a hole in the sand.

Charlotte looked at his head. His hair in the brilliant sunshine was a sort of golden-red. She looked at his neatly set ears and the firm line of his chin and throat. She loved him so much that her eyes filled with tears and a queer sharp pain ran through her heart. She sat up and put her arms round her knees and blinked the tears away. She had known for several days that she loved Rory but until this moment she had not loved him quite like this. It was funny, really, because she had never thought she would fall in love. Other people seemed to, but she had imagined herself to be immune. It was an eye-opener to Charlotte that she could love somebody in this mad way with a wild sweet tenderness that made everything he touched precious to her. Sometimes she had wondered what Rory felt; he was very kind and thoughtful, he noticed if she wanted anything and paid her little attentions—such as sending her the red roses, for instance—but he was kind and thoughtful to everybody. He loved everybody (as it had said in the legend of the Red MacRynne) and was beloved by all . . . except presumably Esther! No, thought Charlotte, Rory did not love her in that very special kind of way, and it was just as well, because even if he did she would not marry him. That was quite definite. It was the one rock in the sea of feelings in which she was submerged. Whatever Rory said or did or felt she would not marry him and become Tessa's stepmother. She would not come between these two people, whom she loved best in the world, and spoil their perfect relationship.

That being so she ought to go home (or rather, since she had no home, she ought to leave Targ) but she did not want to go. She was like Barney (she thought) all she wanted was to be near her beloved, to see him and to hear his voice. Surely it was doing no harm to stay and take that small comfort—just for one more week! One more week and then her visit to Targ would be over and she would never see him again. What harm could it do to anybody if she stayed another week? To herself, perhaps, but she was willing to pay the price.

The children had come out of the water now and were running about on the shore collecting drift-wood for a fire; to them no picnic was "a real picnic" without a fire. They were shouting merrily and chasing one another but in spite of the fun and games they got the fire going and put the kettle on to boil. How good for them this was! thought Charlotte. They were behaving like real children—like children of eight and nine years old—but they had missed their proper childhood. Certainly the Eastwoods had missed theirs; even Tessa had had far too much care and responsibility for her age.

"They want to climb after tea," said Rory after a long silence. "You hate watching, don't you Charlotte? So you had better go home and leave me to do nursemaid."

She hated watching. Rory had assured her that it was not dangerous—not dangerous if you were careful and knew how to do it—but she did not really believe him. When she saw Rory climbing she always thought of the legend of the Red MacRynne. She still had not heard the end of it and still was sure that some frightful fate had been foreshadowed. And what more frightful fate than to fall from a cliff and be dashed to pieces on the rocks below!

"Oh Rory, I wish you wouldn't!" exclaimed Charlotte. "It frightens me."

"I know. That's why I've told you to go home," said Rory smiling. "I must take them climbing this evening; it's a promise—and it's their last day. Barney loves it. He's a born climber with a splendid head for heights. Of course he's not up to a difficult climb, he hasn't had enough practice, so we'll just do some easy ones."

While they were talking Barney had approached to tell them tea was ready and had overheard the last few words.

"Tessa says you climbed that when you were a boy," said Barney, pointing to the cliff. "I don't believe I could ever do it," he added.

It was sheer and steep, a great black wall, which reached out into the sea and sheltered the little bay from the north.

"The Black Cliff," said Rory, looking up. "Yes, it's a stiff climb. Euan and I climbed it with a rope. It would be very dangerous without a rope—especially that piece near the top. Do you see a small rowan tree growing from a shelf? That was the worst part. I tell you what, Barney; next year if you come back to Targ for a holiday we'll get out the ropes and I'll teach you how to use them."

"If we come back . . . " said Barney. His face had suddenly gone white beneath its tan and Charlotte noticed that he was shivering.

"You've been in the water too long!" said Charlotte, rising. "You had better run and put on your jacket and we'll have tea."

She was a little worried about Barney and she watched him as they all sat round and ate sandwiches and drank the slightly smoky-tasting tea. Barney did not eat much, which was unusual, and he took no part in the conversation. She wondered if he had got a chill from being too long in the water, or whether it was the thought of going home to-morrow that was troubling him.

After tea Charlotte and Donny walked back to the castle together; Donny was not particularly anxious to climb and there was packing to be done.

"This time to-morrow we shall be home," said Donny sadly. "I can hardly believe it. Targ seems as far away from Larchester as the moon."

Charlotte had much the same feeling herself, so she could sympathise.

"I shall be able to think about it," continued Donny dreamily. "That will be something."

"It will be a great deal," said Charlotte. "You can think of all you've done and seen, and you can look forward to next year. Try to help Barney, won't you?"

"Barney is awfully miserable. I'm terribly worried about Barney. Of course I hate the thought of going home and so does Harold, but Barney is *awfully miserable*. I wonder . . ." she paused uncertainly.

"What were you going to say?"

"Oh, just I wonder whether it will be different when we

get home or whether it will be the same. Harold thinks it will be different. He thinks we've sort of grown up a bit since we've been here—but Barney won't talk about it at all—and that's funny, you know, because Barney usually talks about everything that comes into his head."

"It will be different," declared Charlotte, trying to speak with conviction. "You *have* grown up. You've shared in a different kind of life so you know what it's like. The great thing is to have confidence in yourself. That's what you lack, Donny."

"I get frightened, Miss Fairlie," said Donny rather miserably.

"I know you do, my dear, but try to face up to your fear and ask yourself what you're frightened of . . . and always remember you have friends who love you."

"Yes, I've thought of that," said Donny quickly. "Tessa wouldn't love me unless I was worth loving, neither would you, nor Colonel MacRynne."

"Of course you're worth loving. We *all* love you," Charlotte told her.

Charlotte said a good deal more in the same vein and Donny listened and agreed and promised to be brave. It was an odd sort of conversation because Professor Eastwood's name was never mentioned and yet the conversation was all about him. His figure was in both their minds.

* 28 *

THE CLIMBERS returned in time for dinner; they were perfectly whole and sound and quite pleased with their exploits. Barney looked better, Charlotte thought. As a matter of fact Charlotte was feeling more cheerful about the future of the young Eastwoods; her talk with Donny had been satisfactory. Perhaps the Professor would find it more difficult to browbeat his children after their stay at Targ.

When she was going upstairs to dress Charlotte saw that the door of the room opposite to her bedroom was slightly ajar, and she heard the gentle hum of a sewing-machine. She looked in; there was a woman seated at a table in the window working industriously.

The woman looked up and said, "Good evening, Miss Fairlie," in a soft pleasant voice: it was Euan's mother.

Mrs. Euan looked so different in neat clothes with a clean white apron and her hair smooth and tidy that until she spoke Charlotte had not recognised her. Meg Merrilies had vanished and in her place was an eminently respectable person.

"May I come in, Mrs. Euan?" asked Charlotte.

"And why not?" returned Mrs. Euan gravely. "It will be a great pleasure to chat to Miss Fairlie . . . if you will not mind me going on with my work while we are talking. I come to the castle one day in every week to look after the linen and do any other mending." She hesitated and then added, "If Miss Fairlie has any stockings to mend I will be very pleased to do them."

Charlotte realised that Mrs. Euan intended her offer to be taken seriously and might be a little hurt if it were refused, so she accepted it with suitable expressions of gratitude and went away to look out some stockings which required attention.

"I will do them now," said Mrs. Euan. "It is easier to talk when I am mending than when I am working the sewing-machine."

There was silence for a few moments while Mrs. Euan searched in her capacious basket for silk of the right colour for her task.

"I wanted to ask you about that prophecy," said Charlotte at last.

"The prophecy about the Red MacRynne?"

"Yes," said Charlotte. "I've been thinking about it. I can't get it out of my head."

Mrs. Euan nodded. "It is a strange prophecy, Miss Fairlie."

"And it has all come true."

"It has nearly all come true."

Charlotte scarcely dared to make her request; perhaps it would be better not to know . . .

"Miss Fairlie would like to hear the end of it," suggested Mrs. Euan in a soft voice.

"I'm—not sure," said Charlotte with a little catch in her breath. There was something sinister about the woman, something frightening. Beneath her quiet gentle manner there was iron strength.

"There is no reason why Miss Fairlie should not hear the end of it," said Mrs. Euan. "I did not tell it when you came to my house because Tessa must not know."

"Is it so terrible?"

"It is not terrible at all," replied Mrs. Euan looking up in surprise. "Some people would say it was a good ending to the story. Look, Miss Fairlie, I will tell you. The story ends by saying that the Red MacRynne will live to be old and honoured—he will be the white MacRynne when that time comes and no longer red—and the walls of Targ will echo to the happy voice of his son. And he, in his turn, will be another Red MacRynne."

Charlotte was silent for a few moments and then she said, "Yes—yes I see."

"It would not be a good thing," said Mrs. Euan in a thoughtful tone. "No, it would not be good at all. Tessa has held her place for too long to give it up easily. It would not be good for Tessa and it would not be good for Targ. There are some who say that the MacRynne should have a son to be chief of the clan when he is gone but I am not one of them. All the people love Tessa and she loves all the people and every stick and stone of the island. Already Tessa has a place in the hearts of the people—you know it is true, Miss Fairlie. We have a woman for our Queen and I have never heard anybody say a man would be better or would do the duties more faithfully. It would be a strange thing to say and untrue as well." She was silent for a few moments, her head bent low over her darning. "So that is the reason," she added at last. "There is nothing terrible about the prophecy."

"No, nothing terrible," agreed Charlotte.

There was no more to be said upon the subject. Charlotte admired Mrs. Euan's handiwork—which certainly was worthy of admiration—and after a few minutes' conversation about other matters she came away.

The children went to bed earlier than usual that evening for the Eastooods were leaving Targ early the following day. Rory cleaned his gun and then sat down opposite to Charlotte at the fire.

"Everything is fixed," he said. "Breakfast at half-past seven. Tessa and I will go over with them to Invergoily and see them safely into the plane. There's no need for you to come, Charlotte."

"I think I should go south with them," said Charlotte in a voice which she hoped sounded steady. "It would be better really. I can look after them and——"

"What!" exclaimed Rory in consternation.

"It would be better," repeated Charlotte. "They aren't used to travelling——"

"But Charlotte, what nonsense! They came up here by themselves without the slightest trouble—in fact they enjoyed it—they'll be perfectly safe in the plane."

"I really ought to go back," declared Charlotte. "There are various things I ought to do. I've had a lovely holiday. I really ought to go back."

"But why?" he cried. "What's the reason? You were going to stay for three weeks and you've only been here a fortnight!"

"I know, but you see——"

"Surely there isn't anything as urgent as that? Can't you write—or ring up?"

"I'm afraid I must——"

"Oh Charlotte—please!" he cried. "I've been looking forward so much to having you here alone—just you and I and Tessa! You don't mean it, do you?"

"Yes, honestly, Rory. I'm afraid it seems rather rude to—to dash off so suddenly, but there are various things——"

"Are you tired of us?" he asked, breaking into her feeble excuses.

"No, of course not."

"What is it, then?"

Charlotte tried to speak but failed. She realised that she ought to have had some water-tight excuse for her departure, but the decision to leave Targ had come to her suddenly. All at once she had felt she could not bear to stay a moment longer . . . it was unbearable to be here with Rory loving him so desperately and knowing that it was hopeless.

"Don't go," said Rory, leaning forward and putting his hand on her knee. "Please don't go away. I want you to stay with me—always."

Charlotte shook her head. Her heart had begun to flutter in her bosom like a wild bird in a cage.

"I love you," said Rory gently, "I love you dearly, Charlotte. I can't do without you."

"No," she whispered. "It's—impossible. We've only known each other for a fortnight—it's impossible——"

"Only a fortnight—but we've been together so much that I know every bit of you, my darling. We've been so happy, haven't we? We've been so much in harmony. The very first moment I saw you I knew exactly what you were like—you didn't seem a stranger—and after that everything you did and said was perfect. You're the one woman in the world—the right woman for me."

She shook her head.

"But you are, my dear," he declared, looking into her face with a grave gentle expression that tore her heart.

"This—this shouldn't have happened," said Charlotte in a choking voice. "I should have—gone away—before."

"But why?" he asked. "It's a beautiful thing to happen . . . and 'happen' is exactly the right word. You happened to me, just as snow happens—or frost or thaw or the bursting of the sun from behind a cloud. Yes, that describes it best of all," declared Rory earnestly. "My world was full of clouds —it was a dreary scene—until you came to Targ. I never meant to love you; it just happened." He paused and then added, "I had begun to hope it was beginning to happen to you."

"We've been—good friends—but——"

"Friends!" he cried. "Love isn't warmth and cosiness; it's fire and glory!"

He had spoken so vehemently that Charlotte drew back a little.

"I'm sorry," he said, suddenly gentle. "I didn't mean to frighten you, my dear. Perhaps it's too soon to speak to you like this, but you said you were going away and I couldn't bear the thought of it. I won't say any more just now—only you mustn't go away and leave me. You won't, will you, Charlotte?"

"I can't marry you," she told him. "I can't—it's final so I had better—go away."

"Is it because of Esther?" he asked in a different tone. "Is it because—because——"

"Oh no!" she exclaimed. "No, you mustn't think that!"

He looked at her in bewilderment and she saw that she must tell him. She must make him understand.

"It's because of Tessa," she said.

"Because of Tessa? But it has been the greatest joy to her, having you at Targ and showing you everything!"

"Yes, for a fortnight. It would be quite different if——" Charlotte stopped. The room seemed to have become hot and airless, but Rory said nothing so she drew a deep breath and went on, "You and Tessa are so close together—so happy together—there can't be a third."

"Tessa loves you dearly."

"Yes, she does—now."

"She loves us both, so——"

"Oh Rory, don't you see that makes it worse! She loves us both, she trusts us implicitly. There's nobody else in her world. If we let her down she would have lost everything."

"We won't let her down," declared Rory. "Why should we?" He hesitated and then added, "I can see you're thinking of your father but that was quite different."

"It wasn't really different," said Charlotte sadly. "He and I were dear friends and good companions until a third person came into our lives. It doesn't work, Rory."

"We would make it work."

"I couldn't do that to Tessa—I couldn't——"

He rose and began to walk about the room. "I ought to have thought of this," he said. "You've got it on your mind. You're making far too much of it, Charlotte. Just because it didn't work in your case—and you got so terribly hurt— you think it will be the same in Tessa's case. It's quite different. It isn't the same thing at all. You and I are different; Tessa is just a child."

"She's a child in some ways but not in others," Charlotte said. "She isn't a child in her love for you, and for Targ, and for all the people here."

"You're making too much of it," repeated Rory, stopping by her chair and looking down at her. "But it's no use arguing like this—it's dreadful to—to argue like this. We're getting farther and farther away from each other with every word we say."

It was true of course; they were almost quarrelling and Rory looked so bewildered, so lost, so utterly miserable that Charlotte was tempted almost beyond endurance to comfort him. It would be so easy to comfort Rory, to hold out her hand and tell him that she loved him . . . but what was the use? It was better that he should not know what was in her heart.

"Charlotte," he said at last. "Do you just feel—friendly? Is it true? Sometimes I've thought——"

"Just very friendly," she said in a low voice.

"But I could waken you," Rory said. He stood for a

moment or two looking down at her and then turned away.

Charlotte rose to go upstairs. "I must go to-morrow," she said a trifle breathlessly. "You see that—don't you? I can't stay."

"You might spare us that at least," he replied in a bitter tone. "If you have no consideration for me you might have a little consideration for Tessa's feelings. What's she going to think about it?"

Charlotte paused at the door.

He continued, "How are you going to explain it to Tessa? She knows perfectly well that you intended to stay for three weeks. She'll think we've quarrelled—and she won't be far wrong."

"Yes," agreed Charlotte. "Yes, I hadn't thought . . ."

"And in any case there won't be a seat on the plane," added Rory.

* 29 *

CHARLOTTE DID not sleep for a long time, she was too upset and miserable, but presently she fell into an uneasy doze disturbed by dreams. She awoke suddenly to hear somebody shouting outside her window and a rattle of small stones flung against the pane. In a moment she had jumped out of bed and run across the room to the window.

It was daylight but still very early. Euan was standing upon the path looking up.

"Miss Fairlie, there has been an accident," he said urgently. "I have been ringing the bell and trying to waken the house, but everybody is sleeping. MacRynne must come at once."

"What is it, Euan?" she asked.

"It is the wee lad—it is Barney. He was on the Black Cliff. We were just setting out to the fishing in Alec's boat and we saw him fall."

Charlotte did not wait to hear more. She seized her dressing-gown and ran along the passage to Rory's room.

There was no difficulty in waking Rory—perhaps he had not been sleeping very well either—he sat up and listened to the news in horror.

"Barney on the Black Cliff!" he cried. "But why! Good heavens what was he doing there at this hour?"

"Climbing," said Charlotte breathlessly. "Euan saw him fall. He wants you to go at once——"

Rory leapt out of bed. "Run, Charlotte," he said. "Waken Mrs. Fraser. Tell her we shall want blankets—waken Tessa too. She'll be useful. Call to Euan to get men—and a door. Do that first. Don't forget the door—he'll understand. Tell him I'll be down in a few minutes." While he was speaking he had thrown off the jacket of his pyjamas and was diving into a shirt.

Charlotte ran back to her own room and shouted the message to Euan, then she sped to the back staircase and met Mrs. Fraser coming down.

"I heard somebody shouting——" began Mrs. Fraser.

"It was Euan . . . " said Charlotte and she explained briefly what had happened.

Mrs. Fraser wasted no time in useless lamentations. "Blankets—yes——" she said. "The big brown ones will be the best—and they'll need hot-water bottles and maybe some coffee in thermos flasks. You get dressed, Miss Fairlie. I'll waken Tessa on my way down. We'll not waken the other two children, they'd just be a nuisance."

Charlotte flung on some clothes and ran downstairs; she found Rory in the hall talking to Euan.

"Have you sent for the men?" Rory was saying.

"It is done, MacRynne," replied Euan. "They are to bring a door and meet us there. I waited for you to show you the place."

"You saw him fall?"

"Yes, we were in the boat. The laddie was half way up the cliff when we saw him. We could do nothing. It would have been foolish to call to him—besides he was climbing well and carefully. In a few minutes he was over the bad bit, where the rock is crumbling, and had reached the top. I thought he was safe and my breath came back to me—then he slipped and fell."

"To the bottom?"

"No, MacRynne. There is a narrow ledge half way down —it was maybe thirty feet he fell—he is lying on the ledge now—unless he has moved. If he was to move there would be no hope for him—none at all. We put back quickly but I knew we could do nothing without ropes. Somebody will need to go down with ropes."

"Ropes—yes——" agreed Rory. He opened the hall cupboard and brought out three coils of rope and a small axe. Euan took them from him and they both ran off up the steep path.

They had scarcely gone when Mrs. Fraser appeared with an armful of blankets. "They will need these," she said. "Will you take them, Miss Fairlie? You can go quicker than me. Tessa will bring the other things. If you would tell the Colonel that Tessa is ringing up Doctor Mackintosh on the telephone."

Charlotte took the blankets and followed Rory and Euan up the hill. She was amazed at the efficiency of the Mac-Rynne household; everybody had known exactly what to do and had done it without fuss. She wondered whether there were many accidents of this kind at Targ . . . or whether it was because these people lived far from civilisation and were obliged to depend upon themselves when things went wrong—instead of calling in a policeman or ringing up for an ambulance. Whatever the reason was they certainly were able to rise to an occasion.

The blankets were an awkward load to carry; Charlotte ran until she was out of breath and then walked and ran again. The path mounted steeply, it was rough and stony. Until now she had not had time to think, but now as she toiled up the steep path she thought of Barney . . . Barney had got up and gone out to climb the Black Cliff . . . but why? Why had he attempted such a feat? He had fallen thirty feet . . . nobody could fall such a distance without being killed! If Barney had been killed . . . She stifled a sob and pulled herself together. It was no good thinking like this . . .

Presently she reached the headland and saw Rory and Euan and several other men standing in a little group. As she approached Rory went down on his knees and crawled to the edge.

"He's still there, thank Heaven!" exclaimed Rory. "There's a small rowan growing on the ledge. It may have broken his fall."

"Will I go down for him?" asked Euan.

"I'll go myself," replied Rory.

"Is he alive, do you think?" asked one of the men who had followed Rory to the cliff's edge.

"Alive! Of course he's alive!" cried Rory, turning upon the man with sudden rage. "He's unconscious—so would you be if you'd fallen thirty feet."

The man drew back in alarm. "And that is true, MacRynne," he said quickly. "It was only—he is lying so still—and his leg doubled up so strangely."

"It was a foolish thing to say," declared one of the other men in a low voice. "There is no need to look on the dark side."

Rory rose and began knotting one of the ropes round his waist. Euan helped him, testing it carefully, the others stood by and waited.

"We shall need splints and more bandages," said Rory suddenly.

Euan signed to one of the men and immediately he turned and ran.

"Tell them to ring up Doctor Mackintosh!" shouted Rory.

"They have," said Charlotte. "Tessa was ringing up the doctor when I left."

"We'll need him," said Rory grimly. "It would be better if we could wait for the doctor before moving him—but we can't wait. Besides I don't see old Mack going down the cliff!"

"He could not," Euan agreed.

Rory turned and went over the edge backwards, letting himself down carefully; Euan crawled to the edge and bracing himself between two rocks began to pay out the rope. Another man stood by keeping the rope in his hands and watching Euan.

It was unbearable to stand there and not know what was happening so Charlotte put down the blankets and crawled to the edge. She saw Rory just below her, spreadeagled against the bare rock-face—it seemed sheer as the wall of a house. Below him was the rowan tree growing from a narrow shelf and on the shelf was the small figure of Barney in a crumpled heap. At the bottom of the cliff the sea churned upon the jagged rocks covering them with white foam.

Barney's position was so odd and unnatural that it was no wonder the man had thought him dead. One leg was doubled beneath him and his arms were spread out; his face, turned sideways a little, was stained with blood. Charlotte shivered involuntarily and dug her fingers into the turf.

Rory was going down very slowly and carefully, feeling for each foothold and testing it before putting his weight upon it . . . then suddenly a piece of rock crumbled beneath him and loosened a small avalanche of stones. For a moment or two he hung like a puppet at the end of the rope and then he managed to get hold of a branch of the little tree and pull himself on to the shelf.

"Are you all right, MacRynne?" called Euan in anxious tones.

"All right!" shouted Rory.

The shelf was very narrow. He balanced himself precariously and knelt down beside Barney.

Charlotte could scarcely bear to watch and yet she must watch; she must know.

In a few moments Rory looked up and nodded to Euan.

"He is alive," said Euan.

"God be praised," said one of the men in solemn tones.

There was a slight easing of the tension and Charlotte began to feel dizzy so she crawled backwards and sat down upon the grass. She was ashamed of herself but she could not help it and it would do nobody any good if she were to faint. While she was battling against the faintness Tessa appeared with a large basket and the men began to explain to her what was happening.

"The doctor is coming," Tessa said. "One of you must take the yacht over to meet him. It will save time. Not Euan—Daddy will need him—Fergus had better go."

Fergus nodded and ran off.

"Make haste!" called Euan quite unnecessarily.

Tessa put down the basket and came to speak to Charlotte. "Oh, Miss Fairlie!" she said in a shaky voice. "Oh, why did he do it! We were talking about it yesterday after the picnic. I mean we were talking about Daddy and Euan climbing the Black Cliff. Barney said 'I don't think I could do it,' and I said, 'I'm sure you couldn't. You'd fall and break your neck' . . . and then he sort of laughed and said . . . " Tessa hesitated. Her lips were trembling, her eyes looked larger than usual in her drawn, strained little face. "Oh, Miss Fairlie," she whispered. "Oh dear, I can't bear it . . . he said, 'If I broke my neck I wouldn't have to go home.' Do you think——"

"People often say things they don't mean," declared Charlotte, trying to speak in a matter-of-fact tone. "Barney was upset, so he spoke wildly. We all do that sometimes, don't we?"

"Yes, but—but why did he try?"

Charlotte could find no answer. She said, "There's no use in thinking about it now. Perhaps you could unpack the basket. That would be a useful thing to do."

There was a lot of talk going on amongst the men. Euan was giving instructions; he was speaking in Gaelic. Two more ropes with loops on the end were lowered over the edge of the cliff. Charlotte felt better now but she realised that they knew exactly what to do and that she would only be a nuisance if she offered to help.

Presently the ropes tightened and bit into the soft turf at the edge of the cliff. The men pulled slowly, watching Euan's hand and obeying his gestures . . . in a few minutes a large bundle rolled in blankets and slung in the ropes was pulled over the edge. Rory followed. He scrambled onto his feet and untied the rope.

"Easy with him," said Rory anxiously. "Lay him on the door—carefully. One of his legs is badly smashed—goodness knows what else is broken. I wish we had not had to move him."

"There was no other thing to do," said Euan quietly.

Charlotte went forward and looked down at the small figure stretched out upon the door. Barney was unconscious, his lips were blue and there was a strange pallor beneath the tan of fresh air and sunshine which he had acquired at Targ. He looked ghastly, Charlotte thought.

Rory had knelt down and was gently feeling the smashed leg; he looked up and said, "It's bad. I can set a simple fracture but I don't want to touch this."

"We could splint it loosely in case he moves," suggested Charlotte. She had done some first-aid training so she knew a little about it and was able to help—holding the splints in place while Rory bandaged the leg.

The men stood round and watched. "His forehead is bleeding," said one of them in a low voice.

"That's just a scratch," said Rory. "There's a bruise on the side of his head which looks more serious, and he may have internal injuries as well. Perhaps the doctor will be here soon."

"Would we be giving him a little whisky?" Euan asked.

"No, nothing," said Rory firmly. "Nothing until the doctor comes."

They tucked the blankets round him firmly and four of the men lifted the door and set off down the hill; they walked carefully and very slowly (it was obvious that this was not the first time they had formed a stretcher party). Rory followed with Charlotte and Tessa.

"Does Donny know?" asked Rory.

"I told her," replied Tessa in a low voice. "I told Harold too."

"It's funny that Harold didn't hear him getting up."

"He did hear him," said Tessa. "Harold woke up when Barney was dressing. It was very early—just beginning to be light. Harold was sleepy so he didn't bother, because Barney often got up early. He thought Barney was going out to see the pony—so he just turned over and went to sleep again."

"Poor little chap!" said Rory under his breath. "He must have been half crazy——"

Now that the tension was over and there was nothing useful to do Tessa broke down and began to sob helplessly. She clung to Charlotte's arm.

"I'm glad you're here," she whispered. "For Donny too. You'll talk to Donny, won't you? I don't know what to say——"

* 30 *

CHARLOTTE SAT beside Barney watching him and listening to his thick heavy breathing. He was still lying upon the door. It had been put upon the dining-room table. They had covered him with blankets and had put hot-water bottles round him, there was nothing more to do until the doctor came. Charlotte was frightened. She knew enough to be aware that the child was desperately ill. Every now and then she felt for his pulse but her own heart was thumping so loudly that she could not count Barney's heart beats. She blamed herself for what had happened. Why had she not spoken to Barney and broken through his reserve? She had known he was unhappy and had done nothing to help him, she had not even tried. She had been so taken up with her own affairs, that she had never thought of comforting Barney. Selfish, thought Charlotte, utterly and completely selfish—that's what I was!

Doctor Mackintosh arrived soon after ten o'clock; he came into the dining-room with Rory, and Charlotte left them there together. She was worried about the other children—where were they and what were they doing? She found Tessa and Donny huddled upon the sofa in the study and asked where Harold had gone.

"He went out with Euan," replied Tessa. "Euan asked us to go too, but we didn't want to. We *couldn't*."

"That's just as well, because I need you," Charlotte said.

"Mrs. Fraser has been too busy to make the beds so we'll do it for her, shall we?"

The girls were somewhat reluctant but they could not refuse so they followed Charlotte upstairs. When the beds were made they dusted the rooms and cleaned up the bath-rooms. Charlotte talked calmly and quietly as they worked and soon they began to look better. Tessa's colour came back to her pale cheeks and Donny stopped shivering.

"Daddy sent a telegram to Professor Eastwood," said Tessa. "It just said Barney had had an accident and they are all staying on. Daddy said it was no use telling Professor Eastwood any more until we heard what Doctor Mackintosh thought."

"The doctor is taking a long time," said Donny in a shaky voice.

"Those taps need polishing," said Charlotte, "Just give them a good rub up with a shammy—Tessa can clean the bath."

They were all hard at work when Rory came upstairs and found them. He looked at Charlotte and nodded approvingly.

"Oh, Daddy!" cried Tessa. "What did he say?"

Donny was speechless. She stood, twisting the shammy in her hands and gazing at him.

"We've got Barney into bed," said Rory. "Doctor Mack can't say much. It will be a day or two before—before we shall know how serious his injuries really are."

"Does the doctor think—he'll—get better?" asked Donny in a whisper.

"I'm sure he will," declared Rory with conviction.

Charlotte wondered if this were true. She noticed that he had not said the doctor thought so.

"We must all make up our minds that he's going to get better," added Rory. "It helps, you know."

"You mean it helps Barney?"

Rory nodded. "Any doctor will tell you that. A patient will get better much more quickly if everybody is cheerful and optimistic."

Charlotte went downstairs with Rory to see the doctor who was in the dining-room having a much belated breakfast, and from him she learned more details of Barney's injuries. His leg was very badly fractured and in addition he had three broken ribs and severe concussion. Doctor Mackintosh would have liked an X-ray of course but that was impossible for it would be dangerous to move Barney.

"We'll just need to wait and see," said Doctor Mackintosh. "It might have been worse—I can find no injury to the spine."

"We must telephone for a nurse," said Rory.

"Yes, and to his parents," added the doctor.

"He has no mother," Rory said. "And I won't have his father here."

"You won't . . . but you must!" exclaimed the doctor. "The child is dangerously ill. The concussion is serious and for all I know he may have internal injuries. Supposing the child dies!"

"He won't die," said Rory confidently. "We'll pull him through. I'll take the responsibility of not sending for his father."

"I don't understand you, MacRynne!" cried Doctor Mackintosh.

"That's because you don't understand the circumstances," said Rory calmly. "Barney would be upset if his father came here and we can't risk that. The man spends his time bullying his children; they're terrified of him. Miss Fairlie will tell you that's true."

"Yes, but all the same I think he should be told," said Charlotte doubtfully. She understood exactly what Rory felt but she was more conventionally minded. Rory cared nothing for convention, he was a law unto himself. He did what he thought best and accepted all responsibility without fear of the consequences.

"I agree with Miss Fairlie," said Doctor Mackintosh. "The child's father must be told. I'll write to him myself if you like——"

"Oh, do as you please," said Rory. "I think it's a crazy idea. The main thing—to my mind—is to keep the boy as quiet as possible and to pull him through. If you stir up that man he'll come here and raise hell—but have it your own way."

Charlotte had never seen Rory out of temper before; she realised that he was exhausted and his nerves frayed by the strain. When he left the room she followed him into the hall and laying her hand upon his arm besought him to rest.

"Yes, I will," he said, looking down at her with a rueful smile. "I'm pretty well done—that was why I was rude to Mack." He hesitated for a moment and then continued in a lower tone, "Charlotte, that child had reached the top of the cliff. When I got to the place with Euan—we were the first on the spot—I could see exactly where Barney had scrambled up. There definite marks of his boots on the soft ground."

"Euan said——" began Charlotte uncertainly.

"Oh I know," agreed Rory. "Euan said that Barney had just reached the top of the cliff when he slipped and fell. That's what it looked like to Euan, who was watching from below. I'm trying to tell you he was actually at the top and over the edge—actually safe."

Charlotte gazed at him in horror.

"We must keep this to ourselves," added Rory with a deep sigh. "The men didn't notice the marks on the ground. Nobody knows about it but ourselves."

"How miserable he must have been!"

"It doesn't bear thinking about."

"I knew he was terribly unhappy at the thought of going home—but I did nothing! I didn't even try to comfort him."

"I'm far more to blame than you are," Rory declared. "It's my fault—every bit of it—if I hadn't been so wrapped up in my own affairs—so utterly selfish!"

"We were both to blame—but it's no use thinking about it," said Charlotte, trying to pull herself together, trying to comfort him. "We've got to go forward and get him better."

There was no more talk of Charlotte leaving Targ, indeed the idea of going away never crossed her mind, and the conversation which had taken place the night before Barney's accident might never have been. She and Rory had resumed their old relationship—they were friends—all they thought about was the child.

Various arrangements were made for Barney's comfort; a nurse arrived from Glasgow and took over day duty; Mrs. Euan came and looked after him at night. But there was plenty for Charlotte to do and to think of; she was in and out of the sick-room constantly, helping to move Barney when necessary.

In spite of their decision to be optimistic everybody knew that Barney was terribly ill and was hovering uncertainly between life and death. There was a shadow over the castle, people went about quietly and spoke in hushed voices and sometimes broke off in the middle of a sentence and listened —and forgot what they had meant to say.

31

O N THE third morning the shadow lightened. There was better news. During the night Barney had opened his eyes and had tried to speak before drifting away into unconsciousness and, very early in the morning, he had come to the surface again and Mrs. Euan had given him some warm milk in a feeding-cup. When Doctor Mackintosh came to see his patient he was better pleased and his report was more optimistic. He did not say much for he knew by experience that the friends and relations of his patients were apt to fly to conclusions. If you told them there was a slight improvement they assumed that the patient was almost well and behaved accordingly.

Doctor Mackintosh was just about to take his departure when the telephone-bell rang and a message came through from the harbour-master at Invergoily to say that a strange gentleman had arrived by plane, had hired a fishing-boat and was on his way over to the island.

"There!" exclaimed Rory. "You see what you've done. It's Professor Eastwood of course."

Doctor Mackintosh looked somewhat alarmed. "Well, it's natural," he said. "It's what any father would do. Maybe the best thing is for me to go down to the pier and meet him. I could have a wee talk with him and tell him that the boy must not be disturbed."

Rory nodded. "Euan will go with you and bring him to

the castle. I'll see him myself in the study; after that he can go and look at Barney if he wants to——"

"I'd like to be there," said Charlotte quickly. "In the study, I mean."

"You'll keep out of this, Charlotte," said Rory. "It's my affair. I shall speak to him alone."

Charlotte said no more but she was very uneasy. She hung about on the upstairs landing, wishing that she knew what Rory's intentions were; wishing she could do something to smooth things over and to make things more comfortable for everybody.

Presently the front door opened and Euan came in with the uninvited guest.

"I will take your coat," she heard Euan say. "Colonel MacRynne will see you in the study. It is this way, please."

Charlotte ran downstairs and met Euan coming out. He shut the door quietly and looked at her.

"Euan," she said urgently. "Don't you think someone should be there? I mean Colonel MacRynne is very angry with him."

"Och, it is safe enough! MacRynne would never soil his hands with a wee runt like him," replied Euan scornfully. He hesitated and then added, "If he was a big man—and young—it would be different."

She had to be content with that for it was now time for her to help Nurse Berry in the sick-room. Barney's leg was in a cradle and it took two people to move him and to straighten his bed. He was conscious this morning and recognised Charlotte with a wan smile but made no attempt to speak. Nurse Berry was very calm and exuded an atmosphere of confidence and authority ; when the patient was comfortably settled she gave him an injection and followed Charlotte to the door.

"It was morphia," she whispered. "The doctor said he

was to have it so that his father can come up and see him without disturbing him. People don't realise how disturbing it is for a sick child to see his parents. That's why."

Charlotte nodded.

Nurse Berry went on chatting. Her manner—indeed her whole personality—seemed to change completely when she stepped across the threshold of her patient's room. Inside she was quiet and competent; outside she was a chatterer, a silly little woman and somewhat indiscreet. Charlotte knew this already, of course, but she never ceased to marvel at the metamorphosis.

It was now lunch-time; the interview which had taken place in the study was over and the whole party assembled in the dining-room. Donny and Harold greeted their father timidly and took their places at the table as far from him as possible. Colonel MacRynne, sitting at the head of the table, was silent and withdrawn; his guest was silent too. If it had not been for Nurse Berry, who had left her patient in the care of Mrs. Fraser, it would have been an extremely silent meal . . . but fortunately Nurse Berry was there and the atmosphere of strain did not worry her. She liked talking and never in all her life had she enjoyed such an attentive audience.

After lunch Charlotte took Professor Eastwood upstairs to see his younger son. Barney was sleeping. His face looked very small, but it still retained the tan of fresh air and sunshine and his cheeks were slightly flushed.

"He doesn't look very ill," said his father in surprise.

"No," agreed Charlotte doubtfully. "He's slightly better to-day—I expect the doctor told you—but one can't be sure that he won't have a relapse."

"I should like to be kept informed of his progress."

"Oh, of course."

"It is impossible for me to stay in the neighbourhood,

Miss Fairlie. Colonel MacRynne invited me to stay—either here or in the small hotel in Targ village—but I have work to do at home. Indeed it is imperative that I catch the aeroplane from Invergoily this afternoon . . . but I should like to be kept informed."

"Yes, of course," repeated Charlotte.

The professor stood and looked at Barney for several minutes but his face was inscrutable and Charlotte had no idea at all what he was thinking. Presently he turned and walked out of the room.

The rest of the party were waiting downstairs to speed him on his way. He put on his coat and suggested that Harold and Donny should come down to the pier with him.

"*Would* you mind if I came too?" asked Nurse Berry eagerly. "Colonel MacRynne has offered to sit with my patient for half an hour and it would be delightful to have a little walk in the fresh air."

Harold and Donny were charmed with the idea and said so warmly (what nice children they were, thought Nurse Berry); the professor seemed less anxious for her company but his objections fell upon deaf ears and they all set off together, Nurse Berry still talking.

Charlottte stood upon the steps with Rory and watched them go.

"Well," said Rory. "I suppose you're sorry for him now?"

Charlotte was—a little. She said, "I think he should have been spared Nurse Berry."

Rory had the grace to look slightly ashamed of himself. "But I never suggested she should go," he said. "And the children were pleased."

"You were pleased, too."

"I thought it was—lucky," he admitted, glancing at her sideways. "I suppose you think I'm ruthless and perhaps I am but it was his own fault. Most children, meeting their father after a month's separation, would have wanted a private talk with him. They didn't. Why should I step in when Providence sent an angel to protect them!"

"You really are incorrigible," said Charlotte smiling in spite of herself.

"But I didn't thrash him," said Rory, smiling back. "You thought I was going to thrash him, didn't you? That's why you wanted to be present. Surely you might have known that I wouldn't lay hands upon a man half my size and at least twenty years older than myself in my own house."

"Yes—I see that now. The fact is I never know what you're going to do. Are you going to tell me what you said to him?"

"I didn't leave much unsaid," replied Rory reflectively. "He began by blustering. He said he had been most unwilling to allow the children to come but Sir Joseph Spinner had assured him that I was a responsible person. It was obvious that I was not. If I accepted the care of children the least I could do was to see that they were properly looked after and not allowed to stray about alone upon dangerous cliffs. He had come north at great expense and considerable inconvenience to arrange for Barney to be moved to a hospital and to take the other two children home, but the doctor had informed him that Barney could not be moved and that the other two must remain here in case Barney asked to see them, so he supposed he would have to abandon his plans. Of course he said a lot more than that—and some of it twice over in different words—but I managed to keep my temper and I remained perfectly silent until he had finished (it wasn't easy because he's a very irritating man). Then I thought it was my turn so I told him that Barney's accident was not really an accident at all. I told him that his son had tried to commit suicide—and I told him why."

"Rory! You said nobody was to be told!"

"I changed my mind," said Rory grimly. "I decided it would be good for him to know."

"What did he say?"

"It shook him properly. He didn't believe it at first—or pretended not to—but I told him I had evidence that it was true . . . and I didn't stop there. He had told me what he thought of me so I felt justified in doing him the same service. I fairly bludgeoned him with words. There was very little spirit left in him by the time I had said all I wanted. It's odd how a bully crumples up when you go for him."

"No wonder he was silent at lunch!"

"And *that* was odd," said Rory. "I mean it was odd that he stayed to lunch. I wouldn't have accepted the hospitality of a man who had spoken to me as I spoke to Professor Eastwood. I wouldn't have eaten his salt."

"I expect he was hungry——"

"Hungry!" exclaimed Rory. "I would rather have starved . . . but of course I'm not really civilised, am I, Charlotte? Professor Eastwood is a very civilised person."

Charlotte was silent. Civilised was not exactly the word; conventional was better but it did not satisfy her completely. She tried to make up her mind whether or not she would have stayed to lunch and eaten Rory's salt.

"Well?" asked Rory grinning mischievously. "What's the verdict?"

"You always seem to know what I'm thinking," complained Charlotte. "As a matter of fact I wouldn't have stayed to lunch. I wouldn't have thought about salt—or at least not consciously—but I would have wanted to get out of your house as quickly as I could."

Rory laughed. "That's good enough," he told her. "I must go upstairs and sit with Barney now . . ."

* 32 *

TARG CASTLE settled down into a regular routine, it was like a hospital with only one patient—the whole castle seemed to revolve round the sick-room. Some days Barney was reported to be making progress, other days he slipped back, but on the whole his condition improved and after a fortnight of anxiety even the cautious Doctor Mackintosh began to talk cheerfully about his patient. It would be a long business of course and the leg was so badly injured that he was afraid it would be a little shorter than the other but that could not be helped.

Barney was a very good patient, he never complained, but lay quietly, flat upon his back, and gazed at the ceiling. Sometimes he listened to the radio and sometimes Harold or Donny or Tessa was allowed to visit him for a few minutes. Charlotte sat with him in the morning while Nurse Berry was busy and instead of talking—which tired him—she began to read to him. She had found *Swiss Family Robinson*, an old favourite of hers, in the bookcase in Rory's study and she tried it on Barney. At first he was a little scornful but soon the story gripped him, as she had hoped it would, and he asked for it eagerly; together they followed the amazing adventures of the Robinson family with profit and enjoyment.

Rory was busy with his usual avocations but he made a point of seeing Barney for a few minutes every morning and if he could possibly manage it he sat with the patient after tea when Nurse Berry went out for her daily airing.

There was plenty for Charlotte to do. Somebody had to look after the other children and keep them cheerful; somebody had to visit the old ladies in the east wing; Mrs. Fraser needed assistance, for the small staff was strained to the utmost with the castle so full of people.

Charlotte and Rory met at meals but they had no opportunity for private conversation. In the evenings Nurse Berry came downstairs and sat in the study with them (having handed over her patient to Mrs. Euan for the night). Nurse Berry knitted industriously and chatted continuously until it was time for bed.

So the days passed and the end of the holidays drew near. By this time Charlotte felt as if she had lived at Targ for years; she was thoroughly dug in and Saint Elizabeth's seemed so far away that it was like a place seen through the wrong end of a telescope . . . but of course she must go back before the opening of term. The three children wanted to stay at Targ until the very last minute so it was arranged that they should follow later.

On the last evening before her departure Rory asked Charlotte to go out with him.

"I want to talk to you," said Rory. "I haven't had a chance of talking to you for weeks. We can't sit and listen to that woman jabbering the whole evening. Come on, Charlotte, we'll nip out before she comes down."

"But Rory——"

"It's about Barney. Hurry up for goodness' sake or we'll get caught."

They slipped out of the front-door like a pair of conspirators.

It was dark and windy. There was no moon. Clouds were flying past high overhead, covering and uncovering the brightness of the stars like veils of tattered lace . . . but the sun had been shining all day and in the little sheltered garden outside the study window there was warmth and stillness and the scent of tobacco flowers. On the seat beneath the apple-tree lay a rug and Charlotte's tweed coat; evidence of forethought which touched Charlotte . . . and amused her a little as well.

"You had laid your plans," she said in a low voice.

"Well, of course! I didn't want you to be cold."

They settled themselves comfortably and Rory continued, "We shall miss you horribly but I expect we shall manage somehow—unless Nurse Berry drives me mad—fortunately it won't be for very long. As soon as Barney can be moved with safety Doctor Mack wants to send him to a hospital near Bath where he can have special treatment."

"Does Barney know he will always be lame?" asked Charlotte.

"Yes, I told him some time ago. It was better for him to know the truth—and he took it very well. I think he accepts it as a sort of punishment," said Rory thoughtfully. "He realises that what he tried to do was wrong."

"He told you——"

"Yes, everything. It was better for him to get it off his chest. The boy was so miserable at the idea of going home that he decided to climb the Black Cliff. He was sure he couldn't do it. He was sure he would fall. When he was telling me about it he kept on saying the same thing over and over again: he was sure he would fall. I could see it was the central idea in his mind; I could see that in a muddled sort of way he felt that if he tried to climb the cliff and failed it wouldn't be his fault . . . at least he would have tried. I think I can understand."

Charlotte nodded.

"So he got up very early," continued Rory. "And he went down to the bay and along the shore. It was a lovely

C.F.   S morning and he felt more and more wretched at the idea of leaving Targ. When he got to the base of the cliff and looked up his heart almost failed him—it looked so big and black and jagged—but he had made up his mind to make the attempt so he started to climb. When he was climbing he forgot everything except what he was doing—all his energies were centred upon the task—all he thought about was how to overcome the difficulties and reach the next shelf. He went up and up. There were one or two bad moments when he thought he was beaten but somehow he managed to hold on. He had no idea he had succeeded until suddenly he found himself at the top. For a moment or two he felt triumphant —as pleased as Punch as he put it—and then he realised that he was safe and would have to go home after all—and he couldn't bear it. So he just—lay down—and rolled over the edge. He wasn't in his right senses," added Rory in a low voice.

Charlotte could not speak.

"He sees that now," said Rory after a little pause. "He realises that it was a wicked thing to do—and he's sorry. As I said before he's taking all the pain and misery as a punishment and bearing it like a man. There was another thing on his mind—all mixed up with his feelings—he told me he had been to the silver wishing-well and had wished that something would happen to prevent him from going home. So he had hoped up to the last day that something *would* happen."

"Oh!" exclaimed Charlotte in dismay. "Oh, Rory——"

"I hate these things," declared Rory. "They do harm. People shouldn't meddle with them. If I had had any idea that the children knew about the well I would have forbidden them to go."

"But you don't really believe in it?"

Rory hesitated. "There's something uncanny about it,"

he said uncomfortably. "I don't believe in it—and yet—and yet——"

"I agree that it's bad for psychological reasons."

"Oh, of course, you're different," said Rory with a little smile. "You aren't Highland. You've got both your feet firmly on the ground. I hate that wishing-well because long ago when I was younger than Barney it gave me my wish."

"It gave you your wish?" asked Charlotte in surprise.

"I've never told anybody about it," he continued. "It's a queer story—rather horrible—and it made a tremendous impression upon me—I was seven years old at the time. My cousin was staying here; he was several years older than I was. He had been ill and was sent to Targ for the summer to recuperate. I was very fond of Alastair, in fact I adored him, to me he was a hero and could do no wrong. We were friends." Rory paused and then continued. "Alastair had a watch, it was a large silver watch with a minute hand, and I wanted a watch too. I wanted it not only because of its usefulness but more because if I had one I would be like Alastair. So one day I went to the wishing-well and I dropped in a silver threepenny bit and wished for a watch. Not long after that Alastair went home."

Rory paused for so long that Charlotte began to wonder if he had finished the story . . . but it was not finished.

"What happened?" she asked in a low voice.

"He died," said Rory bleakly. "He was a very delicate boy—I told you that, didn't I? Alastair died and his mother sent his watch to me, saying she was sure he would have liked me to have it. That's all really—but it upset me horribly. I took the watch the next time we went out in the yacht and dropped it into the sea."

"But Rory—it was just a coincidence," said Charlotte quickly.

"Yes, I suppose so," he agreed.

There was no more to be said about the incident and after a few moments silence they returned to the subject of Barney.

"We've got to think of Barney's future," Rory said. "Barney and I have talked a great deal. I've acted the part of Father Confessor—which is not really in my line at all."

"I think you would make a good Father Confessor."

"No, my ideas are much too vague. A Father Confessor should know exactly what he thinks himself before trying to advise other people. I could only grope about for the answers to Barney's problems. For instance Barney wanted to know how far one's duty to a parent should go. Those weren't his actual words of course but that was what he meant. If your father doesn't love you must you go on trying to love him?"

"I've wrestled with that problem," said Charlotte uncertainly. "I never found the answer."

"I think the answer is no. Why should the mere fact that a man is your father entitle him to your affection and respect?"

"I don't know. I only know it seems wrong if you can't give it to him."

There was a silence for a few moments, and then Rory said, "Look here, Charlotte, am I to send him home, maimed for life, to be the butt of that man's tongue? I can't do it. You see, the child loves me; that makes him my responsibility doesn't it?"

"In a way——" she began doubtfully.

"It does," he declared with conviction. "Not in a way but in *every* way. I said to you before (how long ago it seems!) one could make something good of that boy. He could be made or marred."

"You mean you want to—to keep Barney?"

"Yes, that's what I want. It's quite sensible really. We've talked about it a lot, Barney and I, and he thinks he would like to help me to manage my property. I would make myself responsible for his education and have him trained for the job. By the time Barney was ready I should be getting on, and a factor would be extremely useful to me—especially a lad who knew the ropes and was really keen. You mustn't think I'm being charitable; I *want* Barney."

"I think it's a good plan," Charlotte said thoughtfully.

"It *is* a good plan," declared Rory. "It's sensible. Barney's choice of a career will be limited by his lameness but he would make an excellent factor and he says he would rather do that than anything else in the world."

Charlotte could well believe it. "I suppose you want me to tackle Professor Eastwood," she said.

"How did you guess! Yes, Barney and I decided you were the person. You will, won't you? If I hadn't been so rude to him I might have tackled him myself, but as it is . . . "

"I'll try—if you tell me exactly what to say."

"Just what I've told you," said Rory eagerly. "Just that I want to accept all responsibility for Barney's education. I would send him to a good school and have him properly trained for the job. He would come here in the holidays and learn how things are run. That would have to be part of the bargain."

"You don't want to adopt him?"

"Adopt him!" exclaimed Rory in surprise. "Goodness, no! Just make an agreement with Professor Eastwood——"

"There are snags, Rory," Charlotte pointed out. "Professor Eastwood might change his mind and, until Barney was twenty-one, he could always assert his right to his own son. Your gentleman's agreement would be worthless in point of law."

"But surely he would keep his word! And besides, there's Barney—there's the human element. He couldn't lock up the boy in an attic and keep him there against his will; and I can't see him going to law and having the whole thing exposed. Think of the headlines in the sensational papers: PROFESSOR'S SON TRIES TO KILL HIMSELF . . . and a long sentimental story illustrated with smudgy pictures! Would Professor Eastwood like that?"

"Blackmail," said Charlotte, smiling a little at the thought.

"I don't care if it is," declared Rory. "If I can't get Barney by fair means I'll get him by foul. You'll try, won't you, Charlotte?"

"I'll do my best," she said.

There was silence for a little and then Charlotte rose and said she must finish her packing.

"Don't go yet," said Rory. "You're not cold are you?"

"No, but——"

"Please don't go, Charlotte. We've settled Barney's affairs as best we can but I've got something else I want to say."

She knew what it was. "No," she said. "No—please—— there's nothing more to say."

"Just a minute!" he exclaimed. "Charlotte, you must listen. I shan't see you again alone. I want to talk about ourselves."

"But there's nothing more to say—except that I've been —been very happy here—in spite of everything. I hate going away."

"You needn't go. I mean you can come back," said Rory earnestly. "Oh Charlotte, if only you would!"

"I can't—ever," she replied in a low shaky voice. "You know why. It's no good saying it all over again,"

"I must say it," declared Rory. "Things are changed now.

When we talked about it before I thought you didn't love me; but now I know you do."

Charlotte said nothing.

"Darling," said Rory, putting one arm round her and holding her gently. "Dear beautiful Charlotte, you will marry me, won't you? I want you so much. I love you so dearly. I've been thinking about all that you said about Tessa and I'm sure it will be all right if we're careful. We'll be very careful not to hurt Tessa——"

"We might have a son, Rory."

Rory hesitated. It seemed irrelevant but Charlotte was never irrelevant. "Oh," he said at last. "Yes, I see. A son would cut out Tessa. I hadn't thought of that."

Charlotte had thought of it for weeks. She had wondered whether she could say it to Rory; it seemed an odd thing to discuss with him, but it was important for him to understand. "We might not, of course," she said in a hurried voice. "But if we did——"

"A son," said Rory in a low thoughtful voice. "I've always wanted a son more than anything else in the world. It would be wonderful."

Charlotte felt the same. A little boy with red-gold hair, who would run about the castle and shout, so that the old walls would echo! Another Red MacRynne!

"It would be wonderful," Rory repeated.

"But not fair to Tessa."

"Tessa will marry——" began Rory. And then he paused uncertainly.

"Oh Rory, we couldn't do that to Tessa! We couldn't—put—somebody in her place."

"But we might not have a son. You said so yourself. Have we got to give up everything because of Tessa? Doesn't our happiness matter? Haven't we any rights?"

It had always been Charlotte's creed that young people

should be helped and encouraged—their rights came first—
and her years at Saint Elizabeth's had strengthened this
belief into a rock-like conviction. This was natural of course
because the school was run for the benefit of the young;
their welfare was the first consideration. Charlotte tried to
explain her views to Rory but she was too upset to make a
clear reasoned statement and her ideas came tumbling out in
confusion.

"It's so dangerous to be young—everything matters more
—they can't see things in proper perspective. You can make
or mar a young creature—you said that yourself when we
were talking about Barney. This would hurt Tessa. Even
if we didn't have a son it would hurt her. She would have
to share you with someone else and she has had you all to
herself for so long. She would have to share Targ! Oh
Rory, she loves Targ—every inch of the ground and all the
people. But it isn't only that; I'm thinking of myself too.
I love Tessa so dearly. I knew her and loved her before I
knew you—long before—I should never have come here and
met you if it hadn't been for her. Tessa asked me to come.
Tessa asked me . . . "

"I know, my dear, but——"

"Tessa trusts me! How could I let her down?"

"This wouldn't be letting her down."

"I can't do it!" cried Charlotte in agonised tones. "Oh
Rory, please try to understand! Some people would risk it
but I can't. Some people go through life taking things as
they go along and not bothering about the future, but I'm
not like that—and neither are you. We wouldn't be happy
if we made Tessa miserable. The thing between you and
me is such a big thing that it ought to be perfect."

Rory was silent. This was his own creed. He had always
hated compromise. If a thing were not perfect he had no
use for it.

"You *do* understand," said Charlotte looking at him. "I'm afraid of the perfect thing getting spoilt. We might lose each other—and lose Tessa—and it would be all my fault." She could say no more. She turned and ran into the house and left him standing there.

house and left him standing there.

* 33 *

SAINT ELIZABETH'S was full of stir and bustle when
Charlotte arrived for she had left her return as late as
possible and in three days time the girls were coming
back. All the members of the staff were here already and
were settling into their rooms; they were running about
the corridors and chatting to one another in an unusually
cheerful manner and seemed to be making an unusual
amount of noise . . . but perhaps this was an illusion due
to the fact that Charlotte had become used to the peacefulness
of Targ.

It seemed strange to be back in this place that she knew
so well; she had an odd feeling that she was not really here
at all (it was just a dream and she would wake and find
herself in her luxurious bed at Targ Castle with the gentle
prattle of the burn in her ears). The transition from one
place to the other had been so swift and uneventful; only
this morning she had been in the yacht, slipping across the
water to the mainland and watching the black cliffs of the
island grow smaller and smaller . . . watching them
through a haze of tears and knowing she would never see
them again; only this morning she had said good-bye to
Rory at the airfield, had shaken hands with him and thanked
him for her visit, as a guest should do. She had climbed
into the plane and, looking out of the little window, had
seen him standing there bare-headed with the sun shining

282

upon his hair. Then the plane had sprung to life and carried her southward to her duties and to loneliness.

All the people on the island had said: "We'll be seeing you again soon—maybe next summer?" and this was not just their good manners. Charlotte had realised that they honestly hoped to see her again soon; the people in the cottages, Mrs. Fraser, Euan, Fergus, Miss Mary and Miss Anne—everybody on the island with one exception. Mrs. Euan had not said it. Mrs. Euan did not want to see Charlotte come back to Targ.

But there was no time to think of these things; the moment Charlotte set foot inside the door of Saint Elizabeth's she was beset with questions. "Oh, Miss Fairlie, I've been looking for you everywhere! Could you tell me . . ." "Oh, Miss Fairlie, may I speak to you for a minute?" "Oh, Miss Fairlie, I wondered whether . . ."

Charlotte was no longer Charlotte; she was Miss Fairlie, the headmistress of Saint Elizabeth's, taking up the reins again, making decisions about all sorts of important and unimportant matters connected with the school. She had not been at Saint Elizabeth's more than a few hours before the odd feeling that she was not here vanished completely and the feeling that she had never been away took its place. Targ became the dream and Saint Elizabeth's the reality.

The following day was even busier—and perhaps it was just as well. There was no time to brood, no time to feel miserable.

"You *are* brown, Miss Fairlie!" exclaimed Miss Margetson. "Did you have a lovely holiday?"

They had met on the stairs and paused for a moment to chat. Miss Margetson had been to Belgium and had spent part of her holiday studying the various battlefields for which that war-torn country has been famous throughout the centuries. She had enjoyed herself immensely but was glad to be back and was looking forward to the term's work. "I think most of the staff are glad to be back," added Miss Margetson.

"They seem unusually cheerful," said Miss Fairlie.

"Oh, that's because . . . " Miss Margetson hesitated.

"Because what?"

"Because Somebody won't be here."

They looked at one another and smiled.

"Honestly, Miss Fairlie," said Miss Margetson. "Honestly, you've no idea how dreadful she was. It doesn't matter telling you now—she really was quite *horrible*. She did her best to upset people and make things unpleasant. If she could find something unkind to say, she said it. Life at Saint Elizabeth's will be bliss without that woman. I don't envy that school at Brighton."

"Brighton?" asked Charlotte.

"Yes, that's where she's gone. Pour souls, they don't know what's in store for them!"

"Perhaps she'll be happier there."

"Happier?"

"She wasn't happy here. That's why she was so—so difficult."

"The only time she was happy was when she was making other people miserable," said Miss Margetson with conviction.

This seemed to end the conversation. It was a sort of epitaph—or so it seemed to Charlotte—and what a frightful epitaph! It was all the more frightful because Miss Margetson was a kindly woman and not given to back-biting.

By evening Charlotte was so tired that she was almost speechless; she could not remember ever feeling so tired in all her life—and yet she had often done more. At Targ, for instance, she had walked ten miles over the hills and had thought nothing of it! She decided, as she got ready for bed, that it was this kind of life which was so exhausting; it was being tactful; it was having to think twice before you opened your mouth; it was the constant feeling of being on the alert to keep things running smoothly; it was saying pleasant things when you didn't quite mean them. Never before had she realised her life was so false. She sighed wearily and thought: is there anything else I could do? Is there any sort of job where I could be myself and tell the truth freely? She could think of none.

It was not until the Christmas Term was well under way and everybody had settled down comfortably that Charlotte found time to go and see Professor Eastwood. She had promised Rory to tackle him, and must keep her promise but she approached the interview in a very uneasy state of mind. As she drove into Larchester she thought it all over and tried to decide exactly how to put the matter to the professor; there were so many things she must not mention. She did not underestimate his intelligence; he had his blind spots, but in some ways he was extremely subtle . . . and this interview was so important. Barney's whole future depended upon what she said and how she said it.

When she stood upon the doorstep of Hatton Lodge there was a queer tight feeling in her chest which seriously interfered with her breathing. It was a familiar feeling; she suddenly realised that it was exactly the same horrible discomfort which she had experienced before an important exam!

Miss Hurdstone opened the door. "Oh, Miss Fairlie, how nice to see you!" she exclaimed. "I've been longing to hear all about poor little Barney. It was a dreadful accident, wasn't it? I was so worried when I heard—but I suppose he's quite all right again now."

"Not quite," replied Miss Fairlie cautiously. "He's getting better, but his progress is very slow."

"Oh, I hoped he would be coming home quite soon," said Miss Hurdstone in disappointed tones. "The professor gets letters from the doctor, but when I ask for news he just says Barney is better, so I thought he must be all right by this time. We do miss him so," declared Miss Hurdstone. "It's a *very* quiet house. Harold has gone to board at Bells Hill so of course he and Donny are only here on Sundays."

Charlotte had not known about this; it was a good thing, she thought.

"What a change there is in the children," added Miss Hurdstone as she escorted Charlotte upstairs.

"A change?" asked Charlotte, hesitating outside the professor's door.

"Oh yes, I noticed it at once. I don't just mean they look fit and well, I mean they seem different in themselves. The professor thinks they've got dreadfully out of hand but I think it's an improvement."

Charlotte would fain have heard more about the change in Donny and Harold but Miss Hurdstone had opened the door of the professor's study and was announcing her.

The little chat with Miss Hurdstone had steadied Charlotte's nerves and when she found herself face to face with the professor in his study the constriction in her chest disappeared and she was able to draw a deep breath.

They began by talking about the gradual improvement in Barney's condition (no mention was made of the professor's flying visit to Targ) and then Charlotte took her courage in both hands and explained what she had come for. She did so shortly and clearly and Professor Eastwood listened silently until she had finished.

"Do I understand you to say that Colonel MacRynne

wishes to assume all responsibility for my son's education and maintenance?" he asked.

Charlotte nodded. She had told him so already and it seemed unnecessary to tell him again.

"Why should he do so? He was careful to disclaim all responsibility for the accident."

"He doesn't hold himself responsible for the accident but he does feel responsible for Barney."

"Why?"

Charlotte could not say, "Because Barney loves him," but she gave another reason which was equally true. "Colonel MacRynne is the sort of man who feels himself responsible for everybody," she replied in a thoughtful voice.

"That seems a large order."

"I imagine it is a characteristic inherited from his feudal ancestors," Charlotte declared. She was rather pleased with this. Not only was it true, but it was voiced in the professor's own kind of language. As a matter of fact the professor's language was infectious.

"He must have some reason for the offer. What is his ulterior motive, Miss Fairlie?" inquired Professor Eastwood after a short pause.

This annoyed Charlotte—the idea of Rory with an ulterior motive was ridiculous—but she was careful not to show her feelings.

"As far as I know there isn't an ulterior motive," she replied. "I've explained his reasons already. Colonel MacRynne is offering a career which he thinks would suit Barney. Various other careers are closed to a boy who will always be a little lame, but he could be trained to manage an estate."

"It would be a long time before he was ready."

"But Colonel MacRynne doesn't need anyone at present.

He's looking to the future when he will need a young man to help him. He has a very large estate."

"A very large estate?"

"I don't know how many thousand acres."

"Oh, I see," said the professor thoughtfully.

"And he has no son," added Charlotte.

"But apparently—from what you say—he does not wish to adopt Barney?"

"No," said Charlotte. "I don't believe he could do that even if he wanted to—and I'm sure he doesn't want to— Tessa will inherit everything."

"Quite an heiress," commented Professor Eastwood.

Charlotte agreed.

"Supposing Barney failed to satisfy Colonel MacRynne?" inquired the professor after a short silence. "I will be frank with you, Miss Fairlie. I have no illusions about my younger son. His reports from school are far from satisfactory: I am constantly being informed that he is idle and that his intelligence is below the average for his age."

Again Charlotte was annoyed but she replied quite calmly. "I believe if Barney had a definite goal to work for he would do better. Some children can work for the interest of acquiring knowledge, others can't. That has been my experience."

"Your experience is wide," admitted the professor. "It might well be that Barney requires an incentive. You know, Miss Fairlie, I am inclined to agree to the plan. Indeed I do not see how I can refuse to agree to a plan which appears to offer a future to my son. But I should have to insist upon a written contract to safeguard myself from certain possible eventualities. For instance, Colonel MacRynne might decide to send Barney to an expensive school and then—in a few years time—he might find that the boy was not making satisfactory progress and withdraw his support. It would then be my responsibility to continue the boy's education upon the same lines. My means are limited and I do not relish the idea of spending a large sum upon Barney's education. If he were clever and hard-working it would be a different matter."

"A written agreement would be best," agreed Charlotte. "In fact Colonel MacRynne suggested that himself." She rose as she spoke for now that she had said all she had been told to say there was no need to prolong the interview. (Rory had said the professor was a very irritating man and Charlotte thoroughly agreed with the verdict; whether he was irritating by accident or design she was unable to decide.) "Perhaps you will write and let me know when you have considered the matter," she added.

"Er—well——" said Professor Eastwood. "I—er—think I may say my decision is made—yes, I think so—with reservations, of course. You may tell Colonel MacRynne to make a rough draft of his ideas for the—er—agreement."

"I'll give him your message," said Charlotte, disguising her joy.

"I shall read the agreement carefully," declared the professor as he opened the door. "It is possible that some clauses may not be acceptable to me in which case they will require modification. For instance I must retain the rights of a parent."

This was meaningless of course; it was merely a gesture, but Charlotte replied craftily: "Oh, of course! You aren't giving up your son. You're making provision for his future."

"Quite," nodded the professor. "Quite so . . . making provision for his future . . . which is all the more necessary in view of the fact that the career I had chosen for him will be closed to him on account of his disability. Before this deplorable accident it was my intention that Barney should enter the military profession; it seemed the only possible choice of a career for a boy of low mentality."

Charlotte was furious. Professor Eastwood had out-done all previous records; in a few words he had insulted his son's intelligence and the entire British army. The professor thought Barney stupid and idle, so it was the army for him. Had Professor Eastwood forgotten what the British army had accomplished during the war? Had he forgotten the marvellous expansion and organisation and all the clever ruses and inventions? Had he forgotten that the British army—a mere handful of men and deserted by their allies— had stood up bravely against Hitler's hordes? Had he forgotten that miracle of strategy, the Battle of Alamein; the landing in Normandy and the Mulberry floating harbours? Surely he must have forgotten all this if he thought the army was " the only possible choice of a career for a boy of low mentality! "

The odd thing was that Charlotte agreed with the professor in his conclusions that Barney would have made a good soldier, but this only served to infuriate her the more. Somehow or other she managed to keep her mouth firmly shut and came away as quickly as she could.

difficult.

"Look here, Charlotte," he said, "I must see you. It's
no use saying you can't meet me. If you won't make a date
I shall come and see you at Saint Elizabeth's."

"You can't do that."

* 34 *

SOON AFTER her interview with Professor Eastwood
Charlotte received a letter from Lawrence Swayne
asking her to come to dinner with him at Borley Manor
Hotel. She had not seen Lawrence since the Pageant, she
had scarcely thought of him. Now that she thought of him
with his letter in her hand she felt a trifle guilty. She ought
to have written to him. It seemed so long since he had asked
her to marry him and help him to run Bells Hill and so
much had happened in the meantime that it was difficult
to know what to say. For all she knew he might have
changed his mind—in fact it was more than likely. Surely
if he were still thinking about it he would have done something about it before. Lawrence had told her to think it
over and she had thought of it seriously until she met Rory
MacRynne but now she knew it was impossible. She would
never marry Rory but she could not conceive the possibility
of marrying anybody else. Lawrence's letter must be
answered.

Several rough drafts were written and discarded before
Charlotte found the right words. She refused Lawrence's
invitation to dinner, saying she was very busy, and added in
what she hoped was a light vein: "I don't know whether the
post you offered me is still open but I have decided to stick
to my guns."

There was no need to say more; Lawrence would understand.

The next morning Lawrence rang up on the phone. Miss Post was with Charlotte at the time which made things difficult.

"Look here, Charlotte," he said. "I must see you. It's no use saying you can't meet me. If you won't make a date I shall come and see you at Saint Elizabeth's."

"You can't do that."

"Yes I can. I have a right to come whenever I like. I'm a member of the Board."

Charlotte was aware that although Miss Post seemed to be deeply engrossed in her shorthand notebook her ears were cocked like the ears of an Aberdeen terrier. Fortunately she could only hear one side of the conversation.

"If it's about what you said before it's no use," said Charlotte cautiously.

"It's quite different from what I said before. Shall I come to Saint Elizabeth's or will you dine with me at Borley Manor? "

Charlotte hesitated. Perhaps Lawrence wanted to speak to her about the Eastwoods.

"Which is it to be? " asked Lawrence.

"It had better be Borley," said Charlotte reluctantly.

"Good. I'll meet you there to-night at seven-thirty. Will that suit you? "

She said it would.

Miss Post had heard enough to rouse her curiosity to fever-pitch. Who on earth could the "Old Girl " have been talking to? Certainly not a parent for she had not been very polite.

"You can't do that! " she had exclaimed. "If it's about what you said before it's no use " . . . And then, reluctantly, "It had better be Borley." What had the Unknown said before, wondered Miss Post, and who was Borley? Obviously the choice of two not very satisfactory people. Miss Post thought about it all day trying to find a solution which fitted the three sentences but she failed.

Lawrence was waiting for Charlotte when she drove up to the hotel.

"I'm sorry I had to bounce you into this," he said. "You aren't annoyed, are you?"

"It was a bit high-handed," said Charlotte, but she said it with a smile for it was difficult to be annoyed with Lawrence.

"I had to see you," he said. "I want to explain . . . I thought we might sit on the veranda for a bit before dinner. This place is stiff with people and they won't have a table vacant for about half an hour."

There was nobody on the veranda but themselves, so they chose a little table at the far end which was sheltered from the wind and sat down together. It was dark by this time but a very old waiter appeared and switched on the light over the table. Lawrence ordered cocktails.

"Do you want to talk to me about the Eastwoods?" asked Charlotte.

"About the Eastwoods?" echoed Lawrence vaguely. "No, of course not."

Charlotte waited for a few moments but he said no more. He seemed different to-night. He seemed to have lost his assurance and there was a sort of tension in the air which made Charlotte feel uneasy.

"Is something the matter, Lawrence?" she inquired.

"Yes. I've been a most awful fool. That's what's the matter," declared Lawrence. "I don't know how to begin to explain—and yet I must. Somehow or other I must make you understand."

Again Charlotte waited.

"It's about what I said to you at Copenhagen," said Lawrence at last.

"But you said it wasn't!"

"I said it was different," he reminded her. "And it is—quite different. When I think of what I said to you I could kick myself. I wonder you didn't kick me. Why didn't you? It might have done me good."

"What do you mean?" she exclaimed in surprise.

"I insulted you. I told you I didn't love you and then in the same breath, I asked you to marry me."

"But I understood. We were friends, Lawrence. You were offering me a job. It was far better to be truthful about it."

"Will you forgive me?" he asked.

"There's nothing to forgive," declared Charlotte. "Honestly, I don't know why you're making such a fuss about it. The whole thing is over and done with."

"You think I'm crazy," said Lawrence miserably. "I don't wonder really. I've behaved like a lunatic. I told you I didn't love you and asked you to marry me and help me to run Bells Hill; it was an insult, I can see that now—but I didn't see it *then*. In fact I was so pleased with my offer that I was sure you'd accept it. I thought that all I had to do was to sit back and wait until you had got used to the idea. So I sat back and——"

"Lawrence, please! I've told you——"

"Look here, you must listen! I want to tell you all about it. Then you'll understand. All these months I've been sitting back and thinking about my marvellous plan. I've been saying to myself: When Charlotte comes to Bells Hill I'll put in a new bathroom; when Charlotte comes we'll have some of the older boys to supper on Sunday evenings. I thought we would be sort of partners and it would be fun. It wasn't until I got your letter saying you didn't know whether the post was still open but you had decided to stick to your guns that I realised how much I'd been depending upon your coming. Everything just went flat," declared Lawrence. "There's was no good in anything any more. I found I didn't want you as a partner, I wanted you as my wife."

Charlotte had been listening to all this with growing dismay. "I'm terribly sorry," she said. "I ought to have written before, but I had no idea . . . I never thought for a moment you were depending on me."

"It's different now, isn't it?" said Lawrence eagerly. "You understand, don't you? I want you for yourself. I don't care whether you do a hand's turn in the school. I love you . . . desperately."

"Oh no!" cried Charlotte. "Not that!"

"Not that? But that's the whole point——"

"No—I'm sorry—please don't say any more."

"You mean it's hopeless?" asked Lawrence incredulously. "Couldn't you—think it over?"

"No, it's absolutely hopeless." She was determined to make him understand this time.

"Charlotte, you don't mean there's somebody else?"

She nodded.

"But you said there wasn't anybody——"

"There is—now," said Charlotte in a low tone.

Lawrence was silent for a few moments and then he said bitterly, "So I've lost you! And it's all my own fault. If I hadn't been such a self-satisfied bounder—such a blind fool—we might have been married by this time."

It was true, thought Charlotte. If Lawrence had not been so matter-of-fact, so "sensible" about his offer of marriage, she might have accepted it. If he had followed it up and asked her again—as he was asking her now—it was almost certain that she would have said yes. She remembered that several times she had decided to ring him up and each time something had happened to prevent her. She remembered the night of her birthday, when the Buddha had smiled! If she had accepted Lawrence's proposal she would never have gone to Targ . . . perhaps that would have been a good thing.

Lawrence had been watching her face. He said: "It's true, isn't it? If I hadn't been such a fool you might have said yes."

"I'm—not sure," said Charlotte uncertainly. "But—but it's too late now."

"When are you going to be married? Not that I have any right to ask."

"Never," she replied. "We can never be married, so please don't say anything about it. You won't, will you?"

"Of course not," said Lawrence quickly.

They sat in silence for a little. Lawrence had jumped to the conclusion that the man (whoever he was) was married already and Charlotte left it at that. She felt unable to explain; in fact it was impossible to explain the whole matter to Lawrence.

Presently he leaned forward and said: "Oh, Charlotte, I'm sorry. You're very unhappy, aren't you? What a ghastly mess!"

"Yes, it is—rather a mess."

"I suppose there's no hope for me?"

"No, I couldn't."

"Are you sure? You see, I love you so much! I could take care of you and we could be together. I don't mean now—or even soon—but later on when you feel a bit better."

Charlotte found it difficult to speak but she managed to say "No."

"Let's leave it for a bit," suggested Lawrence. "We'll go on being friends and later on I'll ask you again."

Charlotte was quite willing to be friends—if that was what he wanted—but she was anxious that there should be no more misunderstandings. She tried to explain this but without much success. Lawrence refused to take no for an answer. He repeated all the arguments he had used at Copenhagen; he besought her to think it over; he assured her that in time she would feel quite differently. He would wait for three months and ask her again—he would wait for six months—but Charlotte still said no, and at last Lawrence realised that it really was hopeless.

The waiter had interrupted them during their talk to say that their table was ready and now Charlotte saw him approaching again.

"I must go home," she said, rising as she spoke. "I couldn't stay and have dinner with you. Honestly, I couldn't."

"I couldn't either," said Lawrence miserably. "As a matter of fact I'd forgotten all about dinner. What shall we do? The waiter will think we're mad."

"We'll just—disappear——" said Charlotte, beginning to laugh hysterically. She ran down the steps into the darkness of the garden and Lawrence followed her. When they looked back they saw the old waiter peering about the veranda looking for them.

It was so silly; it was such an absurd ending to their conversation that Charlotte could not stop laughing.

"Now then, steady does it!" exclaimed Lawrence, taking her arm in a firm grip. "Steady, Charlotte! Take deep breaths—that's what I say to my little brutes when they get hysterical."

She did as she was told and found it worked. After a few deep breaths she felt better. They made their way round the corner of the house and found their cars in the drive.

"Are you all right?" asked Lawrence as he helped her in

and shut the door. "Would you like me to drive you home?"

"I'm all right," she replied. "Thank you, dear Lawrence. You're awfully kind and understanding."

"If you ever change your mind . . . "

"No," she said. "I shall never change my mind," She felt battered and beaten. It seemed to her that she had been saying No to everybody for months. All she wanted was to creep away into a deep dark hole and be left in peace.

* 35 *

T HE TERM sped on. There was an entirely different atmosphere in Saint Elizabeth's now that Miss Pinkerton had gone. Charlotte had known that Miss Pinkerton was a mischief-maker but she had not realised to what extent. It was amazing that one woman could have cast such a shadow over the place. The shadow had lifted and everyone seemed cheerful and friendly. If Charlotte had not been unhappy over her private affairs she would have enjoyed that Christmas term.

She was very unhappy.

Charlotte had seen other people knocked off their balance by this queer disease of love and, although she had felt sorry for them, she had felt just a trifle scornful. She was certain that it could never happen to her. Now it had happened; she had been knocked off her balance completely. The malady affected her strangely, ebbing and flowing like an irregular tidal wave. Sometimes she felt better . . . and then if she happened to turn on the radio when somebody was singing a sentimental song her eyes would fill with sudden tears and she would feel worse than ever. She was angry with herself—it was so stupid—but she could not help it. One day when she went to her drawer to get a handkerchief she found a large white one amongst her own small ones with the initials "R.M." embroidered in the corner and she remembered that Rory had lent it to her and she had washed it and forgotten to give it back. She stood with it in her hand and thought: if I could just see you, Rory! If only I could see you!

Of course she ought to send back the handkerchief but it was the only thing she possessed that had belonged to him and she could not part with it.

Work is the best anodyne for a sad heart and fortunately there was always plenty of work . . . and she kept on assuring herself that she would get over it in time and settle down contentedly. She had been miserable before and had got over it, so she would get over this trouble in the same way.

Miss Margetson was the senior mistress now and sometimes in the evening she came to Charlotte's sitting-room on business and stayed for a cup of tea and a chat. At first Charlotte was somewhat chary of making a friend of Kate Margetson, for it was against her principles, but after a bit she realised that it did not matter. Kate Margetson was the senior mistress (so if anybody had a right to be friends with the headmistress it was she) and she was such a natural forthright person that everybody respected her and liked her. Nobody could be jealous of Kate Margetson. In addition she was clever and capable and had a good business head so she was able to be useful to Charlotte in many ways and to ease her burdens considerably.

One evening when they were engaged upon some business connected with the running of the school Kate Margetson looked up and said, "You hate this sort of thing, don't you? Administrative work isn't in your line."

"I prefer teaching," admitted Charlotte with a sigh.

"Why do you stay at Saint Elizabeth's? Oxford is the place for you with your talent for languages. You ought to be teaching undergraduates—not schoolgirls—you ought to be free from all this administrative work."

"I've thought about it sometimes."

"I've often thought about it. You're wasted here. Once or twice before I've thought of suggesting it to you, but——"

"Why didn't you?"

Kate Margetson smiled. "You might have thought I wanted your shoes."

"Do you, Kate?" asked Charlotte.

"Not until you've outgrown them," replied Kate laughing.

This conversation stayed in Charlotte's mind. She respected the opinion of her new friend—Kate was sensible and as honest as the day—it might be quite a good plan if it could be managed. A lectureship at Oxford would be more congenial work and the new life might help her to get over her trouble. Kate would make an excellent head-mistress for Saint Elizabeth's; she would carry the burden cheerfully and would say exactly what she thought without bothering to be tactful. Things would be run rather differently and possibly she might not be very popular but she would be respected and obeyed. Charlotte decided to wait until after Christmas and then go and see Sir Joseph and ask his advice.

Christmas approached slowly and then, gathering speed like an express train, was upon them before they expected it. Everybody said good-bye and the denizens of Saint Elizabeth's were scattered to the four points of the compass, but before the final leave-taking Charlotte saw Tessa for a few minutes for she wanted to hear the latest news of Barney's progress.

"I thought Daddy would have written to you!" exclaimed Tessa in surprise. "Hasn't Daddy written?"

"Not lately. I expect he's very busy," replied Charlotte. She had had a letter from Rory thanking her for tackling Professor Eastwood and saying that the agreement had been signed (it was an impersonal sort of letter) but since then she had not heard from him.

"Oh dear, how funny of Daddy!" said Tessa. "I was sure Daddy would write to you. Well, anyway, Barney is much better. Daddy says the moment Barney heard it was going to be all right about the future he started to go ahead by leaps and bounds. Doctor Mackintosh has arranged for him to go to that hospital at Bath for special treatment— he's to go directly after Christmas. It's lovely, isn't it, Miss Fairlie? Barney will be happy now and he'll be a tremendous help to Daddy."

"Yes, it seems to have worked out well," agreed Charlotte.

"I wish you were coming to Targ for Christmas," said Tessa regretfully. "Daddy says it would be too cold for you—but we always have lovely big fires—and of course there will be parties, so it wouldn't be dull. I expect you found it a little dull in the summer, didn't you?"

"No, not a bit, but——"

"You see we couldn't go about much or arrange any parties when Barney was ill. Oh Miss Fairlie, don't you think you could come for Christmas? It *would* be such fun."

Charlotte said she was afraid it was impossible.

"You've made other plans, I suppose," said Tessa with a sigh.

Fortunately this was not exactly a question, so it did not require an answer.

The fact was Charlotte had made no plans at all for the Christmas holidays. She had decided weeks ago that she could not go to Aunt Lydia's and had written a tactful letter to that effect. She intended to spend Christmas alone and to make it a Christian festival instead of a pagan orgy. She would take a room in an hotel where she would be free to do as she pleased. But Charlotte had not booked a room; she had not even tried. There had been such a rush at the end of term that she had forgotten all about it. (Perhaps "forgotten" is scarcely the word. The idea that she must book a room had slipped in and out of her mind. Where shall I go? she had wondered . . . perhaps Sidmouth . . . she had known Sidmouth when she was a child . . . and then some other problem arose and chased her own problem away.) When the day came for her to leave Saint Elizabeth's she had made no arrangements and she was aware that it was much too late now to go to any of the places she knew. The hotels would be full of visitors, it would be hopeless.

Charlotte put her suitcase into the little car and drove out of the gates. She drove westwards in a leisurely manner for she did not know where she was going so she was in no hurry to get there. It was rather pleasant, really. She felt free. The term's work was behind her; before her was a blank.

At teatime Charlotte found herself in a small village and stopped at an inn called the Green Lion; it was an old-fashioned place but clean and warm and the woman who brought her tea was plump and comely with apple-red cheeks and a friendly manner.

"Where am I?" asked Charlotte.

"Where are you, Miss!" repeated the woman in bewilderment.

"I mean, what is the name of this village."

"Oh, I see!" exclaimed the woman laughing. "You've got lost, Miss! I couldn' think what you meant. This place is called Little Garley. It's quite a small village and strangers find the roads round about here very muddling. That's why you got lost."

Charlotte had not "got lost"—or at least not in the sense that the woman understood the words—she tried to explain but without success.

"It depends whether you were going to Bath," said the

woman, and began to explain all the turnings and cross-roads in detail.

They continued to chat while Charlotte had her tea and in a few minutes she learned a good deal about Little Garley. Her hostess was a widow—Mrs. Philipson by name—and she managed the inn with the help of her niece. There was nobody staying in the house over Christmas and they expected to be very quiet.

"We don't have many guests," said Mrs. Philipson. "There's nothing for people to do or see at Little Garley—except the church of course. It's a very old church, the vicar says it's Norman, and sometimes people come to look at that. If it wasn't for the bar we shouldn't be able to carry on: it's the bar that makes the money."

By the time Charlotte had finished chatting to Mrs. Philipson it was pitch dark and had begun to rain, and when Charlotte went out to the door the outside world looked extremely unpleasant.

"Why not stay the night?" suggested Mrs. Philipson. "We could give you a nice little supper and a comfortable bed. You'll just get lost again if you go out in the dark."

Charlotte agreed at once and Mrs. Philipson hastened away to prepare a room.

* 36 *

THE NEXT day was Sunday—it was the Sunday before Christmas—and Charlotte was awakened by a peal of church bells. It was still quite dark so the church was invisible but judging from the bells it must be quite near. Charlotte lay and listened to them (she would have liked to obey their summons but it was too late to think of that). First there was a cheerful peal and then, after a pause, they began to play a Christmas hymn very slowly, as if the bell-ringers were not quite sure of themselves, but there was something simple and pleasant about the sound.

I might stay here, thought Charlotte.

The idea appealed to her. It was a comfortable house—a little old-fashioned but warm and friendly—Mrs. Philipson seemed kind. All the big hotels would be full; they might provide crackers and paper hats for their patrons and hang up bunches of mistletoe. Charlotte did not want that sort of Christmas, she wanted peace.

By the time Mrs. Philipson's niece appeared at her bedside with a cup of morning tea Charlotte had made up her mind to stay. She would have to write to Jakes (who was the caretaker at Saint Elizabeth's during the holidays) and give him her address so that her letters could be forwarded, and she must write to Aunt Lydia. There was nobody else who need be informed of her whereabouts.

The bells rang again for the Service of Matins at eleven

o'clock and this time Charlotte was ready. Mrs. Philipson told her to go through the garden and across the road; the lychgate which led into the churchyard was only a few yards away. It had been raining most of the night but now the clouds had cleared, the sun was shining brightly and there was a fresh smell of wet earth in the air.

The garden was old and looked a little neglected but there were some fine looking apple-trees and gooseberry bushes in it and several rows of winter vegetables. The autumn had been so mild that there were still some flowers in bloom; chrysanthemums and asters and even one or two dahlias which looked fairly healthy; there were also a few somewhat stunted marigolds. Near the wall, in a sheltered corner, Charlotte saw a solitary primrose, burning like a brave little golden flame in its wintry surroundings.

When Charlotte opened the garden gate she found herself amongst a crowd of country folk with pleasant ruddy faces, and followed them through the lych-gate and up the broad path to the church.

It was dim and shadowy inside the building with arrows of coloured light where the sun poured through the stained-glass windows and struck across the aisle. Unlike some old churches this one was pleasantly warm and reasonably well-filled. The walls were perfectly plain except for the brass memorials. Near where Charlotte was sitting was the stone effigy of a knight in armour stretched out upon a stone sarcophagus; his two dogs lay at his feet and his wife and six children were commemorated in low relief upon the side of his tomb.

The service was suited to the rural congregation and the hymns were old favourites which everyone knew and sang. Charlotte liked the vicar; he looked about sixty and had a fine-drawn face and a mop of silvery hair. Although he was unusually small his voice was deep and musical; his sermon was thoughtful and delivered in plain everyday language with no pretensions to rhetoric.

When she came out of church Charlotte walked round the outside of the building and admired the well-balanced proportions which are such an outstanding feature of Norman architecture. The church was solidly built of grey stone with mullioned windows and a square tower and it stood upon a little knoll surrounded by the graves of dead and gone parishioners. Most of the graves were old with mossy headstones commemorating the virtues of the deceased. Charlotte discovered one which bore her own name and lingered for a few moments to look at the inscription.

CHARLOTTE
Born 25 Oct. 1833—Died 25 Dec. 1853
Enter thou into the joy of thy lord

So this girl had died on Christmas day a hundred years ago! Why had they only put her Christian name, wondered Charlotte, and why had they chosen that particular text for such a young creature. It was a text which seemed more applicable to a man who had lived his full span of years than to a girl of twenty.

Suddenly a voice said, "Well done, thou good and faithful servant!" and looking round Charlotte saw the vicar standing on the path smiling at her cheerfully. He was even smaller than she had thought, and a great deal older. The outdoor light showed up the wrinkles in his face.

"Oh, do you know about her?" Charlotte asked. It seemed quite natural to drop straight into the middle of a conversation with him instead of starting in the conventional manner with introductions.

"I know nothing about her," he replied. "A hundred years is a long time—even in Little Garley—and nobody can tell me who she was. There are several things I should like to know about Charlotte, but principally whether she was entitled to that text. Did her friends choose it deliberately or did they just open the Bible and light upon it by accident and say, ' Here's the very thing! ' You see I'm an inquisitive individual. I like to know all about my parishioners—even the dead ones."

Charlotte wondered if this was a gentle hint. She said: "I'm not exactly one of your parishioners (or at least only a very temporary one) but you might like to know that my name is Charlotte too—Charlotte Fairlie—and I'm staying at the Green Lion."

"I'm afraid I knew that much already," he told her with his ready smile. "The advent of a strange lady causes quite a stir in a quiet country village. The news came with the milk."

Charlotte laughed. She found the little vicar amusing. "I expect they're all wondering why I came," she said. "The fact is I wanted to escape from paper hats and mistletoe."

"I have nothing against paper hats——"

"But surely you don't like mistletoe? "

He considered the question seriously. "Now that I think of it I can see that there is something sinister about the plant. The druids valued it very highly . . . Dear me, I seem to have forgotten how they used *Viscum album*. I must look it up."

"Then it *is* a relic of paganism! " exclaimed Charlotte. "I knew it! There's something quite horrible about mistletoe; I can't bear its queer soft green stalk and its sticky berries . . . and if the druids valued it why should we use it for Christmas decorations? It doesn't seem right."

"You feel very strongly about it! "

"I suppose it's silly," said Charlotte, smiling apologetically. "After all, it's only a plant—but somehow it's a symbol of what I'm trying to escape from: crackers and paper hats and eating too much rich food. I wanted . . . " she hesitated.

"Please go on, Miss Fairlie."

"I wanted to find the real Christmas spirit."

"I hope you will find it here," said the vicar with sincerity. "I hope so with all my heart. I shall see that there is no mistletoe amongst the decorations in church."

"Oh, but you mustn't pay any attention——"

"Oh, but I must," he declared, nodding as he spoke. "You have given me something to think about; perhaps you will allow me to use your thought for my Christmas sermon?"

"Of course—if it's any use."

They talked for a few minutes longer; Charlotte learned that her new friend's name was William Aylwin and that he had been at Little Garley for seven years; he was a widower and lived alone (except for daily help) in the enormous vicarage which had been built to house an enormous family.

"We all have our problems," said Mr. Aylwin with a little sigh. "I should be a great deal more comfortable in a two-roomed cottage—but I love my garden. You have no objections to holly, I hope?"

"None whatever," replied Charlotte laughing.

37

CHRISTMAS TIME at the Green Lion was very quiet; Charlotte had the whole place to herself and could sit and read in the comfortable little lounge beside the fire. She found some old books in the bookcase; *Miss Mackenzie*, by Trollope, was one of them (she had read all the Barchester novels but *Miss Mackenzie* was a new acquaintance and an entertaining one). The letters, forwarded by Jakes, arrived in a few days and included over three hundred Christmas cards, for nearly every girl in the school and all the staff put down Miss Fairlie's name upon her list as a matter of course.

Some of the cards were large and very beautiful: there were dozens of pictures of birds—mostly of wild geese flighting over sedgy lakes—and dozens of pictures of a coach and horses drawn up before an inn. There were pictures of churches in snowy landscapes; there were pictures of children playing in the snow; there were pictures of dogs, pictures of horses, pictures of bells and plumpuddings and candles and holly. There were even pictures of mistletoe.

The recipient of this enormous mail looked through it with interest and enjoyment . . . but it suddenly struck her that the real Christmas spirit was singularly absent. Amongst all the astounding mass of beautiful and artistic pictures she could find only eleven which commemorated the birth of Christ. This seemed rather queer when the festival they were celebrating was His birthday.

"The lady at the Green Lion" was an endless subject of conversation and conjecture amongst the inhabitants of Little Garley and the stacks of letters which arrived for her at the post office, and were delivered by the postman in a special bag, added fuel to the fire. She must be Somebody Important—and yet she did not seem so, for she was not at all "proud" and she had a pleasant word for everybody she met—and wasn't it very odd that a lady with so many friends should be spending Christmas alone at Little Garley?

Mrs. Philipson was a kindly woman; she liked her solitary guest and endeavoured to find entertainment for her. She suggested that Miss Fairlie should go to the pictures in the town (which was only six miles away) and, when this plan was rejected, she invited Miss Fairlie to come to her private sitting-room one evening and listen to the wireless. Miss Fairlie thanked her but said she had letters to write.

"I told you there was nothing to do at Little Garley," said Mrs. Philipson with an anxious frown.

"Don't worry," said her solitary guest smiling. "I'm not lonely."

This was true . . . or at least it was very nearly true. Certainly she was not as lonely as she had been last Christmas amongst a crowd of uncongenial people. She decided that if one had no family—no children to run about the house and prattle excitedly of Santa Claus—it was much better to be alone. Sometimes she wondered what they were doing at Targ. She could imagine them sitting in the comfortable study beside the log fire. Tessa would be reading and Rory cleaning his gun after an afternoon's shooting on the moor —or perhaps tying flies. The room would be quiet except for the far-off rushing sound of the burn and the whisper of the wind in the chimney. The scene was so real to Charlotte that she could imagine herself there.

These dreams disturbed her peace. The easiest way to peace would have been to put away all thoughts of Rory, but Charlotte did not want to take the easy way; she wanted to remember him always. She would be casting away something valuable if she put Rory out of her life . . . if only we could be friends, she thought. If I could see him sometimes! But she knew Rory would not be satisfied with that. He had said love was not warmth and cosiness, it was fire and glory. Rory had made it clear that he wanted all or nothing.

The weather continued mild and pleasant, with cloudy skies and blinks of golden sunshine. Charlotte went for long walks through the woods and fields and came back to the Green Lion ready for the plain wholesome meals provided by Mrs. Philipson; she spent some time in the church reading the brass inscriptions; she walked up and down the terrace behind the church and occasionally if it were warm enough she sat upon a wooden seat which had been placed in the shelter of the tower. There was a delightful view from here; a view of green meadows and brown fields and a wooded ridge of hills.

There were services in the church nearly every day during Christmas week for the vicar took his duties very seriously. Only a few of his parishioners were able to find time to come to church on week-days but that did not worry him unduly. In fact (as he explained to Charlotte in one of their short conversations) if nobody had come he would have carried on just the same . . . but there were always a few and this few came to worship—just as the shepherds had come to worship the babe in the stable over nineteen hundred years ago. Charlotte, as she joined in the simple services, made it her prayer that her heart might find peace and that she might be able to think of Rory without pain.

The mild weather continued. Christmas morning was fine and dry. The stars were fading in the first glimmer of dawn when Charlotte let herself out of the side door and walked across the garden on her way to early Communion. There were other people going too—quite a crowd—walking together in little groups and talking in quiet voices.

"We left them in bed," one woman was saying. "They were opening their stockings. It was a treat to see Bobbie's face . . . he was too small last year to be excited about Santa Claus."

"My two were awake at five," said her companion with a chuckle. "Jim and I were up till nearly two, decorating the tree, so we didn't get much sleep—but there, Christmas belongs by rights to the children . . . "

"That's what I always say," said the first woman. "Christmas would be sort of meaningless without children."

Charlotte paused for a few moments at the lychgate with a pain in her heart. It was true. Christmas without children was meaningless . . . and then she raised her eyes and saw the little church with its lights shining through the stained-glass windows and she realised that there was one child who belonged to everybody . . . or at least belonged to everybody who would let Him come in. The cloud upon her spirits lifted and quite suddenly she was happy and at peace.

One day towards the end of the holidays Charlotte was coming back from a long walk and took her usual short cut through the churchyard. She stopped for a few moments at the grave of the girl who had died a hundred years ago. As a matter of fact she often lingered here, for mysteries intrigued her, and gradually in her usual imaginative way she had dowered her namesake with a personality and a history.

Charlotte was thinking about this—and smiling at herself for being so childish—when she heard the squeak of the lychgate. She turned quickly and saw Rory and Tessa coming up the path. For a moment she could not believe her eyes—they were not real—it was an hallucination —and then Tessa waved and shouted joyfully and came running towards her.

"Darling Miss Fairlie!" cried Tessa, throwing her arms round Charlotte's neck. "You *are* pleased to see us, aren't you? Do say you're not cross with us for coming."

Charlotte was not cross. Her heart soared like a lark in spring. She kissed Tessa fondly and held out her hand to Rory.

"It was Tessa's idea," said Rory a little uncomfortably. "You know what Tessa is like when she gets an idea into her head."

"But it was such a marvellous idea!" cried Tessa. "You see Miss Fairlie, I got your address from Jakes—we went to Larchester to call on the Eastwoods. We went there after we had taken Barney to the hospital at Bath."

"Why tell it all back to front?" asked Rory smiling.

"Miss Fairlie understands," declared Tessa laughing excitedly. "She's clever! I knew she would want to hear all about Barney and it was much better to come here and see her than to write. When people write they never tell you all you want to know."

"We're on our way back to Bath," explained Rory. "Barney is being X-rayed and I want to see the surgeon on Monday before going home to Targ."

"Daddy, listen, I've got a splendid idea! Why don't we stay here for the week-end?"

"I don't suppose they'll have rooms," said Rory hastily.

"We've got our rooms at the hotel at Bath. No, Tessa,——"

But Tessa was enchanted with her latest plan. "We'll ask if they have rooms, shall we?"

"No Tessa, I don't think——"

"Oh, do let's!" she cried. "Please, Daddy! Miss Fairlie would like us to stay, wouldn't you, Miss Fairlie?"

Charlotte was not sure whether she wanted them to stay or not. It was lovely to see Rory, but she had a feeling that she would pay for this joy afterwards—her hardly achieved resignation would have to be won all over again—and what did he want? Did he want to stay or go? It was useless for them to stay if Rory felt unhappy.

"You'd like us to stay, wouldn't you?" repeated Tessa.

"Yes, of course I should," said Charlotte—what else could she say?

"I'll go and ask," cried Tessa joyfully. "I'll ask if they have rooms. It's a gorgeous plan . . . "

She ran off to find out and Charlotte and Rory were left standing upon the path looking at one another.

"I'm sorry, Charlotte," said Rory somewhat ruefully. "It wasn't my idea to pursue you like this and force ourselves upon you . . . but Tessa kept on saying: 'Don't you *want* to see her?' and I didn't know what to reply. Of course I wanted to see you." He hesitated and then added, "It was impossible to tell her that you wouldn't want to see me."

"But I did!" exclaimed Charlotte involuntarily.

"Well, that's all right," he said.

"You understand, don't you? I mean nothing has—has changed."

He nodded. "I understand. As a matter of fact I've been thinking about it myself, and I've come to the conclusion that you're right. It wouldn't be fair to Tessa. We wouldn't be happy. You can't snatch happiness at somebody else's expense . . . but I wondered if we could be friends. If I could see you sometimes, Charlotte . . . "

It was her own idea! "Yes," she said quickly. "Oh yes, I've thought of it often. It would be lovely to have you as a friend. I would have suggested it long ago but I thought you didn't want that."

"Half a loaf is better than no bread," said Rory rather sadly.

There was no difficulty about rooms. Mrs. Philipson was only too pleased to have two more guests for the week-end so the matter was settled and Tessa was as happy as a king. At lunch they talked about Barney and told Charlotte how well he had stood the journey and how happy he was in the hospital; there were several other boys in the ward and they would be company for him. Tessa did most of the talking, her elders found conversation rather a strain. They had agreed to be friends but it was not easy to resume the old relationship when there was so much that could not be said.

After lunch Charlotte took her visitors to see the church and when they had admired the stone knight and his progeny and looked at the brasses and the stained-glass windows they went and sat on the seat in the shelter of the tower.

By this time all the safe topics of conversation had been exhausted and Charlotte could not think of anything else to say. She realised that this meeting was a mistake. If she could have talked to Rory alone—or to Tessa alone—it would have been easier, but with both of them there it was impossible to cope with the situation. How were they going to get through this evening and all to-morrow, wondered Charlotte.

Obviously Rory was feeling the same. He had said that "half a loaf is better than no bread" but he had found that in this case it was not. Rory was quite unlike himself—silent and dejected—and seeing him in this condition made Charlotte so miserable that she could easily have wept. It's no good, she thought. We can't be friends. It would be better not to see Rory at all . . .

The day was fine and still. There were soft clouds in the sky, moving slowly and casting lights and shadows over the peaceful landscape.

"It's a very pretty view," said Tessa after a long silence. "Not beautiful, like Targ, but nice in its own way. It's a very English view, isn't it?"

"Yes, very," agreed Charlotte.

"By the bye, Miss Fairlie, everybody at Targ sent their love to you—specially the aunts. They're looking forward tremendously to seeing you in the Summer holidays."

Charlotte hesitated, wondering what she should say.

"You are coming, aren't you?" said Tessa, leaning forward and looking at her anxiously.

"I don't know—really," replied Charlotte vaguely. "I may be going to—to France." She had not thought of going to France until this moment, but it was a reasonable excuse.

"To France!"

"Yes, I have friends in Paris——"

"But you *must* come to Targ!" cried Tessa in dismay. "You said you would come! I thought it was all fixed. Daddy, you must make Miss Fairlie come!"

"She must do as she likes," said Rory. He was sitting forward on the seat with his hands clasped between his knees gazing out over the fields.

Tessa was silent for a few moments and then suddenly she burst out with a cry of grief, "Oh, goodness, what's the matter? I thought you liked each other! What's happened? Everything's different and—and miserable. I wanted you to get married."

"What!" exclaimed Rory, turning his head and looking at his daughter in amazement.

"I wanted you——to get married," repeated Tessa with a little catch in her breath.

Charlotte rose from the seat; she simply could not bear it.

"Sit down, Charlotte," said Rory. "Please sit down. We'll have this out." He turned to Tessa and asked her if she knew what she meant.

"But of course!" exclaimed Tessa in surprise. "Of course I know what I mean. Miss Fairlie is just the right person. I've known that for ages. That's why I made you ask her to come to Targ. I wanted to see if she would do."

Rory began to laugh and Charlotte joined in, a trifle hysterically.

"I don't know why you're laughing," said Tessa. "It's quite sensible. I had to see if she fitted in—and of course she was perfect! When I saw her talking to all the people I knew I was right. She wasn't a bit patronising—which they would have hated—she was just herself and they all loved her straight off."

"You want me to be married?" Rory asked.

"Well, of course! You can't have a son unless you're married," Tessa pointed out.

Her elders were speechless.

"I thought you liked Miss Fairlie," continued Tessa. "In fact I thought you liked her the very first moment you saw her. You put off going to that meeting at Inverness because you thought she was nice, didn't you?"

"Yes," admitted Rory.

"And you liked her more and more. You gave her roses and—and everything."

"Yes," said Rory. "I liked her so much that I asked her to marry me—I asked her twice—but she said no."

"Oh!" exclaimed Tessa, turning a reproachful glance upon Charlotte. "Oh, Miss Fairlie!"

Charlotte was going to speak but Rory put out his hand and stopped her.

"I suppose it's because—because of Saint Elizabeth's," said Tessa uncertainly. "I suppose that's why you don't want to marry Daddy and come and live at Targ."

"No," said Charlotte in a low voice. "No—it isn't that."

"Oh, but—but if it isn't that—don't you *like* Daddy? I thought you did."

Charlotte was silent.

"Oh dear, this is awful!" cried Tessa in dismay. "You're angry with me! I shouldn't have said anything—I shouldn't have interfered. I thought I was being so clever—and I've just been a fool! But I *did* want it so terribly much—mostly for Daddy's sake, because he's lonely when I'm away, but not only for that. I thought it would be so perfect if I could go away—not worrying about Daddy at all—and then come back and find you both at Targ. That's what I thought," continued Tessa in a shaky voice. "I see now—it was silly to interfere—but I did want it so awfully much—more than anything in the world. I prayed and prayed—and I wished at the Silver Wishing Well and I thought it was going to be all right—and now—every thing has gone wrong." She began to sob. "I'm sorry—I'm sorry I've been so—awfully silly——"

"Leave us, Tessa," said Rory gently. "Go away and leave us to talk." He gave his daughter a little push as he spoke.

Tessa rose at once and went away, walking quickly and not looking back. They watched her disappear round the corner of the tower.

"Charlotte?" said Rory. There was a question in his voice.

"Does she understand?" asked Charlotte uncertainly. She looked at Rory and found that he was looking at her. His eyes were soft and shining and there was the beginning of a smile upon his lips.

"Tessa understands," he said. "Tessa chose you for me and invited you to Targ to see if you would do. My daughter is a very practical person, she leaves nothing to chance . . . and she always says what she means; you know that as well as I do. She wants to be able to go away without having to worry, and come home to Targ and find us there, waiting for her. That's what she wants. Charlotte, please will you marry me?"

Charlotte could not speak. She was struggling with tears.

"Charlotte?" repeated Rory beseechingly.

She put out her hand gropingly and found it seized in a warm firm grasp. They sat like that for a long time without moving.

THE END